The Billionaire's Captive Mistress

Jessica Simmons

Zitr0 Publications

The Billionaire's Captive Mistress * Jessica Simmons

This is a work of fiction. Any character references or likenesses to persons living or dead are completely coincidental. Actual people and places have been added to give the story a sense of reality.

Copyright 2013, ZitrO Publications/Divine Ortiz

All rights reserved. Without limiting the rights under copyright reserved above. No part of this book may be reproduced into retrieval system, or transmitted in any form , or by any means (electronic, mechanical, photocopying, recording, or otherwise) without the prior written consent from both the author and publisher, ZitrO Publications, except brief quotes used in reviews, interviews, or magazines.

For information about special discounts for bulk purchases, please contact ZitrO Publications at:

919-904-8414

zitropublications@yahoo.com

Cover design by Dynastys CoverMe

The Billionaire's Captive Mistress

Jessica Simmons

ZitrO Publications

To my grandfather, for always believing in me.

To my father, for pouring that insatiable urge to write into my veins.

To James and Melody, my reasons for all that I do.

Chapter 1

Michelle lost herself for a moment gazing into the rain falling outside her taxi until the driver impatiently cleared his throat.

"You gonna pay lady? I ain't got all night," he growled, his voice thickly accented by what she was sure was a lifetime in New York. She handed him what was left of the contents of her purse, and sighed as it stared emptily back at her. If she had any hope of making it home, she would have to make Dorian Johnston listen to her.

She stepped out of the cab and onto the sidewalk, and turned her eyes heavenward. A light shone from the very top of Johnston Towers, the intimidating building that professionally housed one of the most ruthless executives she had ever known. Even so late at night, that light did not surprise her.

He often worked late hours; she knew and recalled the many late nights she had waited up for him in the four months she had been his mistress. With a shudder she relived how she fawned after him, how her body had unashamedly responded to even his slightest touch, how she had fallen so deeply in love with him…and how, when he had sent her away, it wasn't long after that she discovered she hadn't been sent away alone…

No, she had taken a very large part of Dorian Johnston with her.

She regretted coming to his office so late, but she had to get home soon and if she was going to do that, she needed to talk to him and catch him off guard. It wasn't like her at all to ask for money, especially not from a man who had so emotionlessly dismissed her from his life four years ago, but she was out of options. Broke with twin boys to take care of, she was desperate.

Dorian Johnston's twins…

Somewhere in the back of her mind, she was reminded of that fact, as she had been when she had kissed them both goodbye three days earlier, much to their tears and pleas to accompany her to New York. Her neighbor Candice had been a lifesaver, volunteering to look after William and James while she was gone. Michelle promised not to be away too long, and had hopped in a taxi, scared all the way down to her toes.

When she had arrived at her cheap motel, she had wasted no time in calling his office and informing his secretary that she needed to see him concerning an urgent personal matter. The wait on the phone had seemed like forever, and when the secretary had returned, she informed Michelle that Mr. Johnston would see her in one week. But she couldn't wait— wouldn't wait—and had impulsively called a taxi to take her to him in the middle of the night, which brought her to her present reality: soaked in the rain and standing outside a building that promised nothing but difficulty inside.

She squared her shoulders and began to walk inside, remembering when her feet had first made the same shaky journey four years previously. Michelle had been just a shy little virgin then, twenty-two and fresh out of college; she had been honored to be considered to decorate the newly established New York office of one of the most prominent businessmen of the twenty-first century.

Their relationship had started as purely business, with him interjecting her daily work occasionally with a personal suggestion or two, which she had embraced and ran with. Every so often he had made a joke and she had cordially laughed, not wanting to seem too uptight in case he considered her for another job. He had hinted that he might have other properties that could use a touch, and it encouraged her to work long hours and show him she could handle the load. For almost a month, they had exchanged little more than cordial greetings when she came in the office in the mornings and the same when he left in the evenings. Sometimes he would bring up a news story and ask her take on it, and gradually they had begun talking more and more about a range of topics. She enjoyed his conversation; he posed thought-provoking questions and interesting ideas, and sometimes she got so into their conversation that she forgot all about her work.

He usually left before she did, as she liked the quiet the nighttime gave her to think and create. One night had been different, though. He had left before she did, like any other night, with a simple "goodnight, Ms. Ortiz" to complete his exit. He had stepped into his personal elevator that led him straight down to the lobby uninterrupted, where no doubt his chauffeur and one of his many leggy blondes he used as arm candy would be waiting. A billionaire in his own right even after his father's inheritance, women literally fell all over themselves to be graced by even a smile. Michelle couldn't blame them; he was stunningly gorgeous, a strong, tall, charming latte of a man, with haunting dark eyes that could pierce the soul. When he smiled even the stuffiest of boardrooms seemed to lighten, yet he could break down the most stubborn of businessmen to do things his way.

    He flashed her one of those devastating smiles before the doors closed, and she took a little time replaying it in her mind before she finally kicked off her shoes and put in her iPod earphones. As Prince's "Kiss" flooded into her ears, she danced around to the beat, moving her hips to the seductive words. Before long she was so into the song that she forgot all about her work, and she raised her arms above her head and let the music take over. She felt the waves in the song flow through her body, and she let the music guide her movements. She had always loved to dance; it was an easy way to escape from the chaotic world she lived in and simply be herself for a moment. There were only a few times when she would miraculously have her small apartment to herself, but when she did, she would turn her stereo up loud and dance throughout the house.

She slinked her way across his plush carpet, the lush feeling between her toes only adding to her simple bliss. It was when she danced that she felt most beautiful, and she danced around his spacious office pausing only to change the song to Melanie Fiona's "Give It to Me Right". She moved from the foyer of his office to his desk, using it to keep her steady while she wriggled down to the floor in a seductive dance. She sang out the chorus as she turned around: "give it to me right, or don't give it to me at all—Mr. Johnston!"

He leaned up against the wall of his office and smiled at her as if he was a lion cornering a gazelle. "Having fun?" he asked in his smooth baritone voice. Color flooded her cheeks as she yanked her earphones out, tripping over her apology. "Mr. Johnston, I'm so sorry…this is so unprofessional, I know, but I thought you were gone for the night. I didn't mean to stop working, I mean…" she stammered as she rushed past him, thoroughly embarrassed. Michelle had barely slipped on one shoe before a strong hand caught her by the arm. She took a breath before glancing up into his gorgeous eyes.

"I really should go," she said, feeling the raw heat of him through her clothes. It had taken all her strength the last few weeks not to push their business relationship, and she wasn't going to start now. She cleared her throat as he let her go, and she quickly put on her other shoe and headed toward the elevator, needing to pull herself away from his gaze.

"Michelle!"

She stopped, and said a silent prayer before turning around. She took a careful breath. "Yes?"

"Have dinner with me."

She blinked once, a slow-motion movement over her suddenly animated eyes. Then she gave a tiny shake of her head, a miniature protest. "No." She turned quickly around and closed the remaining distance to the elevator, making sure not to press the down button too lightly. In fact, it was a wonder she did not push the button clear through the wall. Now that he had her in his sights she had to get out of there as quickly as possible or risk doing something she was positive she'd regret later.

There was a sound of movement behind her, thundering feet across the carpet, and then the stone grip of his large hand wrapping like a shackle around her wrist and forcing her to face him. "That's it?" he questioned. "Just 'no'?"

Even through her clothes his touch felt like a hot iron, sizzling and searing its way deep into her skin, bone-melting heat that threatened her willpower to leave.

She looked down at the hand circling her wrist, so powerful and unyielding against her slender frame. She raised her eyes slowly, determined not to alert him of how much his touch affected her.

"What's the matter?" She challenged him daringly, the spunky side of her she had kept under wraps for her entire duration of employment finally breaking loose and stretching its legs. "Has it been so long since you've heard that word that you've forgotten what it means?"

"You have a date."

She wanted to laugh at his automatic response. Of course, an alpha male like Dorian Johnston would assume a woman would feel incomplete without a man, especially when offered his company. Nevertheless, she didn't laugh—she couldn't—not when the heat pouring from his eyes equally matched that from his grip, setting her skin aflame by the moment. Instead, she battled to get her racing heartbeat under control, while trying to get her breathing more regular.

In the end, she merely shook her head.

"So why not have dinner with me?"

"It's just not a good idea."

"You haven't eaten all day. I know. I've watched you."

Somewhere between his words, he'd relaxed the tone of his voice. It was less potent, more persuasive. And somewhere along the line he'd also relaxed his grip on her wrist, so that his thumb stroked the underside of her arm, making soft circles on her skin. Her pulse raced just under his touch, and she wondered if he could feel it beneath his strong fingers. It was soothing, almost hypnotic, so much different from his steel grip of before, yet no less unnerving. Heat spread like soft sunlight throughout her body, warming her breasts to tingling, before pooling heavy and demanding between her thighs.

She swallowed, not sure how much longer she could keep him at bay. He was like rushing water; his presence ever-present and quite dangerous, yet she yearned for him in a way she didn't know she possessed. She had to keep it together.

"I had a granola bar."

His beautiful mouth curled into a devious smile. God, why did he have to look at her like that?

"Tempting," he acknowledged, still stroking her arm, the circles larger now. "But hardly enough."

"I'll eat when I get home."

"I'll take you home after we've eaten."

"I told you, it's not a good idea."

"Why not?"

She sighed, struggling to find the right answer, because she secretly didn't have one. Every carnal impulse was telling her to take him up on his offer, but her brain remained the voice of reason. No, it screamed furiously inside her head, yet she wasn't sure she was listening as fervently anymore.

"Because I don't want to!" she finally settled for. "And you can't make me." She sounded a bit childish, but she didn't care.

His eyes narrowed. "It's just dinner."

Was it? The words themselves sounded perfectly safe, and yet when did 'just dinner' invitations come with such an animalistic undertone? When did they come with mesmerizing eyes that glistened like deep pools, looking like they were ready to pull her down into tantalizing oblivion, so much so that the idea of sharing a dinner transformed into visions of much more satisfying exchanges? And, if he could make her manic with simply a look, with just one touch, then what more was possible?

Her brain cried out to her, screaming for her sanity. She had to get out of his presence, before she started wanting to find out just how much more he could give her.

"I want to go," she stated as convincingly as she could, hoping her voice didn't betray her when every other part of her was drawn to him, drawn to what she knew would be more dangerous than stepping into a black hole. Somehow, she knew that once he had lured her into his embrace there would be no escape.

No, no, no. She couldn't let that happen.

As if it had read her mind, the elevator dinged, announcing its arrival, the doors sliding open alongside her. She knew she had to move quickly, lest her senses become overrun by lust. She turned away from him, turned away from his heat and towards the welcoming space of the elevator where the air already seemed cooler. Safer.

She jerked her arm away, assuming she would meet with resistance to her dash for freedom, but there was none, and the momentum of snatching her arm from his grasp caught her wrong-footed and sent her tripping sideways towards the elevator doorframe.

She cried out, trying to catch herself on anything that would offer its support; unfortunately the slick wall and open doors of the elevator provided no help whatsoever, and she begin to brace herself for the fall when he caught her in a tangle of limbs and spun her into his arms. Her chest collided with his, which sent the air in her lungs cascading out of her in a deep wave. But she was saved. She dragged in air, content for the moment to rest in the circle of his arms, his lean body lending her strength while she caught her breath.

"Okay now?" he murmured in her ear, his cheek pressed against her hair and his warm breath a silken caress.

She drew in another long breath, feeling the beat of her heart slow and regulate before she felt steady enough to respond.

"Th…thank you," she whispered, finally feeling confident enough to try to push herself away. She raised her hands to his chest and felt the answering thud of his own heartbeat. And in the space of just a second or two she felt it kick up a notch, as though her hands on him caused a momentary spike in his pulse.

The relief that she hadn't crash-landed gave way to a fear that she'd been saved into circumstances much more dangerous indeed.

She edged back and looked at him, and felt the connection with his eyes like a bolt of electricity. They were so intense, so heavy with longing—*longing for her.*

No, she registered from some far-off place. *I can't do this.* Her mind screamed at her in frantic protest.

But for some reason her body didn't want to listen, not with the way his lips hovered so tantalizingly close to her own.

With one hand he lifted her chin, and her lips parted on a sigh in anticipation. His answering moan fed into her senses like a rolling wave of desire, and she barely registered the elevator doors sliding closed behind her, cutting off her escape route.

Except escape was now the furthest thing from her mind, and, just when she thought it wasn't possible to want him any more than she already did, he kissed her. Her mind exploded in a wave of emotions all at once, but a burning need stood out among the rest; a need that threatened all avenues of self-control she possessed, a need for more, much more. His mouth was forceful yet passionate against hers, starting simply at first, but as his hunger for her grew and hers began to reciprocate, he introduced his tongue in a flash of wild abandon. It was then she began to lose all sense of self, and became engrossed in the raw masculine heat of the man who held her trapped in his embrace.

Her spine seemed to melt, her body arching into his, letting herself be supported by his hands as she clung to him, wrapping her arms around his neck and pulling him close, feeding on his male touch and taste even as he supped on her.

Such wide shoulders, such lean, muscular flesh; her hands relished the sculpted skinscape of him. She curled her fingers into the shirt covering his firm flesh, feeling his muscles flex and tighten beneath. He shuddered when she raked her nails across the fine fabric, and pressed his long, lean length closer to her so she could not be in any way ignorant to his arousal.

How empowering. Knowing she could do this to him. Knowing that a man like Dorian Johnston would react to her touch. Knowing that a man like Dorian Johnston wanted her.

His hand scooped its way under her jacket, sweeping the length of her back, setting her skin alight in a sensual massage. Everywhere he touched her burned. Everywhere he touched her sizzled.

He was setting her aflame.

She was crazy, she recognized; she must be crazy. It was the kind of crazy that made all rational thought obsolete, the kind of crazy that took you by the hand and led you into a maze with no foreseeable means of escape, no way of returning to how things were, no way to remedy what had been done after the fact. It was the kind of crazy she had tried to stay away from, but that had her utterly captured. She was stuck, helplessly, yet she wasn't so sure she wanted to be set free; she had to admit there was definitely something to be said for being crazy.

He tilted his head and directed his mouth down the line of her jaw and her throat, his hands moving over her back, his fingers and thumbs seeming to test every part of her flesh, but, she had no doubt, giving much more than they were receiving.

His fingers rounded her rib cage and brushed the underswell of her breast. She gasped, arching involuntarily into the movement, and momentarily lost in sensations so foreign to her and yet at the same time so evocative. It was like a drug, this feeling coursing through her, feelings that simultaneously made her senses sing and turned logic funny. It had taken one kiss and she was addicted.

He cupped one breast with his hand, brushing her nipple with his thumb. Air rushed into her lungs as though he'd switched on a vacuum, and the addict in her craved more, more immediately.

He trailed kisses along her jaw, burying his face in her hair and breathing her in.

"Do you realize how much I want you?"

A tremor shimmied through her. And a flicker of fear. Through the drug-inducing haze of sensation, she recognized this wasn't a good idea. Things had gone too far—too fast—and a kiss had turned into something else entirely.

"Mr. Johnston…"

"Dorian," he purred into her ear.

"Dorian…"

"Stay with me," he murmured, his voice husky, his breathing choppy. The look in his eyes was one she'd never seen, yet it seemed to mimic her own restless needing. "Here. Tonight. I have a bedroom suite in my office."

It was insane, but for a moment she was actually tempted—to feel more of this exquisite rush, to experience more of what he obviously had to offer. But it was madness.

Wasn't it? Or was she just telling herself that?

"I don't think—"

"Don't think!" he urged. "Just feel. Let me have you tonight, Michelle. All night."

"But…Mr. Johnston—I mean, Dorian—I…"

"Michelle—stop talking," he said, and claimed her mouth again. She closed her eyes in willing surrender as his tongue slipped between her softly parted lips in a long drugging kiss.

Finally when she was breathless he raised his head. "I have waited too long for this." He peeled off his jacket and hers as he walked backwards in what she hoped was the direction of something softer than his office carpet.

She felt her breasts swell as his hand stroked one lace-covered breast, his thumb grazing the tip over the fine fabric, and her nipples tightened into hard pulsing points of pleasure. His mouth caught her soft gasp of delight, then moments later he nudged a door open with his shoulder.

She barely registered the bedroom; she had eyes for nothing but Dorian.

Without a word he cupped her face and bent his dark head, covering her mouth with his at first tenderly, then, as she opened her mouth to him, with a fast-growing passion that she returned with helpless fervor. Somewhere in the midst of things he'd removed the camisole she'd been wearing under her jacket, but she had barely noticed beyond her aching lustful need.

"Michelle." He said her name, and lifting his head, he locked his magnetic eyes with hers, full of a hunger, a passion, that burned through to her bones. His hand slid around her back to dispense with her bra and stayed to hold her to him. For a long moment he simply stared, and just his gaze on her naked breasts made her tremble with excitement.

"Exquisite," he murmured throatily as he lowered his head to trace the slender length of her neck with his mouth and suck on the rapidly beating pulse there. After a breath of time that was an eternity, he trailed his mouth lower to her breast, and whatever reserve she had left was shattered.

His tongue licked one erect nipple and the tightened tip engorged at his touch. She cried out as his teeth gently tugged, and her head fell back, her back arching in spontaneous response as she offered herself up to the incredible pleasure only Dorian could arouse. He suckled first one and then the other with a skill that drove her crazy with need and had her writhing in his hold.

She felt her skirt slide to the floor, and suddenly he was swinging her up in his arms and lowering her gently to the bed. She whimpered involuntarily as he straightened up and looked down at her.

"You have no idea how much I want you," he grated, his dark eyes ablaze as he divested himself of his clothes in seconds.

She stared at the wide shoulders, the muscular, slightly hair-roughed chest, the strong hips, the powerful thighs and long legs. Totally naked and fully aroused he was almost frightening in his masculine beauty, and nervously she crossed her arms over her throbbing breasts.

"Let me look at you," he growled and, leaning over her, grasped the top of her miniscule lace briefs. "All of you." He slid them down her long legs and dropped them. Then his hands curled around her ankles and stroked back up them slowly, tracing the curve of her hips up to the indentation at her waist.

She was trembling all over by the time he reached for her wrists and, unfolding her arms from her chest, pinned her hands on either side of her body.

"There is no need to pretend shyness," his words danced over her. "You are exquisite, more than I ever dreamed of." He caught her eyes. "And trust me, I have dreamed. A lot. I can't take my eyes off you, Michelle. When you're here at the office, it takes all my will not to drag you into this bed. But I just can't take it anymore." Taking protection from a side table, he lowered himself down beside her, his magnificent body sliding against her, flesh on flesh.

What followed was so outside what Michelle had ever imagined it was unreal. The odd times that she had imagined the act of love, she had thought it would be some magical meeting of heart, body and soul—sweet, tender love reaching a joyous climax. But the raging emotions flooding through her were nothing like that.

With tentative hands, she explored the width of his shoulders, the strong spine. She shuddered as his dark head lowered and found her pouting breasts once more. No longer tentative, but eager, she stroked up his back and raked her fingers through the silken hair of his head, holding him to her. She groaned aloud as he lifted his head and moaned her delight as he found her mouth again. The sensuality of his kiss made her head spin and her body burn, and as he lowered his mouth to her neck she was completely aware of every exquisite feeling that was coursing through her body.

His long fingers found the moist, hot center of her femininity and a low aching moan escaped her, and she wanted more, much more, her hips lifting, her whole body throbbing. She was helplessly prisoner to the wonder of his experienced touch and her own uninhibited response. She clutched desperately at him and looked up into his taut face, saw the raw passion in his eyes and reveled in it.

Wild and wanton, she caught his hair and pulled his head back to her mouth. She was panting with frustration and an incredible need to feel all of his long, hard body over her, in her, joined with hers. She groaned as he paused to slip on protection and then kissed her. The sensuous pressure of his lips, the thrusting of his tongue, mimicking the sexual act and the fire in her blood turned her whole body into a mess of pure sensation. He settled between her thighs, and she lightly cried out his name, burning with a fever for more. His hands on her hips tightened and she arched up as he thrust home.

Michelle felt a stab of pain and winced. She saw the shock in his glowing eyes as he stilled and began to withdraw. But she could not let him go, not now as the thick fullness of him made her inner muscles clench, and instinctively she locked her legs around his waist, slid her arms around his back. "Please. Please. I want you. Please, Dorian."

She felt the sharp intake of his breath, felt the heavy beating of his heart and the tension in every muscle of his body. Then he moved, slowly thrusting a little deeper, and then withdrawing and sliding deeper still.

Miraculously her silken sheath stretched to accommodate him, and Michelle was lost to everything except the pure physical wonder of his possession. The indescribable sensations beating through her, the sleek skin beneath her fingers, and the heated scent of two bodies joined. The wonder as in seconds she matched the rhythm he set, driving her even higher to some unknown destination she ached...was dying to reach.

Her nails dug deep into his satin-smooth skin as great rolling waves of ecstasy rippled through her, and then roared as he thrust hard and fast. She cried out as her body convulsed in exquisite rapture, and she was thrown into a hot, mindless oblivion. She heard Dorian groan and she forced her eyes open and felt his great body buck and shudder with the force of his own release.

Loosely she wrapped her arms around him as he buried his head on her shoulder. The heavy pounding of his heart against hers and his weight were a solid reminder of his power and passion, and at the time a soft smile curled her lips.

But a smile was the last thing she wanted to do now, and she squared her shoulders and pressed the elevator button, giving a weak wave to the guard as the doors opened and she shakily stepped inside.

Chapter 2

Dorian slammed the phone down after talking to his night guard, who had informed him that a particularly beautiful woman was headed up. After getting a more detailed description, his throat went dry. So, she was here. She had the gall to show up at his office! Unannounced! At least when he had given his secretary a date to give her, he had provided himself enough time to prepare for her arrival; steel himself against her feminine charms.

He hadn't seen her in four years, since he had dismissed her from his sight and his life. Even after all the time that had passed, he hadn't encountered a woman quite like her. She had been beautiful, sweet, energetic, and a willing sexual student. He had unleashed the sexual goddess within, and she had literally blossomed beneath him. He was lucky he had gotten rid of her before she had a chance to get underneath his skin.

He spun around in his office chair and stared out into the rain pouring down outside. Why in the hell was she here? If she was trying to wiggle her way back into his bed for whatever reason, he wasn't sure he'd be able to resist her. He looked over at the door leading to the small bedroom he'd had built in his office—for the nights he was simply too tired to go home—and a small smirk played across his face as he remembered how many times he'd taken Michelle right there after watching her work around his office during the day. He'd even left a particularly frustrating conference call mid-sentence to ravish her after seeing her bend over to pick up some pieces of paper that had dropped out of her hands.

Ever since she had walked into his office four years ago, he had wanted her. She had pranced around the place, putting all of his staff in a wonderful mood with her sunny demeanor. It had been infectious. To add to her amazing qualities, she was diligent. From the moment she had arrived, she had presented him with infinite ideas for his office, all of them innovative and creative. It had taken every ounce of his strength and willpower not to seduce her from the beginning, but he had kept his distance because she was an employee. It wasn't until he had seen her hips wiggling all over his desk that his reserve had broken.

He couldn't remember what had possessed him to come back upstairs after bidding her farewell, but he had gotten to the lobby and stared at the marble floors for a moment before turning around and stepping back into the elevator. As he had ridden the lift up to his floor, he felt his heart begin to race in anticipation, a feeling he found unfamiliar. He prided himself on keeping a level head in tough situations, and he couldn't believe he was getting anxious over a woman. The sight he saw when the elevator doors had opened into his office was enough for him to thank God he hadn't gotten into his limo.

She was dancing all over his desk, and he was almost jealous he wasn't the hunk of wood instead. In the many strip clubs he had sampled in the course of his life, he had never seen a woman with more grace and sexuality. His body had immediately reacted, and as she had turned around and noticed him, he had tried to stay composed.

But his body was on fire for her.

She had attempted to appear reserved, but he could see the hunger in her eyes and he feasted off it. He had taken her to bed and made love to her until they were both senseless, and it had been bliss.

But she couldn't stay. He had learned once before not to let a woman get too close, and he wasn't going to make the same mistake.

No matter how beautiful the vixen.

The same said vixen was on her way up, and if he was going to have any luck keeping her away, he would need to put on his poker face. He turned back around to face his desk, pulled his scotch and a spare glass out of his bottom drawer and poured himself a drink. He had only managed to take a swig before the elevator sounded its arrival. He swallowed hard and sat back in his chair.

The doors seemed to open in slow motion, and she was there. She was dripping wet, her clothes and coat clinging to her figure. And what a figure it was, indeed. He could remember his hands scaling up and down those luscious curves…plowing inside her sweet warmth while she wrapped those mile-high legs around his waist…

"Dorian." His name seemed to reverberate throughout the quiet office, and he let the sound simply hang in the air for a moment. She spoke his name in her usual honeyed voice, and he realized how much he had missed hearing it whispered repeatedly in his ear as she climaxed beneath him.

"Michelle."

She took a step forward. "I know it's late and I'm a tad bit unannounced, but—"

He cut her off. "And dripping on my carpet."

"Yes…but I had to see you. You see," he watched as her chest rose and fell as she took a deep breath, "I'm desperate."

So, she *was* trying to wiggle back into his bed. He should have known she'd come crawling back sooner or later. Oh, this ought to be good. He took a slow sip, and then spoke.

"Please, continue."

"Can I sit?" she gestured to one of the chairs in front of his massive desk.

"Please."

She slowly took off her coat and hung it over the chair furthest from her, then sat down in the opposite one. Hell, could her curves be any more defined? It was as though she'd been carved by angels.

"So, Michelle, why are you here?" As if he didn't know.

"Well, I'm in a bit of a bind. I've had some…uh…family problems to arise, and my finances are a bit depleted. Now, you are the last person I'd consider coming to for money, but—"

"You're desperate." He finished off his drink. "So, what are you proposing? You want your old job back?" The question came out of nowhere, rolling off his tongue before he could think twice about it.

"Well," she said as she looked around his office, "I'd say I did a pretty good job last time I was here, wouldn't you say? I mean, you kept everything as I left it, I see no reason to change it. Now, if you have other properties that need work, I'd be happy to…"

She trailed off as his abrupt laughter erupted throughout the room. How could she possibly think he was talking about her platonic job when there was one much more satisfying?

He walked around to the front of his desk and sat on the edge, her dark eyes shifting to look up at him. God, she was beautiful.

"Not that job, Michelle. I'm speaking of a much more fulfilling job. How about it?" He traced the curve of her cheek with his finger. "Just how desperate are you?"

He watched her dark eyes widen in recognition. "You mean, as your mistress?"

"Is it so unimaginable? If I remember correctly, we were pretty damn amazing together. Wouldn't you agree?"

Color flooded her cheeks, and he was already somewhat satisfied. "Look, Michelle, I'm only in New York for the next couple weeks, and then I'm flying back to London for a while. During this time, I will need an escort to society events and parties. Do that for me without complaint and I'll write you a blank check. How does that sound?"

He could see she was contemplating it as she slowly spoke.

"What exactly does 'being your escort' entail?"

He grinned. "You would be my arm candy at these events. The men would be so focused on you they'd forget the fact that I'm taking over their companies piece by piece."

"And that's it, right?" she asked cautiously.

How could she deny him what he knew she was craving? The tension between them was like electricity; neither of them could run from it.

"We'll see," he finally responded.

"Only two weeks."

"It should be, yes. Why, do you have someone at home waiting patiently just for you?" He felt his stomach tug at the thought of another man taking her to bed every night, but he wasn't quite sure why. His hunger for her was so powerful, so all-consuming; whenever he would take her to bed, he would possess her entirely. The thought of a man even looking at his marked property made him sick to his stomach. Lord, he needed to get her out of his system. He wouldn't be able to think straight until he did.

"Not exactly."

"Ok, then."

She sighed. "So, when do I start?"

"Tomorrow." He looked at his watch. "Well, this evening, since you decided to come here at three in the morning. I have a business dinner with a couple of my clients. I'll send my car for you at seven thirty. Where are you staying?" He flipped to the appointment log in his phone and out of the corner of his eye watched her hang her head as she fiddled with her fingers. He could sense something was wrong, and he looked up from his phone.

"What's wrong? Where are you staying, the Hilton? Plaza?"

She cleared her throat. "The Budget Motel."

He nearly choked. How could she even imagine staying in a hovel like that for the next two weeks? *She must be in a terrible financial bind*, he thought to himself. For some odd reason, he immediately felt a sense of protectiveness—what was she going through that could bring her so low? She had such a vibrant life about her when she was with him; how could life throw her such a curve ball that she couldn't smile her way out of its path? He picked up his office phone and punched in a set of numbers. After someone finally picked up, he spoke into the receiver.

"Charles Morgan, please."

"What are you doing?"

He ignored her. "Charles, it's Mr. Johnston. I have a dear friend of mine staying with me for a couple of weeks. Will you prepare my guest suite? Thank you."

He hung up and she immediately began to protest. "No, Dorian. I'll be fine, really. It's only a couple of weeks. I'll be ok. I don't—"

He cut her off. "Nonsense. You are my escort and therefore you will act the part or I'll have no choice but to send you home even worse off than you started. Understood?" Her reaction was a mix of shock and defeat, a pair of emotions he had seen many times as he laid down the law to one of his clients. She slowly nodded her head. He called his car for her and watched her leave, noticing her plump bottom still had its amazing shape. He moved to the window just in time to see her run out to the car, and slowly it drove away.

He hated being so harsh to her, but he had to play this right and be in control if he wanted her to do things his way. She would come willingly back into his bed, and damn, he couldn't wait.

*****

What in the hell was she doing? She had sworn long ago that she would never put herself back under his control, and yet here she was, at his mercy. She rode back to her hotel in defeated silence, dreading the car that would surely be there at the promised time that evening. Instead of worrying herself sick, she decided that when she got back into her hotel room she would take a much needed and deserved nap. She thanked Dorian's courteous driver as they pulled into the parking lot, a man who seemed unaffected that a woman was being sent away from Dorian Johnston's office in the middle of the night.

Wearily she climbed the stairs and opened the door to her room, her surroundings staring dismally back at her. Somehow, she managed to take off her clothes and climb under the covers, and she welcomed the sleep when it quickly came to claim her.

She had never slept so hard, nor was more angry when her body made her awaken. She yawned and stretched her arms above her head, making herself remember why she was there in the first place, so she wouldn't be tempted to roll over and pull the covers over her head. The last few hours seemed like a horrible nightmare, as if her mind was playing a terrible joke on her. She couldn't believe where she was or why she had agreed, and the thought of her sons barely sustained her as she climbed miserably out of bed and lifted the telephone receiver. As she dialed Candice's number, she didn't know how she was going to explain the situation to her, and briefly contemplated lying and thinking of something creative. But she quickly reconsidered, remembering that Candice was doing her a favor and deserved to know the truth. Michelle only wished the truth didn't sound so ludicrous.

Michelle involuntarily held her breath while putting on a fresh pair of jeans and a shirt, and Candice answered on the third ring.

"Hello?"

"Hey, Candy, it's Jess."

"Hey! Are you at the airport? I didn't recognize the number."

Michelle took a long breath before she spoke her next words.

"Um…no, I'm not at the airport…"

"Ok…what's wrong?" Candice asked, concerned, and Michelle placed the phone on her shoulder for a moment. How would she even begin to elaborate on what was happening with her? Hell, she couldn't even make sense of it herself.

"I have a little snag…"

She explained the situation to Candice, and finally told her the truth about William and James' father. She felt as though a huge burden had been lifted, being able to finally tell someone the truth.

"I thought you said he was some guy at work!" Candice said, completely aghast. "You never mentioned that he was the boss!"

Candice laughed heartily, and then quickly lowered her voice as she remembered the boys were down for a nap. "Look, Michelle, you take all the time you need. The boys and I are doing just fine. I'm happily retired; where am I gonna go?"

Michelle breathed a sigh of relief, and told Candice to give the boys her love before disconnecting the call. She sat back on the bed and barely had a chance to gather her thoughts before there was a knock on her room door.

Cautiously she stood up and began to walk towards it, not knowing if her emotions could take any more unpleasant turns in her life. But as she slowly opened it and found herself staring into the face of Dorian's driver from earlier that morning, she knew he couldn't possibly be the bearer of any good news. He spoke with the voice of a man who, in his profession, was not surprised by anything anymore.

"Ms. Ortiz, Mr. Johnston has asked me to escort you and your belongings to his guest suite at the Waldorf-Astoria. Are you all packed, or shall you need assistance?"

Her jaw couldn't have dropped any lower if the floor had opened. How dare Dorian think he could just boss her around! She was not some weakling threatened by his every move! She opened her mouth to tell the driver exactly that, but she quickly remembered why she was there in the first place, and she sighed deeply. She looked behind her and eyed her suitcase, which held her pajamas, some jeans, a sweater, her toiletries, and underwear. Also inside was her textbook for her business management class, and she made a mental note to call her professor and explain her upcoming two-week absence. Luckily, she already had an 'A' in the class.

She had not packed too heavy because she had not planned to stay long, and quickly realized that the next two weeks were going to be hell. The driver cleared his throat. "Ma'am? Do you need help with your luggage?"

"No, thank you. I'll manage."

Michelle grabbed her suitcase and slid into her shoes, leaving her room key on the nightstand as the receptionist had instructed her. Dorian's driver was waiting for her in the hallway, and she followed somberly as the elevator arrived and they quietly stepped inside.

The silence gave her a quick moment to compose herself. She had been 'sent for' many times when she was Dorian's mistress, as he often loved to take her in the middle of the day or after a frustrating board meeting. At the time, she had loved being his stress relief, and thought it an honor to be so highly thought of by such a desirable man. However, looking back, it sickened her that she had let him have that much power over her. He had dictated her every move; he had called for her at all hours of the night...she was almost at his beckon call. She had fallen so madly in love with him that she had failed to see he didn't reciprocate the feelings, and on the rainy night that he had abruptly ended their affair, she had felt as though the world had stopped turning.

She'd had a car sent for her that night, too, and as she had climbed happily into the back of the limo, she had no idea what was waiting for her at the top of Johnston Towers. It had begun raining on the way, and as she ran into the lobby and quickly stepped into the elevator, she had tried to minimize the damage the rain had done to her hair.

She had suspected something was wrong by the way he had greeted her. He hadn't lifted her into his arms, as usual, but instead hugged her and gave her a quick kiss on the cheek before asking her to have a seat in front of his desk. When he had slid a box to her, she thought he was taking things to the next level. God, had she been mistaken. He looked at her for a long time before he spoke his heavy words.

"Michelle, look, it's been fun, but..."

She didn't hear the rest of his words, since she already knew what he was saying. She had seen it happen to so many women before, read about it in the gossip magazines, how Dorian Johnston had "broken yet another girl's heart". He had said something about long distance that she barely registered, and hoping that her professionalism wouldn't change, but she knew it to be nothing but a load of bull. He hated commitment, which she saw clearly, and she had already started mending the pieces of her broken heart before he had finished speaking.

She had continued to work until her project was done with minimal interaction with him, while he buzzed about the office as though breaking hearts was something he did daily over lunch. When she was done with his office she quietly turned in her resignation, and had moved to Maine to be closer to her mother. When she had found a job nearby that she not only loved but that utilized her skills, it had only sealed the deal. It wasn't until a few weeks after she had moved into her apartment that she realized that Dorian and she would be connected forever.

She had gone to the doctor with complaints of nausea and tenderness in her breasts, but after peeing in a cup and having a fetal heart monitor placed on her belly, she had walked out with surprising news: she was pregnant. And not only was she pregnant, she was carrying twins. She remembered standing out in the sunshine and feeling as though she'd been cast out into a tornado: completely lost.

The patient driver cleared his throat, and Michelle realized that she was standing in the middle of elevator doors, leaving them wide open. She quickly grabbed her suitcase and followed him outside to the waiting limo. They rode in silence all the way to the hotel, and she felt quite defeated as Dorian's driver opened her door and a different man called out her name.

"Ms. Ortiz?"

She said thank you to the driver and took her suitcase from his outstretched hand, turning her attention to the man speaking to her.

"Yes, that's me."

"Follow me, please."

Quietly she followed behind him past the lobby and bar, and into an elevator where he pressed a button, swiped a card attached to his belt, and they were sent straight up, uninterrupted. It halted at what Michelle assumed was the top floor, and the doors slowly opened. She found herself staring at a pair of double doors, with large golden spheres for doorknobs. The doors were wooden and glossy, and she could almost see her reflection. Despite loathing her current situation, she was almost glad when she opened the door with the key the polite man handed her to see that brunch had already been sent up, and she promised herself she would eat as much as she could keep down after she had a nice, long shower. She smiled and thanked the bellman, and he closed the door behind him as he left.

It hardly felt like 11 in the morning, and Michelle sighed as she realized that only 8 hours earlier her life had taken a turn she hadn't been prepared for. She once again wished she had never come in the first place, but her boys' faces ran through her mind for the millionth time as a constant reminder of why she had to stay. As she tossed aside her clothes outside the huge bathroom's door, she hoped the fresh water would be able to give her a fresh outlook on what she was in for.

*****

It was on a sheer whim that he'd had her picked up that morning, and Dorian couldn't figure out why. It was as though he had to know where she was at all times, so he could make sure no other man even thought about coming after her. He couldn't bear thinking about another man laying his body over hers, her moans falling on ears that were not his own. He hadn't slept well, as she had kept filling his head with her voice and her body. He intended to tell her exactly what she could do with that voice and body, and the thought drove him wild as he rode the elevator to his suite.

The top two floors of the hotel were his, with his personal suite sitting underneath his guest suite. The elevator could go to either floor, but they were connected by a set of stairs inside. He liked it this way, but he had never invited any woman to stay for an extended period. A night, maybe, when he was feeling generous, but never a couple of weeks.

Then again, Michelle was not any woman.

She was the one woman who had refused to get out of his system. Every time he had cautiously entered yet another relationship (much to the delight of the media) to get her out of his mind, he had always found himself comparing whomever he was dating to Michelle, and it had driven him crazy. He avoided commitment like the plague, but he vowed that if he found a woman who put Michelle out of his memory bank he would marry her.

But so far no woman had, and the paparazzi anxiously awaited his next "playboy" move. Dorian hated that term, "playboy", but he couldn't deny his heinous reputation, and the playboy smiled as the elevator doors opened to his suite. Unlike the guest suite, the elevator doors opened directly into his room, accessible only by his key. He had complete control, which was how he preferred it. He had liked having total control since his father had retired and left him in charge of the company. Though the board members had expressed their disbelief that the reckless youngster could manage an international company, Dorian had shocked them all by taking the lead and steering them in a direction that had increased revenue by over seventy-five percent. But his father was starting to realize his age, and whenever Dorian called he received the same question from the old-timer: "son, where are my grandchildren?"

Dorian involuntarily cringed at the thought, and as he poured himself a drink to wait for Michelle, his mobile phone began to ring—and the bearer of the question that made his stomach turn was on the other line. He slowly answered.

"Hi, pop."

"Dorian, son, how are things?"

"As well as can be expected. Did you get the copy of the prospectus I sent you for the Armatti deal?" The Armattis ran a bank that was slowly going under, and Dorian had single-handedly proposed a contract that would add another 1.8 billion to the company's pockets through a tactful merger. The dinner that evening to finalize the deal would be vital. Dorian smiled as he thought about the ace card he held. A very curvaceous ace, he might add. He returned his attention to his father.

"Yes, yes, I got it. Stop trying to change the subject from what you know is coming."

He braced himself and steeled his spine.

"When in God's name are you gonna calm down and bring a nice girl around here?"

"Dad, I—"

Dorian paused because a pair of very wet, very delicious legs were descending the stairs in front of him. His breath caught in his throat as he watched Michelle carefully slink downstairs in only a towel, dripping wet. Somewhere in the back of his mind he heard his father speaking to him, but all his comprehensive thought was lost as Michelle's legs had him transfixed. She was coming down slowly and quietly, stepping lightly on the balls of her feet. Apparently she didn't notice him, and from where he stood behind the stairs made only of metal and carpeted flat planks, he had a wonderful opportunity to just watch her. He definitely wasn't prepared for her to be there already, and he found the wheels spinning in his head and his mouth moving before he even realized what he was saying.

"I have to go, Dad. My fiancée just walked downstairs."

At the sound of his voice, she jumped and fell off the last stair, landing on her butt with a soft thud. The towel she had carefully wrapped around her delicious body had slipped open, and she frantically grasped at it as she looked up at him, horrified. Her clutching at the towel did not help; he had already seen enough and his body was already responding rapidly. He pocketed his phone and walked over to where she sat, silently stunned.

"Are you alright?" he asked, holding out his hand to offer his help. She slowly took it and stood, the electricity between their hands making him smile.

"What are you doing here? I wasn't expecting your car until seven-thirty. A situation I actually need to talk to you about, after you explain to me this 'fiancée' mess." She re-tucked her towel and saucily put her hands on her hips. He was happy to notice that the action jutted out her beautiful breasts, and he watched her respirations for a moment before speaking.

"Why are *you* here so early? I was expecting you to pack. Don't you women usually take long to pack?" he said, cleverly changing the subject.

"That's what I needed to talk to you about. I don't have any clothes here, and no money to buy anything. So I don't think this dinner is such a great idea."

"Don't try to wiggle out of it. Why didn't you tell me you didn't have anything to wear? I'll have to pull some strings, but we can get you ready in time." He pulled out his phone and punched in a few numbers while she stood with her hands on her hips, flabbergasted.

"Andrew. It's Dorian. Look, I know it's short notice, but I need a huge favor." He made arrangements for Michelle and turned back to face her. "See? Problem solved. Now, go get dressed in what you do have and we'll head out." He started to turn around to take a sip of his drink, but a slender hand grabbed him by the forearm and forced him around. He turned to face her questioning eyes, and resisted the urge to pull her into his arms.

He had to be patient.

"No, no, no. You are not dismissing me that easily. You still have not told me what this mess is about me being your fiancée. Who were you talking to?" She folded her arms over her chest.

"My father. He's been asking me for months when I'm going to bring a nice girl to meet him. And since you're my escort for an extended amount of time and you can be nice when you want to be—"

"Wait, wait, wait," she said, throwing her hands up. "You said only a couple of weeks! And you said nothing about lying to your father and passing me off as your fiancée!"

"Are you saying no? You do remember, do you not, that I can choose to send you home empty-handed, right? You act like you've got to rush home for something."

"Yeah, my life! It's nothing compared to yours, but I do have one."

He sighed. What life could she possible have that could compare with what he was offering her? He knew women that would kill to be in her shoes, being flown to London to meet his father. What was wrong with her?

"Look, we're just gonna go, stay for a bit, then I'll tell him some urgent business has come up and we need to leave."

"I just—"

"Look, we're helping each other out here. I am helping you, obviously, but you are helping me by showing my father that I gave it the good ol' college try and it didn't work. Once your time is up, I'll write your check and tell my father that things didn't work out. Everything will be fine, I promise. Now, go get dressed."

She opened and closed her mouth a couple times as if about to speak, but she slowly turned around and walked back upstairs. His phone rang, and he frowned as he saw his dad was calling him again.

He pressed 'ignore'. *Later, dad.*

Chapter 3

Michelle couldn't believe what she had been told downstairs. Commanded was more like it, she acknowledged, since he held her survival in his masculine hands. She sighed as she plopped down on the edge of the bed, yet again realizing that her life had been taken out of her hands and led in a direction she didn't agree with. She couldn't understand how she could be such a strong-willed person in every aspect of her life, but when it came to him, she was more like warm dough. How in the world she managed to go from merely coming to ask him for money to somehow agreeing to fly halfway across the world to be presented to his father was beyond her scope of comprehension.

He always had that affect over her, merely having to hint at a suggestion contrary to hers and she would abandon her idea and latch onto his own. It was his energy; his pure, raw, masculine life force simply took over her mind and ensnared her senses. One word, one touch, and she was lost. She couldn't explain it, she couldn't escape it; it was as though someone had laced her with puppet strings and given them to Dorian to do with as he pleased. She slowly undid the towel around her, let it fall to the bed, and looked over towards her suitcase. As she slowly got dressed, she once again questioned what he had in store for her, and with legs that were not as steady as she would've liked, she headed back downstairs.

Even before she saw him, she knew he was waiting for her. It had been that way when she was his mistress, too: often before she turned the corner, she knew he would be on the other side. He smiled at her as he put his phone back into his pocket, and walked to meet her at the bottom of the stairs. She could feel the heat radiating from him as he neared her side, and she closed her eyes for only a moment to collect her thoughts. Her feet hit soft carpet, alerting her of the end of her descent and time to face her new reality. She dared herself to speak.

"Do I look alright?" she asked tentatively.

"No. But that will soon change. Are you ready?" She gasped at his blatant put-down, and silently nodded.

"Good. Now let's go get you into something more presentable." He quickly led her out of his suite, and as the elevator doors closed behind them she noticed her dismal expression. Apparently he noticed as well, because he looked up from his phone as he spoke. "Don't look so melancholy, dear. Not many women can brag that they have my undivided attention. You should consider yourself lucky."

Before she could offer a retort, the elevator doors opened and they stepped into the cool air of the lobby. The sound of her cheap flip-flops sounded quite inferior when paired with the expensive 'click's of designer stilettos, and she was suddenly very aware of her contrasting appearance. She was also very aware of the whispering woman at the front desk who kept peering in her direction, as if to question her right to even exist dressed in jeans and a t-shirt. There were two fashionably dressed women at the bar having afternoon martinis, and as she passed by they suddenly found something extremely funny. She vaguely heard something whispered along the lines of "charity case", but she ignored it and followed Dorian out the revolving door and into the fresh air.

The doorman looked a little perplexed as he called for the car, but in his profession he had learned not to ask questions. He simply bid them good day and held open the passenger side door for her. She quietly said "thank you" and slid inside the car, where Dorian was already waiting, ready to drive off.

The tension inside the car could be cut with a knife. She didn't want to be the first one to speak, so she quietly stared out the window as they rode through the city streets. Everything seemed to pass in a blur, as if she had been taken out of her real life and was looking over someone else's for the time being. Nothing seemed real, but even as she said it in her head, she became aware of Dorian's presence beside her as he shifted gears. Just as she was getting used to the silence, he cleared his throat. She braced herself involuntarily.

"So, what have you been doing these last few years? Is there a special man in your life?" She noticed the slight tightness in his mouth as he said the last few words. She smiled internally. Jealous, perhaps? She wished she could tell him that she had a pair of special men in her life thanks to him, but she instead quietly said, "no, no husband."

She noticed his shoulders relax. Why had he been tense in the first place? She had every right to move on, there could be no doubt about that, she just hadn't. She adjusted herself in the seat.

"What about you? Has there been a woman in your life?" she asked, as if she didn't already know.

"Several." He didn't miss a beat. She didn't know why she felt mildly disappointed; she knew all too well he had a plethora of women in and out of his bed. No doubt he had several of said women on speed dial right now, all of them ready to drop their worlds if his name were to pop up on their caller IDs.

"Will one of them be waiting patiently for you to come home this evening?" she inquired carefully.

"Now, now. No need to worry. I believe in fidelity, even if the relationship is not serious. So no, no one will be waiting at home."

She felt herself breathe a small sigh of relief, and she cursed her weakness. What was it about him that made her lose herself? The way he casually dismissed her should have turned her off him, instead it only fueled her lust for him. She just didn't understand. She dared herself to steal a glance at him through her peripheral, and when she did she felt herself involuntarily shudder. His stern face showed no emotion, as if he were deep in thought. His dark eyes held no clue to his mood, and as she continued to sneak glances at him, she found herself licking her lips.

"Is something tempting you, my dear?" he asked, apparently noticing the action.

She searched her mind for something to say. "Not these days, no." Right after she said it, she regretted it. She quickly started to correct herself. "Not that—"

"I see you came back into my life right on time, darling. I can definitely be of service."

She heard the promise in his voice and knew she was treading on dangerous ground. For the rest of their car ride she remained silent, not daring herself to speak. The city passed by in a haze, and she barely registered the people on the sidewalk, blissfully oblivious to the trapped feeling she felt inside the powerful car.

When they arrived at their destination, she immediately recognized the name. She glanced at Dorian, astounded. Did he not realize where they were? Surely, it was a mistake.

"Neiman-Marcus? *This* is where you're taking me?" she asked, stunned. Already someone was appearing out of nowhere to park their car, a service reserved only for the VIP clientele.

"Yes. Is there a problem?" he asked, opening his door and handing the smiling gentleman his keys. He stepped out, not even waiting for her answer. Such arrogance would have been sickening on any other man, but for Dorian Johnston it fit like a glove. His overpowering masculinity somehow excused his character flaws, and every woman who found herself in his presence was lost. She knew that all too well.

As she stepped out of the car and into the chilled air of yet another dreary day, the weather reflected her mood. She couldn't believe he had brought her here, of all places. Looking up at the store's name in dramatic, slashed writing, she was suddenly taken back to a much happier time, when a small box with the same slashed writing on it was slid across a desk to her in the middle of a rainy night.

At the time, she had been delighted to receive something from the famous boutique. Had she known it would be a parting gift, she wouldn't have accepted the diamond earrings she found inside. Her mind began to vividly relive the memory in spite of herself.

She had sat down at the desk and simply looked at him for a time, sensing something was wrong. When he had quietly slid a small box to her without saying a word, she had smiled and opened it. Before she could thank him, she saw him take a preparatory breath and knew he was about to speak. She put the earrings in while he began.

"Look, Michelle, it's been fun, but I think our arrangement has run its course." She immediately thought he was firing her, but she soon realized it was something much more devastating. She had let her hands fall into her lap as she took in what was happening.

He was breaking it off. A ball of lead began to form in the pit of her stomach, and she was suddenly nauseous.

"I'm constantly moving from here to my other offices. I don't want to start anything long distance.

But I do hope your professionalism won't change, though."

She couldn't say anything. Her mouth couldn't even begin to form words that would explain how she felt. Piece by piece her world was crashing around her. She felt as though she were gasping for air, but couldn't seem to get enough oxygen. Instead, she had gotten up and slowly walked to the elevator, hoping the lift would not take long to arrive. By some magic it opened as soon as she pressed the button, and she kept her eyes downcast as she rode it down to the ground floor. She only hoped no one saw her tears as she hurried outside into the rain.

Bringing her mind back to the present, she barely registered Dorian was speaking to her. She steeled her rampant emotions and focused.

"What did you say?"

"I said, would you prefer somewhere else?" he asked impatiently. He was holding the door open for her, silently daring her to object. She quickly prepared herself for the battle of wills that was sure to come. She stepped forward and smiled sweetly, noticing his initial shock as he saw her changed mood. "No, thank you. I'm fine."

*****

Dorian couldn't believe where he was. And why was she smiling up at him like that? What did she have up her sleeve? In his life, he had learned not to trust women who put on pretty smiles to get their way. He had seen his share of them, using their beauty as a pawn in their ridiculous mind games. He sighed to himself. If only they knew it did them no good.

But Michelle was different.

From the moment she had stepped into his office, he had known she would not be like all the other women he'd let in his life. She was a brunette, for starters. He seemed to attract only blondes, and though he hated the stereotype, he couldn't argue that there was a reason for it. Ditsy, empty-headed, and always very flirtatious, they flocked to him in the hopes that they would snare him and his fortune. Michelle had been the complete opposite. She hadn't cared about his money, even before she had become his mistress. Working for him, she had challenged any foolish ideas he had—like putting an ugly fern by his desk—with a spirit that thrilled him. When she was passionate about something her face lit up, and he started making her laugh just to watch the glint in her eyes. He found himself starting to look forward to coming to work, just to engage her in conversation.

On the few occasions that they talked about something other than work, she was energetic, smart, and could hold her own in their conversation. It was a refreshing change from the men and women he dealt with all day, who were afraid to merely speak to him.

Gradually they began to talk more and more, until finally their topics had nothing to do with work. When he had made her his mistress, he was delighted—and pleasantly surprised—to learn that she was not interested in what he could give her, and often shunned the expensive gifts he bought her. So now, to see her smiling broadly as they walked into Neiman-Marcus was quite a change.

He held the door open for her and she walked in past him, filling his nostrils with her exquisitely feminine scent. The smell itself reminded him of the times he had inhaled her intoxicating aroma while she lay in his arms, thoroughly spent from their lovemaking. He smiled to himself and focused on the present. He heard Michelle gasp, and he turned to her.

"It's so big...how do you find anything?" she asked him. The boutique was open and airy, but still held a stuffy attitude that could only be accomplished by a large amount of rich people in one place.

He began to answer, then realized he honestly didn't know. Whenever he called in a favor from Andrew in the women's department, it would always be to have something sent over. Never once had he stepped inside, so he had no idea where they needed to go. Not wanting to look foolish, he directed her attention to a young woman sitting at a desk.

"Let's ask her," he said, taking her hand.

Her hand felt so warm in his, when they got to the desk he almost didn't let go. He finally did, and he noticed her quiet sigh. She was almost his, he knew it.

The redhead who sat behind the large wooden desk turned her attention to both of them. Dorian watched her assess Michelle's casual t-shirt and jeans, then turn her attention to him. She smiled a sweet smile.

"May I help you?" Her voice was dripping with practiced flirtation, and he was suddenly very annoyed. Did every woman try to use her looks to get what she wanted?

"No, you cannot. Andrew, however, can. Where is he?" he asked, putting as much authority in his voice as he could, and her tone quickly changed.

"I'll call him for you, sir. Your name?"

"Dorian Johnston. Tell him it's urgent."

Immediately her eyes widened, and she began to fumble over her hasty apology. "Mr. Johnston, please excuse me, I didn't realize it was you..." She trailed off as she lifted the receiver, punched a few numbers, and waited. After a moment, Dorian heard Andrew's voice on the other end, though he couldn't make out what he was saying. The woman at the desk spoke into the phone.

"Andrew, it's Jade. Dorian Johnston is here at the front desk for you. It's urgent. Ok, bye." She turned her attention back to the pair. "He'll be just a minute, Mr. Johnston. Sorry for the wait."

He laughed to himself at how quickly the mention of his name earned him total respect. Once people knew his name they became overly helpful, doing whatever he asked at the drop of a dime. He loved the power, but it almost always guaranteed no one was sincere.

He noticed that during the entire conversation Michelle remained quiet, and he couldn't tell by her expression what she was feeling. Standing beside him she seemed so vulnerable, and he had the urge to wrap his arms around her. Such a feeling was so alien to him, he had no idea where it had come from. The only woman he had ever wanted to protect was his mother, and in the end, it had done him no good. Before he had a chance to delve into hurtful memories of his past, however, his attention was drawn to a flamboyant man strolling toward them.

He was power walking, holding his arms stiffly by his sides in excitement as he approached them with a smile. Tall and thin, his immaculate black pinstripe suit hung on him as though it were still on the hanger. He had accented it with a peach-colored shirt and black tie, everything color-coordinated flawlessly, and his diamond cufflinks sparkled in the light as he came closer. His jet-black hair—complete with subtle blond highlights—was cut in a fashionable short style, falling in angular pieces. Altogether, he looked like a Vogue spread; and appeared completely comfortable in his surroundings.

"Mr. Johnston! I see you've finally climbed out of that stuffy old office. And who is this?" He took Michelle's hand and kissed it, and a smile spread across her face.

"I'm Michelle," she answered for him, and Dorian made the introduction. "Michelle, this is Andrew, my consultant. He—"

"I help him find the right thing, whether it be a diamond or a dress," Andrew interjected. "Has anyone ever told you that you have the darkest eyes they've ever seen?"

Andrew was right. Her eyes were like velvety pools, endless black lakes that threatened to consume whoever drew too near. It was the first thing he had noticed about her, and his favorite feature. When she was happy, they twinkled like stars against the backdrop of a midnight sky. When he was bringing her to heights of intense pleasure, however, they glistened like uncut onyx. He had never seen such eyes, and they constantly mesmerized him. She blushed slightly at Andrew's compliment, and her eyes sparkled.

"Yes, actually, a couple of times," she sweetly replied.

"Well, you do. So, what's the occasion?"

"Business dinner with clients, Andrew. Make it classy yet seductive."

He needed his clients at least comprehensive during dinner, not transfixed by Michelle's amazing figure. He saw Andrew's face morph into deep concentration, then he took Michelle's hand and led her away. He spoke over his shoulder to Dorian.

"Find a seat, Mr. Johnston. It's gonna be a while."

Dorian smirked, and suddenly he was hungrier than he'd ever been.

*****

"I think black and strapless for you, missy. To go with those gorgeous eyes of yours. You're lucky we have a salon on-site, or you'd be in a world of trouble! You can't be on the arm of Dorian Johnston looking like this!" Andrew said to her. He was leading her through lines of clothes and deeper into the store, and she felt almost like a rat being led in a maze. She felt completely out of place, and not even Andrew's reassuring tone could soothe her as she tried to keep up with his rapid gait in her flip-flops.

Once again Dorian Johnston, with his sheer, raw masculinity and power, had come into her life and caused a typhoon of her senses, driving her to the point where she gave up her freewill. She knew in her heart that he could probably make her do whatever he wanted without saying a complete sentence, and that thought sickened her. He seemed to embed himself in every part of her being, causing chaos all the way down to her soul. No matter how hard she tried, she just couldn't seem to get him out of her system; he flowed into her like a powerful river that couldn't be kept at bay. He invaded even the smallest crevices of her soul, and knowing that he'd fathered her children only made the feeling stronger.

She realized Andrew had stopped walking, and they were standing in the section designated for evening gowns. All around her were swirls of exotic colors, and she was sure that just one of the gorgeous gowns would cost her a few months' rent. As she looked around, the names of famous designers popped out at her. Jason Wu, Chanel, Versace, Vera Wang, Balenciaga…each exquisite gown more and more expensive. She didn't understand how people lived so lavishly; people who were able to get whatever they wanted when they waved their money around. She thought of Dorian. It was exactly the kind of man that he was. Whenever he had a problem, he simply threw money at it until it went away. He blew the equivalent of what she paid in rent for a year on trinkets and baubles for his slew of women, while she had to scrape every penny just to keep two hungry, growing toddlers fed and clothed.

Somewhere in the back of her mind, she held a deep-seated anger at Dorian for not being present in her sons' lives, but her logic reminded her that it wasn't entirely his fault. She had tried to contact him for a couple months but after so many dodges she had given up, so it wasn't as though he had neglected them, he simply—a thought struck her. He had no idea he had fathered two beautiful boys; how was she going to keep that from him? If he did win their battle of wills, he would take her to bed and surely he would find out; he wouldn't be able to miss her C-section scar, a telltale sign of her pregnancy. Deep down inside she knew he would either win or she would surrender, and a cold chill of anticipation traveled all the way down her spine. So, she would have to find a way to stop him from examining her too closely. But even as she thought it, she knew it would probably be impossible.

She focused her attention back to Andrew, who was thumbing through a rack of gowns. He was mumbling something to himself, and as she stepped closer, she could make out what he was saying.

"Where are you…where are you…just saw it yesterday…come on—aha! Found it!" He looked at her. "What are you, a fourteen?"

She was amazed. "Yes, how did you know?"

"Girl, please. I make it my business to know." He flicked through a few more until he found the gown in her size, then pulled it from the others. Black, strapless, and utterly gorgeous, Michelle took it in for a moment before taking it from Andrew's outstretched arms. It hung to the floor in a smooth material that she was sure would hug her curves, but the hemline did not stay there. It shot back up the leg in a daring thigh-high split, and for a moment she wondered if she had the legs to pull it off. The neckline did not stay in one place, either; it dropped sinfully down in a thin slit, to show a glimmer of cleavage instead of an eyeful. Near the top a white streak started, one that coiled around the dress from the neckline down to the hem. It gave it a bold, daring look, and Michelle was ready to try it on even before Andrew spoke.

"I thought it might make the subtle shimmer in your eyes pop, having two contrasting colors." He came closer to look over it, and she could see he was truly in his element. "It's from Vera Wang's new collection; we just got it in last week. Let's try it on!"

Michelle moved as if to look for a dressing room, but Andrew spoke quickly.

"Um, wait. What do you have on underneath there?" he asked, motioning toward her jeans and t-shirt. Had it been any other man asking her the same question, she would have slapped him. But somehow she had a feeling he wasn't interested. She looked down, and was quickly reminded of how out of place she looked.

"A bra and panties, why?"

He scoffed. "That's it? Honey, please. We need to put you in some *lingerie*." He roamed his eyes over her, paused to think for a moment, then excitedly said, "stay here, I'll be back in a jiff."

She watched him speed off, and turned to look at herself in a nearby full-length mirror. The woman who stared back dismally at her was not the woman she saw every morning. That woman was strong-willed, determined, and full of perseverance when it came to overcoming obstacles. The woman she looked at now was but a shadow of her true self. All of her freewill had been snatched away by a man who cared nothing for her. How in the world she had ended up in front of a mirror at Neiman-Marcus was unbelievable to her.

Andrew's reappearance snapped her out of her reflective trance. "Ok, when you try the dress on, take these with you." He handed her a black lace bra and panty set, something she never would have bought for herself. The panties were boy shorts made of sheer lace, with a small black bow perched in the middle of the front of it, adorned with a single pearl. The half bra that accompanied was also made of the same lace, with only an underwire for support.

Out of habit from years of watching every penny, she started to look at the price tag. Quickly Andrew spoke up.

"Oh no you don't! Don't worry about how much it is. You're not paying for it, remember?"

A thought struck her. For once, money was not an issue. A strange feeling began to percolate through her. She wondered if the way she was feeling was the same as Dorian's other mistresses; the feeling of having unlimited funds at her disposal was quite thrilling once she let it sink in. What a liberating feeling, indeed. She decided to stop worrying and have fun. She smiled, and Andrew was instantly excited.

"See, there you go!" He looked at his watch, and his eyes widened. "Oh my goodness! It's already two o'clock! Ok, hurry and try on your dress, but trust me, it's gonna look great. We still have to find you some shoes, do your nails, AND hair and makeup. It's gonna be cutting it close, but here goes nothing!"

Chapter 4

For what seemed like the millionth time, Dorian looked at his watch. What were they doing? He didn't have time for this. He needed to be prompt with the Armattis if he wanted to buy them out, and he didn't have time to wait for—

An exquisite beauty coming towards him derailed his train of thought. She floated forward as though she walked on air, and his breath caught in his throat for a moment. He briefly contemplated introducing himself until she met his gaze and smiled, and he then instantly recognized the glint in her eyes. But when had Michelle transformed? She looked like a vision from an exotic dream, with her dark hair cascading around her shoulders in bouncy curls. He never noticed how long and luxurious it was, since she always kept it pulled back. But seeing it loose, he vowed to never let her put it up again.

The black dress that she wore deliciously accentuated every curve she had from her beautiful breasts to her hips, then stopped at her waist to fall straight to the floor. When she shifted he caught a glimpse of leg, and he prayed that she would cross her legs during dinner. Andrew came from behind her and stood beside him, looking thoroughly pleased with himself.

"Nice, huh? The dress was my idea."

"Very nice indeed, Andrew, how can I ever repay you?"

"With a check, plastic, or cash. Oh, we'll be sending you the bill." Andrew laughed heartily, gave Michelle a quick hug, and then strolled off, saying, "God, I'm good!"

Dorian watched Michelle smile and shake her head, then he offered his arm. "Shall we?"

After a moment's hesitation, she looped her arm through his. "I suppose," she said, and together they stepped outside into the chilly evening air.

As he closed Michelle's door and walked around his car to get in, he glanced at his watch. If he applied a little creative driving, he could get to the restaurant with some time to spare. As he slid inside his car, he felt Michelle put her hand on his knee. The spark he felt as she touched him electrified him all the way down to his loins, and he tried to slow his heartbeat as she began to speak.

"Thanks for everything, Dorian. Really. That's the most fun I've had since…well, I can't remember."

He noticed her hesitation and was tempted to investigate further, but he had no time to delve into her personal life. So he offered a quick "you're welcome" and sped off.

During the entire ride she stayed silent, simply looking out the window at the rapidly-filling streets of New York. Had she not been breathing, he would have forgotten she was there. He didn't like the silence, but he wasn't sure what to say to fill it. He finally opted for the obvious.

"You look beautiful."

She looked down, as if she didn't believe it herself. "Thank you. Andrew did everything. I just stood there."

"He did a wonderful job. Now, just be your beautiful self at dinner and we'll be in business."

"Got it."

He watched her turn back to the window and sigh deeply, making her breasts rise and fall. Just that small movement drove him almost mad with need, and he vowed to take her that night. Waiting be damned. He had to have her or he was going to explode.

Although he did feel a little guilty for taking her freewill away so harshly, he had to keep control. He wanted things his way; it was how he had always been, and people close to him knew it. Even if it did portray him in a negative light sometimes, no one could argue that it got the job done.

They pulled up in front of Masa, a Japanese restaurant where he often took his clients. The fine dining and Zen-like ambience seemed to win people over as much as his charm and smooth words. As he put the car in park, he stole a glance at his watch for the umpteenth time that day. Unbelievably, they had still made it on time, and he smiled as he handed the valet his keys. A smiling man was opening Michelle's door for her, and Dorian watched her smooth, fluid movements as she took his outstretched hand and slid out. She had legs that seemed to go on forever, and he was so grateful Andrew had chosen a dress that showed them off.

As he came around the car to offer Michelle his arm, their eyes locked for a moment and his mouth became suddenly dry. She was looking at him with a bit of lust in her eyes, as if she also knew what was inevitable between them. He recognized the same feeling in himself and smiled knowingly as he gently took her hand in the crook of his elbow. He noticed she looked a bit nervous, so he dipped his mouth to her ear and whispered, "don't worry. You look stunning. Just be yourself." He saw her shoulders slightly relax, and he ushered them inside.

A tuxedo-clad man waited at a podium by the door, looking down at his reservation book. He looked up as he began to speak, but Dorian knew he would not need to give his name.

"Reservation, please—Mr. Johnston! How good to see you again. Your table is ready, sir." He looked over his shoulder and snapped his fingers twice, and a waiter immediately appeared to usher them to their table. He could feel Michelle smiling beside him, and he noticed that every table they passed had at least one man who was grinning back at her. He liked that feeling, knowing that others wanted what he possessed. And even though she wasn't a powerful sports car or a valuable piece of real estate, she was still his.

No matter how hard she tried to deny it.

He looked over at her as the waiter pulled out her chair; how she smiled and thanked him gracefully as she sat. Her movements were so effortless, almost like a dance, making him transfixed. She did not know it yet, but he would soon make their undeniable attraction very clear. Then, when the time was right, he would ask her to be his mistress again for an undisclosed amount of time. He smiled to himself at that. He was quite ready to get her out of his system, no matter how long it took to accomplish that feat.

As he finally sat, the waiter spoke up. "Shall we start the evening off with a bottle of wine or something from the menu as we wait for your guests to arrive?" He indicated toward four flat menus on the table, and he saw Michelle pick one up and her eyes widen. Having frequented the establishment, he already knew what he wanted.

"A bottle of your 84 Haut Brion La Mission, please. Chilled. As well as the Masa toro rolls with caviar, to start." Out of the corner of his eye he watched Michelle scan the menu, apparently looking for what he had ordered.

"An excellent choice, sir. I'll return momentarily with your wine." The waiter hurried off, and Michelle leaned towards him.

"That's a three-thousand dollar bottle of wine!" she whispered. "Why does it have to be so expensive?" He took a moment to stare at her cleavage before grazing the back of his hand over her cheek. He noticed the small flush in her dimples.

"I accept nothing but the best," he told her.

"Well, aren't you two cozy?" a voice boomed from behind them. Dorian turned to see the Armatti brothers, Marco and Joseph, walking towards them. It was Joseph who had spoken, and Dorian stood to accept his handshake. He shook Marco's hand as well, then stepped to the side and put his hand on the small of Michelle's back. She stood and smiled as both men took one of her hands and kissed it.

"This is a dear friend, Michelle, I've asked her to join us. Michelle, these are the Armatti brothers, Marco and Joseph," he informed her, and she beamed up at them, clearly working her charm on his behalf.

"Pleased to meet you," she said sweetly.

Marco spoke first. "The pleasure is entirely mine, dear."

In an unexpected bolt of wit, Michelle replied, "now, don't keep all the pleasure for yourself, Mr. Armatti. That wouldn't be fair." Dorian noticed the subtle flirtation in her voice, and he could almost feel the evening ending well. He made a mental note to repay her the first chance he got.

"A little spitfire you got here, Johnston. Might wanna hold on to this one. She may teach you a thing or two."

Besides both being Italian, the Armattis were two very different men. While Marco was tall and slender, Joseph was a bit shorter and stocky. They both were intelligent men, but Joseph had a habit of making rash, impulsive decisions that put their family-owned bank in trouble.

They both wore black suits, but Marco wore a blue sweater vest underneath while Joseph had opted for a traditional white shirt and black tie. They both sat, and their waiter appeared to pour them all a glass of wine. He left the bottle in a bucket beside the table, set the caviar rolls in front of them, and addressed the entire party.

"Now that you've all arrived, are we ready to order?"

Marco and Joseph lifted their menus, but Dorian was ready with his usual. "I'll have the wagyu beef tataki, with black truffle fried rice." Sensing that Michelle might not know what to order, he began to order for her as well. But before he could open his mouth, Michelle spoke.

"I'll have the barbeque lamb, with calamari and mushroom fried rice."

Michelle looked over at him. As Marco and Joseph gave their orders she leaned into his ear, her breath sending electrical pulses throughout his body.

"What, you thought I was gonna let you order something for me? I'm not completely helpless." She sat back in her seat, smiling, and he suddenly remembered why he had made her his mistress in the first place. It was her fiery spirit, her passion. He knew that although a tiny flame may show on the surface, a mighty conflagration roared just beneath. All he needed was the right spark to set her aflame.

"Yes, ma'am," he said jokingly, and turned his attention to the Armattis. Joseph spoke first, addressing Michelle.

"So, do you belong to this man, young lady?" he asked bluntly, and Dorian felt a momentary surge of protectiveness over her, as if he blamed himself for not warning her about Joseph Armatti's complete lack of tact. But Michelle didn't miss a beat.

"I belong to no man, Mr. Armatti. But he does have a certain charm that makes it fortuitous to keep him around."

Joseph was surprised and so was Dorian, something that didn't happen too often.

"Ha! I like this one!" Marco said, joining the conversation. He put his forearms on the table and leaned intently toward Michelle, and Dorian could only imagine what was about to come out of his mouth. He braced himself.

"So," he began, pointing at Dorian, "why should my brother and I go into business with your friend here? I've already heard all he has to say, maybe a third party can convince me."

Dorian's heart skipped at least three beats. She did not know it, but the fate of a billion-dollar deal had just been placed squarely in her beautiful lap. He only hoped he would not regret what she was about to say. Michelle sighed.

"May I be frank with you, Mr. Armatti?"

"I wish you would. And please, call me Marco."

"You wouldn't be considering a partnership unless you were at the end of your rope. Frankly, you're dealing with one of the sharpest financial minds in the world. I mean, seriously, who else are you going to call? Rockefeller and Simpson are dead."

Dorian's brain could not comprehend what he had heard. How had she come up with that brilliant response so fast? Not only had she answered the question beautifully, she had even worked in a compliment for him. God, she was good. Without a word from him, she had basically sealed his deal. Paired with Joseph's next words, he didn't have a doubt.

"I couldn't have said it better myself. I like how you think, missy! We could use a dozen just like you! You ever consider a career in banking, Michelle?"

"Actually, I'm an interior decorator."

"A damn good one, too," Dorian spoke up, wanting to have at least some part of the conversation. He also wanted to thank her for her amazing performance, even if it was just that: a performance. She certainly was working hard for that blank check. He returned his mind to the conversation.

"An interior decorator, eh? You got any experience with banks?" Marco asked.

"No banks, but offices are my specialty," Michelle replied, casting an eye at Dorian, and he smirked.

"Well, I'll have to keep you in mind, young lady," Marco said, then addressed his attention to Dorian. "Well, that settles it, Mr. Johnston." He extended his hand, and Dorian almost couldn't believe what was happening. He reached out and firmly clasped Marco's hand. "I'm sold. I'd be happy to go into a partnership with you."

Dorian couldn't have smiled harder if his mouth was made out of elastic. One of his largest business deals had also been his easiest, and already he couldn't wait to get Michelle back to the hotel room and properly thank her. He shook Joseph's hand as well, and a waiter returned with their trays of food. He watched Michelle breathe in the aroma, before picking up her fork and digging in. She took a bite, chewed, and swallowed it, and only then did she notice he was watching her. Her cheeks flushed and she smiled, making her eyes twinkle.

He couldn't wait to find out what the next two weeks had in store.

*****

Michelle breathed a sigh of relief as she sat back on the leather seat. The evening had gone so well; she could hardly believe it. The things that had managed to come out of her mouth had shocked even her, and she was so glad she had made Dorian look good. Even though she knew it could not be true, she felt almost as though she belonged there, by his side. Somehow she naturally seemed to complement him, as if she was made for no other purpose. As soon as the thought crossed her mind, however, she shunned it. She was there for only one reason, and she had to remember that. She couldn't go getting emotionally attached to something that would only last two weeks. She turned her attention outside the window and watched the landscape go by, and she began to get lost in her own thoughts when Dorian cleared his throat.

"You were amazing tonight, really," he said, not taking his eyes off the road. "Where did you get a wit like that? I've never seen anything like it," he said, sounding impressed. Michelle laughed to herself. Impressed? Ha. Probably shocked was more like it. She tried to think of a particular source. Growing up she had simply used it to deflect her tough emotions, but she wasn't about to let him know that. The less he knew about her life, the better.

"It came naturally, I guess," she finally decided on. "Glad it got you your deal," she added at the last minute, and let it sit in the air for a moment.

"Oh, I would've sealed the deal without you," he said matter-of-factly, "but you helped."

Instantly her pride was shattered. So, her presence had not made a difference, after all. Either that, or he simply did not want her to think she was important to him. Perhaps he didn't want her to get a big head and start making demands. Well, there was no chance she was going to do that! She quickly changed the subject.

"I can't wait to get back to the room and climb into bed," she said, yawning. As soon as she said it, she began to regret it. But before she could start to correct herself, Dorian quickly spoke.

"Oh, is that right?" he questioned, looking at her out the corner of his eye. She saw one dimple rise, and she knew he was smirking.

"I didn't mean it like that," she offered, too late.

"Oh come on now, Michelle. Why are you denying what we both know is fast approaching? You cannot fight me forever." He said it with no doubt in his voice, as if he had just sealed her fate. She couldn't believe it, but she actually began to consider the possibility that it *could* happen. That it *would* probably happen. The thought alone shook her all the way down to her stiletto-clad toes. But she couldn't let him know that. She had to stay in control of her emotions if she was going to survive the next two weeks with any dignity left. She swallowed hard before she spoke.

"We'll see where things go," she slowly said, not daring to meet his eyes.

"I suppose we shall," he replied, turning smoothly into the hotel's entrance. He handed the waiting valet his keys, then walked around to open Michelle's door. She took his hand, and noticed the heat that passed between them. But she didn't say anything, lest he act upon the feelings she was sure he was experiencing as well. She didn't want to give him a head start to the inevitable finish; he already had too much ground as it was.

The walk to the elevator was intensely quiet, and as he pressed the 'up' button, Michelle felt her stomach involuntarily tighten with anticipation. She already knew what was coming but did not want to admit it to herself, as if she felt more denial would suppress her stomach's somersaulting butterflies. The ride up seemed to take forever, slowly leading her to her fate. She tried to walk to the doors of the room as slowly as she could, but she seemed to almost sprint to the glossy wooden doors of her suite. She only hoped Dorian had not noticed.

"Excited, are we?" he said, sliding the key into the lock. She chose not to respond, but simply breezed past him and went towards her bathroom. He did not follow her but went downstairs to his suite instead, and she found she was a bit disappointed. Instead of moping, however, she slowly unzipped her dress and let it fall to the floor in an expensive heap. She sat down on the edge of her bed and bent over to take off her shoes, when she heard a quiet shuffling noise. Her breath caught in her throat as she realized what it was. She hoped he did not notice how eerily still she had become, but his smooth words to her proved she was wrong.

"Don't let me disturb you," he purred at her, and she felt a shiver go down her spine. "I just came up to say goodnight. But I see you were expecting me."

She tried to calm the flush in her cheeks as she sat up. She nervously cleared her throat. "Actually, I was heading to bed. So, goodnight." She turned off the light, hoping that it would suffice, but she was mistaken.

"Look, we need to talk," he said, coming to sit beside her on the bed. Luckily, he chose not to sit too close to her, or she would have had to scoot over. She wasn't sure she could trust herself to feel his body against hers, not with the way she was already feeling. The tension flowing between them was almost unbearable; she could hardly stand it.

"We've been dancing around the issue, my dear," he almost whispered, putting a stray piece of hair behind her ear. The simple motion nearly undid her, and she was almost panting when Dorian's lips claimed hers.

Her mind exploded in a wave of emotions. She had forgotten how good he felt, how naturally their lips fit together. It was as though the final decisive piece of her puzzle had been clicked into place. She inhaled his scent; his masculine aroma intoxicated her senses. The world seemed to evaporate as their kiss deepened, becoming hungrier and more desperate. When her mouth parted to receive his eager awaiting tongue, their passion intensified.

    He slowly tilted her back onto the bed, guiding her with his hand on the nape of her neck. As her head hit the soft comforter, she felt Dorian slide his hand down her stomach. He did not take his eyes off her as he hooked a thumb in her panties and softly tugged. "Take these off," he whispered in her ear, but she was not about to allow him to have her that easily. She softly shook her head.

    "You do it," she pouted, running her fingers lightly over his chest. The instant darkening in his eyes gave her the satisfaction she had sought. He slowly moved over her, taking one side of the sheer lace that covered her femininity in each of his hands. She shivered a bit involuntarily, and he kissed both thighs as he hooked the flimsy material off her one remaining shoe.

    She couldn't quite put words into the intense feelings that were running through her, both physically and emotionally. She had not felt a man's touch since he had had her in his bed so long ago, and her body was starving to have more of him pressed against her; buried inside her. She ran her fingers through his hair as he traced his hands up her sides, finally bringing his lips up to meet hers again. Before she could urge him on further, a strange buzzing sound halted her movements. She felt Dorian tense, then breathe a heavy sigh and reach for the case on his belt to answer his phone. He put a finger up and mouthed, "don't move."

    He got up and walked across the room to take the call, and she took the opportunity to compose herself and slowly slide under the covers. She was shaking from the sheer, raw emotion she was feeling. She had practically begged him to take her, and she couldn't believe how she had acted. It was completely out of character for her; she would never have thrown herself at any other man. But something about Dorian Johnston made her lose all sense of self, as though he dictated the very path of her soul. By the time he turned around to speak to her, she had collected herself.

    "That was the office. Just need to finish some last-minute paperwork before the start of business tomorrow. It shouldn't take long. When I get back, you'll be the first to know."

    She tried to appear unaffected, as though she was left in billionaires' hotel rooms on a daily basis. "That's fine," she said, putting her head on the pillow and closing her eyes. She was nowhere near sleepy, but she hoped the gesture would shut him out. It did, and she heard him head downstairs, gather his things, and leave. She waited until she heard the elevator doors close before turning on the light, walking over to her suitcase and taking out her schoolbooks. If she was going to be awake, she was at least going to be productive.

*****

Dorian swung his powerful car into the parking structure. Usually he did not park his own car, but he didn't feel like waiting for the after-hours valet. As he turned each corner to climb higher and higher into the parking deck, he tried to calm the heat searing in his loins. At least now he was certain that Michelle reciprocated his feelings, so the next opportunity he got he knew she would come to him willingly. She seemed to get deep under his skin every time he was near her, as if she had a permanent place in his physical memory. No matter how hard he tried he could not get her out of his system, but he looked forward to trying. The thought made him smile as he stepped into the elevator to his office, and he was grinning by the time the doors slid open on the top floor of his building. He reached his desk, then reached for the phone receiver and dialed his father's number. When he answered, Dorian immediately got down to business.

"What is going on? Why am I getting frantic calls from Gwen talking about how the McAnderson contract is incomplete?" he questioned, turning on his laptop.

Gwen, his personal assistant, had been in his employ about five years, and she played a vital role in his office. He had hired her because of her impeccable organizational skills as well as her glowing references, and after he had established she'd never sleep with him (on his first flirtation attempt she had quickly shut him down, proudly stating she was happily married), they had settled into quite a comfortable friendship. Without her, he'd never be able to keep his appointments straight, and he had never missed one thanks to her. She probably knew more about him than he cared for, but he didn't mind. Her confidentiality—or her loyalty, for that matter—had never come into question. And even though she was eight months pregnant and as big as a house, her productivity had never slowed—no matter how many times he had told her to.

As he put in his password, his father began to explain. "Well, Thomas McAnderson is claiming that since he's missing some documents in the partnership agreement, the contract will be null and void if you're not at the next board meeting here to discuss things with him. He won't sign off on it unless you're here, in person."

Dorian should've known the McAndersons would try to weasel their way out of the deal. When his takeover of them four months ago had become hostile, they had tried everything to renege and back out of their contract. He could have expected they would try a stunt as outrageous. He would not let them get the upper hand. He printed off the McAnderson file and put it in his briefcase.

"When is the board meeting?" he asked, already beginning to get ready to leave.

"Friday," his father responded.

"I can be there tomorrow afternoon," he replied, anxious to get off the phone and back to a certain beautiful woman waiting for him in his hotel room. His father derailed his train of thought.

"We still need to talk, young man. Fiancée?" he said, reminding Dorian of why Michelle was there in the first place.

He didn't miss a beat. "Later. Bye, dad." He hung up the phone and sat back down at his desk for a moment. Looking around his office, he realized Michelle had placed everything there, in some way. Her presence resonated in every corner of the entire floor, and he concluded that she was quite talented. Whenever the stresses of the day got to him, he retreated to his office; it gave him peace in his chaotic world. Somehow, he knew Michelle had designed it to be that way.

He couldn't wait any longer; he had to get back to her. He missed her touch so much he was aching for the feel of her hands on his skin, and when he got inside the elevator, he was almost shaking with longing. What on earth was she doing to him? The sooner he had her under him, the better. He couldn't wait until he was plowing inside her sweet warmth, re-familiarizing himself with her every curve. His mind could only think of her as he navigated his way to the hotel, and he found himself almost running to the elevators when he had finally gotten back.

When he reached his floor and his room at last, it seemed he could not get upstairs fast enough. Every step seemed to be a mountain he had to trek just to get what he wanted, but he hopped up each one like a skilled Everest climber. But before he could take full advantage of his boundless energy, a sight stilled him in his tracks.

Lying on the bed, under the covers, surrounded by books and paperwork, was Michelle. She looked like a vision, so peaceful, as though she had been painted by Da Vinci himself. He knew what lay just beneath the sheets; the soft, curvaceous piece of Heaven between her thighs was mere feet away. But his curiosity was piqued by the things that surrounded her, and he quietly tiptoed to the bed and picked up the large textbook that lay spread open in front of her.

"Business Management," he read the title aloud.

She was taking a class on business management? He had not known she was interested in a degree in business, nor had he known she had been actively pursuing it. He put the heavy textbook on the table beside the bed and began to pick up the papers individually, examining them. They were past tests, as if she were preparing herself for a final exam of some sort. As he was looking over them, he noticed that a bright red 'A' was placed neatly in the top right corner of every page. He looked over at Michelle, who was still sleeping peacefully. It was hard to believe that beneath her exquisite beauty lay an intelligence that was just as remarkable.

He gathered the papers in a pile, placed them on top of her textbook, gave her a soft kiss on the forehead, and headed downstairs to pour himself a drink. As he filled a crystal tumbler with scotch and took a seat on the couch, he let his mind wander.

During the four months he had taken her to bed over and over again, he had never even inquired about her life. He had no idea about her hopes, her dreams, her aspirations; in a stark realization he concluded he knew almost nothing about her. He had navigated his way through her most intimate of crevices, yet he knew nearly nothing about her as a person. In the times they had talked she hadn't brought up anything about herself; it was a major difference from the overly-chatty blondes he seemed to attract, who prattled on and on endlessly about themselves non-stop.

He looked into his glass, and did not realize he had finished off his drink. Closing his eyes, he leaned his head back on the couch. How had he nearly fallen for a woman he knew almost nothing about? He let the thought sink in. If he wanted her to be connected with him fully when he reacquainted her to the passion of their lovemaking, he would have to learn at least a little something about her besides how she liked to be caressed.

He stood to pour himself another drink. He made a promise to himself that he would take more interest in her personal life, starting with their trip to London in the morning. With a new resolve and a powerful new outlook, he downed his drink and made his way to his bed. But as he looked at the oversized bed with its warm, inviting covers, he noticed it seemed horribly empty. Without a second thought, he headed back upstairs to where Michelle lay.

She was still in the same position she had been in when he had left, and he took a moment to simply look at her. She truly was a remarkable sight. The soft light from her bedside lamp cast a warm glow over her face, making it appear golden and angelic. Her full, long lashes lay in sooty fans across her dimples, and her lips came together in a slumberous pout. But he knew underneath that heavenly exterior lay a tigress waiting to be unleashed. He only had to open the cage.

    He never quite understood why he pursued her ruthlessly. With every smile, every light laugh, she got deeper and deeper into his system and he knew soon it would take even more and more to fully get her out of it. But he had to stay in control, or risk another...no, he was not even going to think of it. His beautiful Michelle could not have a deceitful bone in her body. She was only in her predicament because misfortune had befallen her; otherwise, he reckoned she would have gone on with her life.

    With that thought, he pulled back the covers from her voluptuous form, noticing her involuntarily shudder from the sudden coldness. Before it could wake her up, however, he scooped her into his arms. He noticed how easily she snuggled into his chest, and he had to mentally stop himself from rousing her awake the best way he knew how. He did not want her forced under him, in no way. With personal restraint he did not know he possessed, he turned and carefully started down the stairs. As he got to solid ground, she slightly stretched and put her arms around his neck, an action that nearly undid him. He quickly closed the gap between him and the bed, and lay her softly down on one of the pillows. She sighed in her sleep as she settled down into it, and Dorian stripped down to his boxers and slid beside her. He wrapped his arm around her and pulled her into him, inhaling her scent. A strange feeling washed over him, a familiarity that caught him by surprise. He felt almost as though she belonged there, encased in his arms, as if he'd wrapped himself around her every night. The way she naturally curled into his body, so at ease...she almost seemed to fit. Her soft curves against him triggered an expected reaction, and he pressed the blatant evidence of his arousal against her. His breath stilled as she snuggled back into him, and he planted a soft kiss on her earlobe before finally drifting off to sleep.

*****

Michelle awakened to a strange feeling of elation in the pit of her stomach. She hadn't slept so soundly in a long time, and felt as though something had kept her safe throughout the night. When she opened her eyes and stretched, however, she did not recognize her surroundings. With a shock she realized she was in Dorian's bedroom, and she quickly sat up. Upon realizing he was not there, she relaxed a bit and began to think.

How had she gotten downstairs? She remembered falling asleep upstairs, so the only way she could've gotten to where she presently sat...no. Had Dorian actually sought her out, picked her up, and brought her to his bed? It was the only logical explanation, yet it didn't make any sense at all. Why had her presence mattered that much to him? Refusing to let herself think she was more important than she knew she actually was, she concluded it must have been for a more physical reason. But they had not had sex, that she knew for a fact. She could never sleep through Dorian Johnston's lovemaking.

With her mind still wrestling, she lay back on the soft pillows. But before she could let her mind truly duke it out amongst itself, she noticed a crisp white card folded in half on the bedside table. Slowly she reached out and picked it up, reading the sprawling handwriting inked in black. The words formed a heavy lead ball in the pit of her stomach.

I've had Andrew send some clothes over, with luggage. Pack your things. We leave for London as soon as I get back.

D.

She gasped. He didn't even have the decency to sign his full name as he dictated her life! She threw off the covers and stood up, furious. She knew this moment was coming, she just didn't think he'd tell her so impersonally or so matter-of-factly. And what did he mean by Andrew sending some clothes over? She looked over at the clock. It was only a little after nine; how had he gotten all that done so early in the morning? But even as she thought it, she answered herself. *Because he's Dorian Johnston. Plain and simple.* She picked up the card and re-read it. It truly brought home the lowliness of their relationship, if it could be called that. In just a few short sentences, he had solidified her inferiority to him. The realization hit her as if Dorian had thrown it at her himself. But what choice did she have? She had to see this through, or she was never going to be able to support two little boys who needed her. With a sigh of resignation, she headed upstairs.

As her foot touched the top stair, what she saw before her was unlike anything she had ever seen. Boxes upon boxes were stacked around the bed, all with familiar black writing on top. On the bed were two open suitcases, as if someone had known she'd be needing them. She made a promise to send Andrew a thank you card.

Upon opening a large rectangular box and finding a full outfit inside, she concluded that the rest of the identical white boxes must hold the same thing. As she opened another one to find linen khakis and a purple halter, her theory was confirmed. In his utter brilliance, Andrew had also included shoes and accessories, and she almost squealed as she examined each box. She slowly counted them. Fifteen in all. How was she going to fit such a massive amount of clothes into two suitcases?

As she crossed to the other side of the bed she noticed three more large suitcases, as well as three larger black boxes with a Versace emblem spread across each. Lord, what had Andrew gone and done? She carefully lifted the lid off the top box.

Opening the white tissue paper delicately, she saw a pool of midnight blue fabric. She set the box on the bed and lifted it out, in awe of the beautiful creation. A halter dress, it had miniscule straps that looped around the neck. In the middle of the neckline sat a beautiful circular diamond broach that sparkled from the sun coming in through the windows. As far as she could tell, the dress looked pretty form fitting until it reached the hips, where it fanned out. Knowing she did not have time to examine what she was sure were two other equally beautiful gowns she began to pack.

Miraculously all the clothes fit into the luggage, and she still had room to pack her toiletries and schoolbooks. As she was placing the last bag by the door she heard the key slide in the lock, and her heart fluttered. God, why was she getting this way about a man who didn't care for her? She wore the jeans and tank top she had changed into after he had left the night before, but she still found herself smoothing back her hair quickly before the door opened.

The door seemed to open forever, then with a devastating smile he was there. It almost felt like days since she had seen him, and she found herself almost longing to touch his hand as it sat perched on the doorknob. His initial smile turned serious as her surveyed her.

"Good, you've packed. I am so glad you're not one of those women who takes forever to pack, especially with the extensive choices Andrew provided you," he said, closing the door behind him and coming towards her. He moved with the powerful grace of a hunting lion, and she felt almost like prey as he quickly closed the gap between them and raised his hand to trace a single finger down her cheek. She briefly closed her eyes, and her breath came out less steady than she would have liked. The small notion put a smile on his face, and he removed his hand to look at his watch.

"Ugh, I did not realize what time it was. I already had my bags sent to the plane this morning. I would have been here when you woke up, but I had an emergency meeting with my staff at the office." He called the front desk to have a luggage trolley sent up, and a thought struck her.

"Sent to what plane?" she inquired, sure she had heard wrong.

"Mine, of course," he chuckled.

So, she had heard right, after all. Although, she supposed she should have known a powerful businessman like Dorian Johnston would need his own transportation to and from continents at will. She swallowed the sudden lump in her throat, and proceeded to ask her next question.

"Where is it?"

"Oh, I keep a Boeing grounded at Kennedy at all times," he said, as if he were talking about keeping a spare pen on hand.

"Is it yours? And don't they mind, you parking your plane there?" she questioned.

"Of course it's mine. Even has the company logo on it. And I pay the airport for the space, as well as use of their command center." There was a brief knock on the door, and Dorian went to open it. The baggage carrier that loaded their suitcases smiled excessively, as if begging for a good tip. Knowing she had nothing to give him, she smiled sweetly and slipped on the flip-flops she had left by the door. She walked out into the hallway with Dorian close behind, and she almost jumped as he reached around her to press the down button.

The closeness of him, the feel of his chest against her back, sent waves through her. She crossed her arms quickly in front of her to hide the fact that her nipples had gotten hard, and was relieved when the elevator doors opened so she could put some distance between them. She hurriedly stepped inside, desperately trying to get away from the heat emanating from Dorian's body. When he stepped to the opposite side of the elevator and the trolley pulled in between them, she breathed an involuntary sigh of relief.

As they rode down, she noticed the stark contrast between them. She was dressed casually, while he wore a three-piece suit as easily as some men wore sweatpants. He seemed so at ease when he was dressed for business; he wore his finest like a second skin. The crisp cut lines seemed to accentuate his manly physique, as though each stitch of fabric were made especially for him. She was sneaking glances at him through the elevator's mirrored doors, and he did not notice her as he scrolled through something on his phone. He was always completely focused on his work even when he didn't mean to be, and it was rare something could pull his mind completely away from it.

Well, not TOO rare…

She blushed as she remembered the certain times when business had been the last thing on his mind. With that thought the elevator doors opened and they stepped out, heading towards the door where Dorian's limo was waiting.

"Have a good day, Mr. Johnston," the doorman called out as Michelle was sliding inside. Dorian had one foot in the limo as he responded. "I'll definitely try."

They rode in silence all the way to the airport, Dorian looking out the window as though in deep thought. She was tempted to ask him a question, but afraid to open her mouth. They took an exit into the airport that did not take them to a main terminal, instead looped around the entire airport to what Michelle was sure were the private hangars.

Sure enough, as they turned a final corner, there neatly sat ten hangars. All were empty except one on the end, which held a pristine white plane emblazoned with a blue 'J' in elegant font. Her breath was almost taken away as the limo pulled to a halt and she stepped out, coming face to face with Dorian Johnston's largest mode of transportation. She barely heard his voice over the plane's powerful engine.

"Beautiful, isn't she? Wait until you see inside." With that remark, he grabbed her hand and led her towards the carpeted stairs that ascended to the plane. She felt almost like a fairy tale princess being led away by her knight in shining armor to his castle in the sunset, but she knew better than to let those kinds of ideas take root. As she reached the top stair and crossed the threshold onto the plane, she was blown away by the luxury spread before her.

The interior could be compared to the nicest of apartments. There was a desk that Dorian clearly used as a workstation, a kitchenette, as well as several couches and chairs. She let go of Dorian's hand and walked towards a closed door near the rear of the plane, and upon opening it she found a fully furnished master bedroom. The large bed caught her eye, and she blushed as she closed the door.

Turning back around, she saw him take a seat behind his desk. He was so powerful, and Michelle caught herself staring at his impressive frame. He looked up after he'd settled in, and she quickly darted her eyes away. With a chuckle, he said, "please, take a seat." He motioned toward a black couch opposite his desk. A small bell was heard throughout the plane, and Dorian turned his attention toward the cockpit.

"We'll be taking off momentarily, Mr. Johnston. Please put on your seatbelts." Michelle looked beside her on the couch, and sure enough part of a seatbelt lay just under her. She tilted her hips to retrieve it from under her thigh, and as she clicked it into place across her lap, she looked up to find Dorian staring at her. She felt her cheeks blush, and quickly looked toward the floor.

The plane began to roll and rise slowly and Michelle felt a weird sensation in the pit of her stomach. It could have been her ascent at a sideways angle instead of the standard forward facing, but she soon realized that her tummy had butterflies from the man across from her. He exuded confidence, and wore his arrogance proudly. He was a commanding and strong-willed man; he backed down to no one. Once he set his sights on something he pursued it with a fervor that almost scared her, and she knew that as long as he wanted her he would stop at nothing to have her. The very thought alone sent a chill of excitement down her spine and into her toes.

As they leveled out, Dorian unbuckled his seat belt and leaned back in his chair. He simply stared at Michelle for a moment, and she was not sure she could keep his gaze until he spoke.

"So, what do you think of it?" he said, looking up and down the plane. Since he had broken the intense eye contact Michelle felt safe to move, and she slowly unbuckled her seatbelt.

"It's beautiful. Very spacious."

"I accept nothing but the best."

"I see," she said, taking a closer look around.

The soft couches and chairs were upholstered in black, with white pillows to offer a stark contrast that was just as dramatic as the man who sat in front of her. Each pillow had the same 'J' she had seen on the side of the plane, stitched in royal blue. They looked so soft and inviting, and she was tempted to lay her head on one for a moment. Dorian's desk was a deep mahogany, and was coated with a gloss that made his figure reflected in the top of it. The entire experience paired with the surroundings made everything seem so dreamlike, as if she expected to wake up any moment. If it all was a dream, she secretly prayed to never awaken. For although being in his presence was intimidating, it was also unbelievably exciting.

Chapter 5

Dorian chose his words carefully, as if trying to find the right combination to open her up to him. Just as he thought he had the perfect opening sentence, she slowly crossed her legs and leaned back on the couch. The entire set of movements took every sensible word from his mind, and he took a moment to compose himself internally before speaking.

"So, I didn't know you wanted to be involved in the business world," he finally said to her. He saw the shock in her eyes.

"How did you know that?" she asked, her eyes wide and her eyebrows questioning.

"I noticed your books," he explained, letting the realization hit her. Her eyes narrowed as she put two and two together.

"So you DID move me last night!" she said, pointing at him. "Why? I was perfectly content upstairs, you know." With a mock pout she crossed her arms, and Dorian was appreciative of how the action make her breasts pop in the skimpy tank top she was wearing. He found the action cute instead of annoying as he usually did, when the experienced spoiled brats he dealt with attempted the same maneuver as a means of seduction.

"Well, my bed seemed so empty. Who better to fill it?" he replied, noticing the rose color that flooded her cheeks. He quickly changed the subject.

"How much longer until you get your degree?" he asked, genuinely interested.

She cast her eyes heavenward, thinking. "Well, once I finish this term and pass my final, I'll have my master's."

He was slightly impressed, until he thought of a small snag.

"Wait, am I keeping you out of class?"

She laughed a light laugh that floated over his ears like feathers.

"Yes, but I've spoken with my professors already. Luckily I'm already passing by a large margin in all my classes, so a couple of weeks are not gonna hurt too badly."

She then leaned her head back and closed her eyes, and in a wave of emotion he felt slightly selfish. He had actually pulled her out of a degree program to satisfy his carnal lusts? In the back of his mind he figured he couldn't blame himself, as he did not know she was pursuing her degree. The small consolation did nothing for his conscience, and his mind turned cloudy with the possibility of sending her home early. But a small, impish voice begged for her to stay, and he could only concede as Michelle stretched out on the couch. But before she could get too cozy, he quickly spoke up.

"Why don't you go lay on the bed? It's much more comfortable."

She looked concerned. "Well, what about you?" she asked, sitting up.

"It's just a 7-hour flight. I'll be fine."

"Ok, if you say so," she said, walking towards the back of the plane. Once she got to the bedroom she closed the door behind her, shutting her body out from his mind and giving him a chance to think.

What was he doing here? He never let a woman have too much power over his body and senses. But with one word, Michelle could set his loins on fire. It was the way she lightly flirted, innocently not knowing how provocative she truly was. She was unlike any other woman he had met before, a true challenge to his willpower. She seemed to hypnotize him with her personality, and every moment he was around her, he seemed drawn to her presence. He was tempted to follow her to the bedroom, but he knew he had work to catch up on and left her to rest.

As soon as he'd settled himself in front of his laptop after a bathroom break, his desk phone shrilled beside him. Rolling his eyes, he saw that his father was calling him again, and he reluctantly picked up.

"How did you know I was flying?"

"It's the only time you don't answer your cell phone. Now, to the real question: did I hear correctly? Fiancée?"

Dorian smiled and thought of his 'fiancée', sound asleep in the bedroom. "Yes, dad."

The sudden eruption of laughter on the other end caught him off guard. "Oh, son, that is wonderful. Why didn't you tell me?"

"I tried to keep it a surprise until you could actually meet her," he quickly improvised. He leaned back in his chair and closed his eyes, trying to remain focused. His father had a knack for detecting deception; the smallest inconsistency would completely foil his plan.

"Hmm," he heard his father say. "A surprise, indeed."

"I'm bringing her with me, so behave."

His father chuckled, and they stayed on the phone a bit longer before finally hanging up, Dorian blowing out a relieved breath. They were clear for now, and he only hoped Michelle could keep up the charade.

After some time his pilot announced their soon descent, and Dorian could not resist his impulses any longer. He slowly got up from his desk and walked towards the rear of the plane, pausing at the closed door. Hearing nothing inside, he slowly turned the knob. Michelle lay on her back with her arms above her head, her cheek falling softly onto one shoulder. She had one knee bent which jutted her hip out, making her tank top rise over her stomach. How she could sleep so naturally beautiful amazed him. He quietly tiptoed to the bed and sat on it, reminding himself that they did not have much time to do what he yearned so much. He wanted to bury himself inside her sweet warmth but they were landing soon. He would have to be content with just a kiss, if it could be kept at just that.

He leaned his head over hers and stopped mere inches from her lips. After taking a moment to inhale her scent, he brought his lips down onto hers softly. He felt as though he were kissing rose petals. He could feel her sharp intake of breath as she awoke, but she did not push him off of her. He opened his eyes to see hers staring back, wide in shock. But instead of protesting she wrapped her arms around his neck, closing her eyes with a sigh.

Every ounce of her passion for him was reflected in the kiss, and he had to place a hand on the bed for support. The fire exchanged between their lips was soul-consuming, and it obliterated every rational thought he had. When her eager tongue found his, it was almost as though an explosion had gone off in his mouth—one that blew his mind and incinerated his senses.

Her breathy moans and sighs under him were more than he could handle, and as a familiar 'ping' rang throughout the plane, he raised his head with an unsteady breath.

"Please put on your seatbelts, we will be beginning our descent shortly," the pilot informed them.

Dorian slowly stood, and Michelle looked at him with longing that would have crippled a man with lesser willpower. With reserves of self-control, he said, "no seatbelts on the bed, darling."

He walked to his desk and took a seat, fastening his seatbelt as he tried to get his raging hormones under control. He thudded an angry fist on his desk. He was not supposed to feel like this; he felt like an out-of-control teenager who couldn't keep himself in check. He couldn't seem to get near

Michelle without losing all his inhibitions. It was something he just couldn't figure out.

Michelle strode from the bedroom, taking a seat on the couch opposite his desk and fastening her seatbelt. He dared not to meet her eyes, and as they landed he steadied his breath. When the plane smoothly touched down and coasted to a stop, he couldn't help but notice how swiftly she unbuckled her seatbelt and moved to get off the aircraft. It was as though she was running away from the insatiable passion she knew existed between them, and he smiled to himself. How could she ever run away from that?

As the stairs touched the ground, they barely had time to settle in place before Michelle was halfway down them. He realized she truly was terrified by the intensity of her lust for him. He'd have to learn to restrain himself if he didn't want to scare her off. When she blossomed yet again beneath him, he wanted her to have climbed in bed all by herself. She couldn't keep denying what he knew she felt. Sooner or later she was going to have to surrender. The thought excited him like the anticipation of an upcoming merger.

In a way, it was.

When he de-boarded he noticed her standing by the parked limo, as if waiting for him. She had her arms folded over her chest, and wouldn't look at him as he walked over. He smiled and opened the door for her.

"Shall we?" He asked it lightly, as if trying to make her feel more at ease about what happened by ignoring it. She smiled up at him and slid inside, and Dorian was sure she had put their moment of passion behind her. He couldn't wait to see what the rest of the afternoon held.

For minutes they rode in silence, until Michelle finally spoke. "So, where exactly are we going?"

"My father's. That's where we'll be staying."

"Oh, and where's that?" she asked, sounding curious.

"My father lives just outside a beautiful borough in Richmond-upon-Thames."

"Your father lives in the Richmond Borough? I heard that was only for the mega-elite," she said quietly, as if in awe. She turned to stare out the window, looking around so intently as if trying to mentally snapshot everything she saw. He smiled to himself at her childlike wonder. It was so refreshing when compared to the vain, selfish women with which he usually found himself surrounded.

"He accepts only the best," he said, turning his attention out the window.

"Like father, like son," she commented, and he could hear the smile in her voice. He loved her sense of humor; it came so naturally, as if joy ran through her blood. Her personality was so infectious, he could almost get lost in it. She had a way with people; a way of connecting with their inner good so that she gained their trust. She made herself readily open and easy to talk to, so that one couldn't help but bare it all to her without fear of ridicule. *I could definitely get used to that*, he thought to himself.

He shook his head quickly. What was he thinking? Such thoughts hadn't even crept to the backburner of his mind in over four years, since a certain conniving blonde had rid him of all notions of having a family of his own. She had swept in and out of his life like a dangerous tornado, spreading her malice and viciousness to every corner of his world. By the time Michelle had come into the picture, he'd been scarred so bad she didn't even stand a chance.

He looked intently at the scenery passing them, the evil woman's face now flashing in his mind. He hoped he would not run into her while Michelle was with him. She was there, somewhere in the city, lurking like a poisonous snake ready to strike at any man who let himself get too close. He knew her venom: coy flirtatiousness in the beginning, followed by empty, meaningless sex with false affection tied to it. It was all in the hopes of becoming the future Mrs. Johnston, a task which many women had tried at and none succeeded. She had come the closest, though, springing a bombshell on him so large that he almost asked her to marry him.

He shuddered. Thank God he had found it all to be not true.

Looking over at Michelle, he realized the dramatic differences between the two. She could never stoop so low; she was genuinely good from inside out. She was giving, caring, and completely unselfish. The day she manipulated someone would more than likely be the day hell completely froze over.

As always, his mind wandered to business. Looking through the calendar on his phone, he contemplated his upcoming business functions. The first one was in three hours: a business gala to celebrate the merger of one of Johnston Inc.'s sister companies to an international banking corporation, a merger which Dorian himself had facilitated. He was glad he told Andrew three dresses, as he remembered the charity auction he had committed himself to the next day. He couldn't wait to see how Michelle looked in them.

For once, he had accepted a social invitation, a formal birthday party for a young CEO who Dorian played tennis with. He longed for any excuse to show Michelle off on his arm. If he was going to have her at his disposal, he was definitely going to get his money's worth. In the bedroom and out. But even as he was looking forward to the next few days, a tiny dark cloud began to creep into his mind: there was a possibility of an unpleasant confrontation with an evil devious blonde. A very real possibility.

Because somewhere out there, Nicole was waiting.

*****

Michelle was lost in her thoughts yet again. She seemed to have stepped outside of her reality into an alternate universe where nothing made sense, and where she was no longer in control. Although she had to admit she loved the freedom, not worrying about mouths she had to feed or backs she had to clothe. She could almost relax and enjoy herself, if there wasn't the smoldering heat passing through her and Dorian. It was something she was going to have to come to grips with, and she was beginning to think it might be sooner rather than later. Try as she might, she couldn't seem to stay away from his magnetism that kept pulling her back. She had found that out on the plane.

She had known it was him when he had opened the door, but she had stayed still and kept her eyes closed. She had tried to keep her breathing steady, and not let it reflect her raging heartbeat. She could feel him coming closer and finally sit on the bed, and she knew what was happening even before his lips claimed hers.

Her mind had exploded in a fury of emotion, and her eyes flung open in shock of the raw need she felt at his touch. When she connected with his and saw the same need staring back, she lost all reserve. She had curled her arms around his neck and darted her tongue in his mouth, doing everything in her power to pull him on top of her. If it hadn't been for the pilot's interruption, she was sure she could have had her fill of him right then and there. Once he had left she had taken a moment to calm down, then had gone to the bathroom to straighten herself out. When she saw herself in the mirror, she had to do a double take. Her lips looked as though she had been ravished, and her hair showed no argument to the contrary. She looked as though she had been made a notch in Dorian's bedpost, and she was instantly furious.

How could she completely lose herself over one kiss? The way he made her feel was ludicrous. She'd combed through her hair quickly with her fingers, slipped on her shoes, and had resumed her seat in front of Dorian's desk, fuming. She didn't even want to meet his eyes, and when the plane had come to a halt she had gotten off as fast as she could. She just couldn't trust her hormones around him. But she didn't want to seem like she was running away—although she was—so she had waited outside the limo for him. He had sauntered over and opened the door, like the moment had meant nothing to him. She then decided that if he could brush it off so easily, then so could she. She would have to if she wanted to survive the next two weeks. She would have to distance herself. So, she had smiled broadly and slid inside, already trying to forget it.

If only she could.

The moment played over and over again in her mind, placed on a taunting loop by her psyche. A couple of times she darted her tongue over her lips to see if they were still searing from his touch, and she could almost taste him there. She tried to focus out the window, but she could picture nothing but Dorian. When she finally couldn't stand the silence anymore, she asked a simple question. The answer she had received, however, was not one she had been expecting, but it didn't surprise her.

She had heard of the Richmond Borough in design school, using photographs of some of the lavish houses' interiors as inspiration in her class assignments. Residency was reserved for the super wealthy, as it housed not only designer shops at its center but beautiful London countryside around each manor. That paired with available waterfront housing on the river Thames, it made for premier real estate.

She was suddenly anxious about meeting Dorian's father and being able to pull off their charade. She had no idea how she was going to explain how or where they met, and she decided they needed to get their stories straight. She turned from the window to look at Dorian.

"If you expect us to pull this off, you might want to figure out our back-story," she said lightly. He answered without hesitation.

"You worked for me years ago, we reconnected and now we're engaged," he informed her. Apparently, he had given it a great deal of thought. Not wanting to press the issue any further, she turned her eyes toward her lap, where her hands were clasped. It was then she noticed something missing that was vital to their scheme. As she realized it, she let out a small involuntary gasp. She hoped Dorian had not heard it. But as she quickly looked out the window, his next words revealed the contrary.

"Yes, I know you don't have a gaudy diamond to wiggle in my father's face. Don't worry," he said, patting her leg, "it's all been taken care of, darling." His hand on her thigh seemed to burn through her clothes and into her skin, scorching the flesh beneath. Just that one touch, and her entire body had started to respond. As he lifted his hand her thigh tingled, as if begging him not to go. She felt the same way. Her body needed his, cried out for it, like a refreshing

drink of water in a blazing desert. She wanted him to touch her so bad she almost yearned for him, and she knew she was falling right back in love with the man who had so carelessly cast her aside without so much as a second glance. It was a hard truth, but she had to face it. Try as she might, she couldn't outrun it anymore. She was head over heels in love with Dorian Johnston.
Again.
Dammit!
Just then, a thought struck her. However, by the time she opened her mouth to ask what he meant by 'taken care of', they pulled in front of a large gate. Black cast-iron and very tall, it opened down the middle with an elegant 'J' on each side. A small security station sat in front of it, but they did not stop to verify their identities. The company limo was unmistakable. They paused only to let the gate slowly creak open, and as they rolled inside Michelle became even more worried.
They rode onto a large driveway, but try as she might she could not see the house. But even without it, the landscaping alone was breathtaking. Tall weeping willows hung over the road, and gave the feeling of going through a whimsical tunnel. The grass was kept neatly trimmed and perfectly green, and she imagined it took quite a large staff to keep everything looking so immaculate. As they took a smooth curve, a house spread out before her that dropped her jaw.
It could not be called merely a house, for the space it occupied could fit several average houses.

What Michelle saw was unlike anything she had ever seen before.

    A beautiful mansion sat perched on top of a perfectly green hill, as if it had been painted there. With large windows, dramatic rooftops, and cobblestone facings, it looked like something out of a fairy tale.

    How fitting for her situation, being brought by the dark prince to meet the king.

    As they pulled up to the door, a man quickly came to the car. He was neatly dressed: black slacks paired with a dress shirt and sweater vest, and Michelle assumed he must work for the family. He opened the door on Dorian's side, leant to him and said, "it's just arrived, sir." He then handed him a teal box, a color Michelle knew well. There was no mistaking a Tiffany's box; every woman wanted to be presented with one.

    So when Dorian thanked him and handed her the tiny blue parcel, her breath caught in her throat.

    "What is this?" she asked, tentatively taking it. She had an idea of what the box held but she didn't want to say it aloud, lest she jinx it.

    "Put that on the appropriate finger," he said, getting out and leaving her to marvel at the perfect ring that sat in her hands.

    A brilliant square diamond sat in the center, held up by pristine white gold. The band itself boasted five smaller diamonds on each side, all sparkling. She took it out of the box slowly, weighing it in her hand before finally slipping it on her ring finger. Had the ring been from anyone else, it would have been an extraordinary symbol of love. But Michelle knew better: Dorian Johnston was marking his territory.

The added weight on her finger felt alien to her, and she lifted her hand to see it against her skin. She found that it matched surprisingly well, and she almost smiled as she exited the limo. But as soon as she had said thank you to the man holding her door open, a thought struck her. She raced to Dorian's side, out of earshot of the staff. She did not want to blow their cover.

"What are we supposed to do with this thing when this farce is over?" she asked in his ear, on tiptoes. He turned his head so that they were almost nose-to-nose, and her heart skipped a beat as she lowered herself. The smile that spread across his beautiful mouth melted a pool of lust deep in her belly.

God, how she wanted him!

His voice brought her out of a terribly erotic fantasy that had started in her mind. "Keep it," he said. "Consider it a severance bonus." With that statement he grabbed her hand and led her up the marble steps to the enormous wooden front door. A large brass knocker hung in the center, and Dorian grabbed it.

Knock. Knock.

There was a squeal inside, and the door was heaved open. On the other side stood a stout woman, with an easy-going face that could make a person want to curl up beside her. She smiled a warm smile that spread from ear to ear, and her voice matched the wisdom apparent by her gray hairs.

"Well, who could this be? By, lad, I think you've grown! It's been too long, dear." She spoke with a slight Scottish brogue. She pulled Dorian into a bear hug, and he returned it with a sincerity that shocked Michelle. She didn't even know he could be so genuine, since he always peered his nose down at her.

As he let go, she turned to look at Michelle. "So, this must be her, huh?" She raised her hand and brushed it softly against Michelle's cheek. "Well, isn't she a gorgeous lass? Such natural beauty," she said in awe. Michelle blushed at the sincere compliment.

"That's so kind of you, um…" Michelle paused as she realized she did not know the gentle older woman's name.

Dorian quickly spoke up. "This is Eliz—"

"Call me Mama Liz, lass," she spoke, pulling Michelle into a tight hug. "Everyone else does." As men unloaded their bags from the trunk, Liz took her by the hand and led her inside.

The grandeur inside matched the outside, with two sweeping staircases that led up to a balcony. She knew upstairs held countless rooms, and that one of those rooms she would have to share with Dorian later that night. To her right a set of double doors stood open, revealing a massive library. Michelle let out a sigh of relief. At least she'd be able to get some work done in peace. She didn't trust herself to actually study in Dorian's presence. He could probably pull her away from the holy gates with only a word and a look. She melted like butter in the sun whenever she was around him. It was inexplicable.

She felt horribly out of place; if she were actually there with an authentic fiancé instead of running a scam, she would have felt more at ease. But knowing she was only there for show did not help settle any discomfort whatsoever. Still, she would have to endure it, and she put on her biggest smile to at least LOOK happy.

"So, are you hungry, darling?" Liz asked her.

"We have dinner plans," Dorian said behind her, and put his hand on her shoulder. "Which you need to start getting ready for," he said, addressing her. "We're leaving in a couple hours."

The announcement of their upcoming dinner engagement was a surprise to her, but she could not show it. Instead she looked up at him and sweetly said, "of course, darling." She reached on tiptoes to give him a light kiss on the cheek, much to Liz's delight.

"Now, that's a sight I've waited to see!" she exclaimed, clapping her hands excitedly. "Oh, God be praised!"

"Indeed," a strong, authoritative male voice said. Michelle turned to see an older version of Dorian walking towards them, who she assumed was his father. He was smiling broadly, showing off his perfect teeth. She could definitely tell where Dorian had gotten his good looks; the older gentleman still radiated the charm that Michelle was sure overwhelmed young women in his youth. Had Dorian's mother gotten lost in those deep eyes, the same mysterious eyes he had passed on to his equally gorgeous son? She looked up into those endless, unyielding eyes as she waited for an explanation.

Dorian smiled back at her, reassuringly. As he turned her towards the still unidentified man he said, "Michelle, this is my father. Dad, this is my Michelle."

She outstretched a hand and he firmly took it, pulling her towards the door from which he had emerged. "Edward Johnston," he said, his baritone voice sounding strangely familiar. She soon realized it was the same caliber of voice she heard repeatedly in her mind whenever she thought of Dorian, yet another family trait passed from father to son. "Let's have a chat, shall we?" he asked, disguising his order as a question. She knew the tactic all too well, and it only cemented the similarities between the two powerful men.

Dorian started to protest, but Edward quickly cut him off. "I'll only have her for a second." He put a gentle hand on her back and led her forward, and she could hear Liz quietly say, "uh oh."

As soon as they had both stepped inside he closed the door, and Michelle took a moment to survey the enormous office.

A large black 'L' shaped desk sat in the middle, almost looming, foreboding, as if an inanimate personification of the ruthless man who used it. Two bookcases sat to one side against a far wall, filled to the tops, but Michelle could not make out the titles. Various papers lay scattered about his desk while his laptop was still propped open, leading her to conclude he had still been working when they had arrived.

He was definitely the busiest retiree she had ever met, and certainly Dorian's father. They shared the same work ethic: never-ending.

Besides a small desk lamp, the only light coming in was from the floor-to-ceiling windows, which displayed a sunset just outside. It cast a golden glow in the room, making it feel otherworldly. Edward took a seat behind his desk, motioned to one of the chairs in front of it and said, "please. Sit." She noticed his tone of voice had changed, more serious, less inviting, and she felt a bit uneasy. Slowly, timidly, she did, and perched herself on the edge of the seat. She almost felt as though she was there for an inspection, and she became even more aware of her casual appearance.

Why was she so nervous? She was only here for a short while, and then she'd never have to see this man again. And certainly after Dorian explained their parting he wouldn't remember her; she quickly be forgotten, like so many of the papers laying about on his massive desk.

She watched him lean forward and put his elbows on the desk, taking a breath before speaking to her.

"So, why are you here? I am sure my son has done nothing to win your heart. So, how much is he paying you?"

The question took her aback, and she was immediately on the defensive. Was his precious son so much out of her league that he could not possibly be genuinely interested? Was he so used to his son being seen with unbelievably gorgeous women that she just didn't measure up? On the other hand, could his question be rooted in a more sinister thought: did he assume his son so cruel? Even though he *was* paying her, she didn't want his father to know that. She had to keep to the façade to the end.

    She sighed. "Your son may be a lot of things, but he's not paying me." She tilted her head as she began to think about Dorian's good qualities. God, she was so in love with that man, no matter how he portrayed himself to the outside world. She had seen him genuinely laugh, an act that lit up his entire face. She knew the magic in his eyes; the passion with which he held her in his arms. It was in there, locked inside, even if no one else could see it.

    "Underneath that cold, rough, extremely intimidating exterior, there's a man who can be so—what?" she asked, noticing the broad smile that had suddenly spread across his face. He chuckled.

    "My God…you're in love with my son, young lady," he concluded, leaning back in his chair with a satisfied look on his face.

    She flushed. Was it that obvious? She knew she loved him, but could someone really tell just by the way she spoke of him? The love must radiate in her voice. He did overpower her heart, after all. "He means a lot to me. He tries to act as though he needs no one, but I know it's a bunch of malarkey. He's rough around the edges, but that's what I love about him. He's not perfect, but I don't want him to be." She paused as she realized she was saying too much.

    She cleared her throat. "I'm still adjusting to my feelings about your son, sir," she said.

"Call me Edward," he quickly replied.

She noted the change in his tone of voice and felt a bit more at ease. Maybe he was warming up to her, after all.

"Well, Edward," she said, trying to word things carefully, "to be perfectly honest, we're not a typical couple. Dorian and I are—"

"Going to be late," a powerful voice announced behind her. His hands on her shoulders had abruptly cut off her words, the action sending a prickling down each vertebra individually. Just one touch, one simple piece of contact, and she was on fire for him already. She quickly stood up, needing to break the contact between them.

"Excuse me, Edward," she said sweetly, and rushed out of the room.

*****

Dorian watched her go, her lush bottom swaying as she turned the corner. How much longer could she keep running away?

God, he did not want to find out.

He faced his father. "What was that all about?" he asked, referring to his private word with the woman who was his supposed fiancée. Had he figured them out? Had he interrogated Michelle into telling him of their charade? He felt a bit of instinctive protectiveness, and hoped his father had not crossed any lines. To Dorian's surprise, his father merely smiled, pointing his finger towards the door from which Michelle had just exited.

"I like that girl," he assessed. "She's honest. To the point. Hang on to that angel," he finished, turning towards a stack of papers. Dorian recognized the action from childhood as dismissal and left, closing the door behind him. He walked to the adjacent library, immediately heading to the wet bar to pour himself a drink. He slowly sipped the smooth scotch and tried to think.

He had only heard his father use 'angel' to describe a woman twice: for his mother, Abigail, and Liz, who had been with their family since before he was born.

He could understand his mother's angelic description: she had met his father when he had nothing, barely living on a waiter's salary and going to school, and together with love and patience, they had built the powerful empire Dorian ran today. Her smile was radiant, her laughter infectious; she had lit up every room she walked in.

He could also agree with calling Liz an angel: she had brought his father back from the brink—not once, but twice—of a drunken downward spiral after his mother had died. Without her, their family legacy would have been in shambles. He remembered as a child not understanding why she would pour full bottles of amber brown liquid down the sink all the time, but now that he was older he realized the favor she was doing them.

But what had Michelle done in such a short span of time to earn being called an angel? She had truly left an imprint on his father's heart, just as she seemed to do with everyone else. Even his PA was still talking about her.

He stayed in the library for quite some time, getting lost in his thoughts, until finally he finished his drink, rinsed out his glass and placed it upside down on the bar. Straightening his jacket, he left the library and waited in the foyer for Michelle. He looked at his watch. He hoped she was not one of those women who took forever to—

His train of thought was derailed by a vision coming towards him. Her hair long and bouncy in voluptuous waves, Michelle floated to him in a blue gown that hugged her deliciously. It had small straps that looped around her neck, with a tight bodice that emphasized her marvelous bosom. When it reached her oh-so-thick thighs, it fell to the floor in a material Dorian was sure he wouldn't mind running through his fingers. It was slick and smooth, just like the exquisite femininity he knew lay between those endless legs.

She held a railing with one hand and the end of her dress with the other, so as to prevent herself from falling. She looked so natural, as if she had descended the stairs just as beautifully countless times before. He couldn't understand it, it was as though this was where she belonged.

As she reached the bottom stair, the hunger in her eyes paired with the smile she presented lit a fire deep in the pit of his stomach—starting as a sizzle, then quickly growing into a raging wildfire. It took all he had not to drag her back upstairs. Instead, he flashed a charming smile.

"Before you even start," she said, holding her hands up, "this is not all my doing. By the time I got upstairs, Liz already had my dress laid out and the curling iron heated. The woman's phenomenal," she concluded.

"I'll have to tell my father to give her a raise, then. You look amazing," he said, holding his hand to her. Without hesitation she took it, and he noted how easily their hands clasped. He did not begin walking right away, but instead took a moment to simply look at her. Her light makeup added a soft glow to her skin, instead of washing out her features. He noticed that most women looked so pale after applying makeup; he sometimes wished they wouldn't wear it at all, but he knew some women would rather die than walk out of the house without the proper cosmetics. Michelle could go either way: she had such natural beauty, it was only enhanced when she applied her makeup. She truly was breathtaking.

"Something wrong?" she questioned, sounding concerned. She self-consciously looked over herself, as if trying to find a flaw that did not exist. He merely smiled, lifting her hand to press his lips gently against her knuckles. He noticed the large diamond that rested on her ring finger, the one he had put there, and felt an unfamiliar tug at his heart. He felt her soft skin against his lips; how he longed to take her back upstairs and feel the rest of her delectable skin up against him.

Patience Dorian, he thought to himself.

"Nope. Nothing at all," he said, leading them outside into the night air. His driver held open the door, and he watched Michelle slide in smoothly before getting in himself. He noticed that she did not sit on the opposite seat as she usually did, but remained on his seat and looked out of the window. That small action, seemingly insignificant, was the first glimmer of hope that he was wearing her down. Slowly but surely.

He was surprised when she spoke. "So, where are we going?"

In that tiny statement, Michelle brought a wave of guilt crashing down on him. He hadn't even had the consideration to inform her where they were going to be, yet he expected her to follow him blindly. What was wrong with him? Blinded by lust, he couldn't even consider the woman he wanted so badly. He cleared his throat.

"A business gala. Pretty boring, actually. Champagne, brandy, pretentiousness..." he trailed off.

"So, why are you going? Sounds pretty horrible," she commented, still looking out the window.

He looked at her profile, so serene, as if lost in thought. Honest and to the point, his father had said to describe her, and he was right on the money. She didn't bite her tongue for anyone. Plus, she did make a valid point. Business functions only served as another way for everyone to sneer down their noses, and Dorian hated the snobby air that seemed to hang like a raincloud over the room. To make matters worse, he had an endless supply of brainless beauties pressing themselves against him, all vying to be the heiress to the Johnston fortune. He smiled as he thought of the curvaceous beauty who would be on his arm. Let those vapid women try anything tonight. The evening promised to be eventful, indeed.

As the car coasted to a stop in front of a luxurious hotel and the door was opened, Dorian let the cool air clear his head. He had to keep his focus if he was going to make it through the night with his wits about him. He noted the crisp air and looked at Michelle's beautiful bare shoulders. He hoped she would not be cold. He stepped out, then leaned his head into the limo.

"Are you going to be cold? It's pretty chilly out here," he said, concerned. She smiled up at him as she got out.

"No, I'll be fine. I stay hot, usually," she said smoothly, stepping onto the pavement. She smoothed out her dress as she stood, and already she looked as though she was supposed to be there. She slid her arm through the crook of his arm and he let himself relish the intimate touch before walking inside.

The reflective lights from infinite diamonds shimmered throughout the ballroom on the necks of some of London's wealthiest women. It only added to the dazzling excessiveness of the event itself, complete with pompous waiters floating about with various expensive finger foods. A large glass chandelier hung from the ceiling, adding an elegant touch as it dangled over the dance floor. High round tables stood scattered about, serving as a place to rest drinks or a gathering point for conversation.

As he was offered something slimy on a cracker from a smiling waiter, he noticed the slight shift of interest as he walked in. He knew it could not be because of his presence only, but because of the radiant woman who stood beside him. She shone like a beacon amongst darkness, even in her navy gown. He was quite sure the socialites couldn't wait to get on their phones and gossip about Dorian Johnston's mysterious date for the evening.

He caught quite a few looks of jealousy from some of the other women there, and quickly felt a mixture of pride and protectiveness. They looked at her as a newcomer who didn't belong there, and he scowled back at them. He dared them to say something; welcomed the opportunity to put them in their place. He felt Michelle tense beside him, and he squeezed her hand in reassurance. He leaned to whisper in her ear. "Don't worry. You'll be fine. You look beautiful," he said calmly. She looked up at him and smiled weakly.

"Thanks. I needed that," she confided. He felt her loosen up. Placing a hand on the small of her back, he led her forward. A waiter approached them, offering glasses of champagne. They each casually took one, and Dorian watched Michelle take a long sip. As he began to take one himself, a familiar figure began to approach them.

Alex Williams, the CEO of Williams' Financial Solutions—now, international, thanks to Dorian—walked towards them. He was beaming, a large grin stretching to cover both sides of his golden face. A few years older than Dorian, their families had grown up together amongst New York's elite. Bold, daring, and willing to take risks, he proved himself a force to be reckoned with in his father's company. So when his father had suddenly passed, there was no doubt in anyone's mind that Alex would lead the company to a whole new level.

And he had. Adopting a more modern approach and making some risky calls, he had raised their revenue eighty percent in only two years. So naturally the next step had been to pursue an international partnership. That's where Dorian had come in. He had set up a meeting with one of Japan's biggest banking firms, who owned businesses in both Japan and the United States. Using his razor-sharp knowledge of the business, Alex had easily sealed the deal.

When he had finally popped the question to his long-time girlfriend and settled down, it had only added icing to the cake.

If only Dorian had such luck. But "Mrs. Right" seemed to be endlessly preceded by "Mrs. Wrong". He looked over at Michelle, who seemed to be lost in her thoughts yet again. He had never truly given her a chance, had he? How could he assume her as being Mrs. Wrong without giving her an opportunity to be at least Mrs. Maybe?

Before he let his mind wander into dangerous territory, he focused on the man who had his arms outstretched.

"Dorian! Aren't you a sight for sore eyes! I didn't think you were gonna make it!" he exclaimed, wrapping him in a tight hug.

"This party is a little late, isn't it? This merger happened like six months ago!" Dorian remarked, after they had let go of their embrace.

Alex flashed yet another beaming smile. "We've been busy," he said, pulling a petite figure from where she had been standing behind him. Dorian recognized the smiling woman as Alex's wife, Lucy, who immediately came in for an embrace.

Lucy was a petite brunette who had captured Alex's heart with her sweet demeanor early in their relationship. He had asked her to marry him on several occasions but she had turned him down repeatedly, stating that he was 'too wild to marry.' It had taken him years to convince her that he had calmed his wild ways, which is exactly what she had wanted in the first place. When she had finally said yes, everyone in their circle of friends had been overjoyed, including Dorian. He was happy at least someone had found lasting happiness.

As Dorian wrapped his arms around her small frame, something hard came in contact with his stomach. He quickly pulled her away, looking down into a rather large baby bump. His eyes widened as she grinned and nodded, putting a tiny hand on her swollen belly.

"About six months now," she informed him, before he could ask how far along she was.

It was then that Alex noticed Michelle, and he looked to Dorian for an explanation. He smiled and took her hand, pulling her forward.

"I've been busy too," he said, bringing her in close, "this is my fiancée, Michelle."

The mixture of shock and joy on Alex and Lucy's faces gave Dorian a tingling of happiness that he did not expect. He was suddenly quite proud of the beauty that stood beside him, and as Lucy reached out to grab Michelle's left hand for confirmation, Alex clapped him on the back.

"Well, it's about time!" he said, laughing.

Lucy moved Michelle's hand into Alex's view. "Do you see that? Looks like someone finally came to their senses," she said. She looked at Michelle, smiling. "Congratulations! I guess it just took the right woman to tame him, huh?"

He watched Michelle smile and blush. "I'm just hanging on for the ride with this one. You never quite know what's going to happen next," she said, putting her arm around his waist. "But I like it that way. Keeps me on my toes, huh, honey?" she cooed smoothly, looking up at him. The subtle flirtation in her voice filled him with so much anticipation he nearly moaned. He smiled instead, turning his face to look at her.

"Every moment of every day," he said, and he hoped that included later on that night.

Chapter 6

"Well, would you look at that," Michelle heard Lucy say, and it brought her out of her daydream. She had been envisioning this same scenario, only wishing it had been true. How she longed to be on his arm for real, to truly have captured his heart. She knew she meant little to nothing to him besides to serve as his arm candy, yet she was still smitten with him. She felt almost like a love struck college student: pining after a gorgeous professor that she knew had no interest in her.

He occupied her every thought, and she often found herself daydreaming about him when he was not near her. Every moment that passed in his presence threw her deeper and deeper in love with him.

Even if he did not feel the same way.

The rest of the evening passed in a blur, which Michelle was thankful for. She wasn't sure how much she could take, having to pretend to be Dorian Johnston's fiancée. Oh, how she wished she was!

After they had met the host and his plump-bellied wife, she had been introduced to countless people. She remembered herself somehow holding her own in their conversations, even getting a laugh now and then. Before she knew it, they were saying goodbye well after two and getting into the limo.

She was vividly aware of Dorian's presence beside her, and she began to let her mind wander. She truly loved him. So why was she resisting him with such fervor? She had two weeks with no responsibilities, so one final fling couldn't possibly hurt. When it was all said and done she would put it behind her and move on, and she was sure he would as well.

She couldn't believe she was actually considering it! But quickly an impish voice spoke up from the back of her mind, egging her on. What harm could it do? After this brief time they'd be spending together, they'd never see each other again. It'd be like it never happened, plus she'd be walking away with enough money to get her and the boys straight.

Her mind resolved itself, and suddenly her blood surged with heated anticipation. Her breathing became increasingly shallow as she realized they were almost back at the house, and she would soon have to face the music. And although she had laid out the sheet music herself, she was still quite anxious to see how the song would turn out.

She sneaked in a glance at him in her side vision. His chiseled features seemed to be set in stone as he looked out the window in deep thought. He seemed so alone on top of the business world all by himself. She was sure he had no confidantes, no one to bring into his tortured psyche for advice or council. She couldn't imagine what that must be like, the feeling of utter loneliness...well, not Dorian Johnston. She was sure he felt anything but lonely.

They pulled smoothly into the drive, and Michelle soon found herself staring at the front door. Dorian led her upstairs without a sound, taking her to her side of their connecting suites that Liz had shown her to earlier. He walked her just inside the threshold, took her hand and kissed it, and softly said, "goodnight, Michelle."

He began to walk out, and she could feel a gaping hole beginning to form in her body. It was almost as though he was taking a piece of her with him as he left. She couldn't stand him not being there; not touching her in some way. The door was almost closed when she came to her senses. She yanked it quickly open.

"Dorian!" She called after him, and she could hear the need in her voice. He had not gotten down the hallway, but instead stood only mere feet from the door. Their eyes locked and she could see her eagerness reflected in his eyes. He did not have to say another word, because as soon as their gazes locked he understood. He closed the space between them and took her face in his hands.

"God, I want you," he breathed, just before his lips claimed hers. The raw statement paired with the passion in his kiss nearly undid her. The world dissolved into nothing around them, and she became swept away in a whirlwind of emotion as their kiss deepened.

She felt her knees give way beneath her, and she thanked God for Dorian's strength as he quickly placed a hand around her waist to support her. In unison they moved towards the bed, their bodies moving as one to satisfy the same aching need. She felt the bed on the back of her knees, and she sat to give her legs a chance to strengthen. Feeling bold, she reached for the buttons on his dress shirt. She slipped a hand inside, feeling the warmness of his skin against the back of her fingers. She looked up at him, only to find him staring hungrily back at her.

One by one she undid the buttons, taking her time so as to savor the sensual moment. She could tell his appreciation: before she had gotten halfway down he snatched the fabric from her fingers and ripped it open, scattering the rest of the buttons. The action only excited her, and she stood and turned to have her dress unzipped. He took her hair and lay it over her shoulder, exposing her back to him. As he pressed soft kisses to her skin, she could have sworn her heart was going to leap out of her chest.

Her pulse was racing as she felt the dress fall, leaving her in only her bra, panties, and heels. Suddenly she felt very erotic, and her nipples formed into hard peaks. Slowly he took her shoulders and turned her around, sitting her softly on the bed. His eyes roamed over her body hungrily, the action sending chills down her spine. Daringly she leant back on her elbows, giving him a better view.

"Just let me look at you," he said huskily. His deep voice traveled over her body in sultry waves, covering her like a warm blanket. He moved to turn the light on, and Michelle remembered the scar that was proof of her pregnancy. Quickly she grabbed him.

"No," she pleaded. "Leave it off." He smiled and came to stand in front of her, and she tilted her head back and let her hair fall down over her shoulders. In his presence she felt so wild and abandon, as though all her inhibitions were taken away with a simple look from him. He seemed to have that irresistible magnetic power, the kind she could completely lose herself with.

Which isn't necessarily a bad thing, she thought to herself.

She could do this. She could have this meaningless fling and walk away when the time came. But that time was not now, and she had no intention of backing down. She had started it, and she was surely going to finish it. Even if it took all of her soul with it.

He took his time roaming his eyes over her, seeming to take in each inch of her semi-naked form. She watched as he slowly undid the zipper on his pants and let it down, revealing his black boxers and the blatant personification of his arousal. When he smoothly pulled them down over his muscular thighs, she felt her heart flutter as his powerful manhood stared back at her. She could not pull her eyes away. Her lips went dry, and instinctively she darted her tongue out to wet them. A sultry smile spread across his lips.

"See anything you like?" he questioned, holding his hands out.

She scooted herself up on the bed, bent both legs, and let her knees fall out to each side. His facial expression gave her the satisfaction she had sought.

His eyes grew dark with desire, and she had barely said her soft 'yes' before he almost leapt on top of her. He softly pressed his body against her skin, running his cheek gently down her neck. She closed her eyes and reveled in the intoxicating feeling. When he began to press light kisses down her collarbone, she couldn't be sure if she'd be able to hold on for much longer. Not when everything in her body called out for this man to be near her.

    She dug her fingernails in his back, feeling his smooth skin. He sucked in his breath sharply and nipped at her ear because of it, and she softly giggled. Slowly he moved his mouth down her body, stopping when he came to her erect nipples to lightly lick each one in turn. This action only aroused her further, sending a sudden bolt of cold lightning down her spine. He ran the backs of his hands down her sides and to her thighs, taking his kisses lower down her belly. When he reached the bud of her femininity, aching with desire, he slowly licked it. She let out a small gasp, and lay back on the soft pillows to fully enjoy the experience.

    She closed her eyes. How she had missed this…how she had missed being able to reach out and touch him, to feel his skin beneath her fingers. She moaned as he gently slid his tongue inside her, darting it in and out. For a moment she became dizzy with raw passion, and she felt herself being taken higher and higher to the peak of ecstasy. As Dorian toppled her over the edge, her orgasm took her by surprise and flung her into oblivion.

She could definitely get used to mindless bliss being distributed on a daily basis by one of the sexiest men alive. It was exhilarating; knowing a man like Dorian Johnston craved her. It set her hair on edge, feeling the pure electricity emanating from him.

He took his sweet time tasting and exploring her, and when he lifted his head and smiled sinfully, she could not take it any longer. A voice she did not recognize as her own called out to him.

"Dorian...please..."

He pressed the head of his shaft near her slick opening; she was already prepared for him. He leaned into her ear.

"Please what? Tell me what you want."

His voice was low and almost growling, and all sensible thought left her. She barely realized the voice that so hungrily spoke was hers.

"Please...take me now..." she pleaded, barely breathing in anticipation.

In a moment that was a breath too long, he entered her smoothly. It took only one fluid movement, and he had filled her to capacity physically and emotionally. Her body was on fire from the inside out, and as he began to slowly withdraw, she clamped her legs around his waist. She could not bear him leaving her in any sense, and she met his eyes with an intensity she did not know she possessed.

"Don't...just—"

He cut her words off with a powerful thrust. Followed by another, even more aggressive, and her hips matched his rhythm in a dance that proclaimed familiarity. Together they rocked with such force it threatened to shatter her sanity. When she thought her heart could not take yet another deep lunge, his movements slowed, deliciously teasing her orgasm into focus. As he tenderly stroked in and out, she felt as though molten lava were inching closer to the surface by the moment, ready to explode in an instant. She raised her head from where it had been buried in his shoulder, and felt him do the same. Their eyes met in recognition of their fiery passion, and it threw her off her crumbling foundation. She was completely swept away in a tornado that took her breath away, and she watched his face as his release took over him.

As he lay down beside her, trying to catch his breath, there came a soft knock on the door. Barely giving her time to sit up and cover herself, Dorian bellowed, "come in!" He smiled an impish grin as the door slowly creaked open.

Liz peeked her head in, and Michelle relaxed a bit. She barely took one glance inside then flung the door open, stepping cheerfully into the room. She cleared her throat.

"Well, at least you're both decent!" She laughed, sending echoes throughout the large room. "But, if you don't mind…" She flung the curtains open with a flourish, pouring daylight into the open space. "Breakfast is ready. Again." With that, she left, smiling.

Was it morning already? Where had the time gone? But before the question could root in her mind, she answered herself. The hours ticked away in a breath when she was encased in Dorian's arms, just as the world dissolved and scattered into infinity when she exploded beneath him. It was inevitable.

And she loved every intoxicating, breathless moment of him.

*****

Dorian could only smile to himself. He had not had to wait long for Michelle to come back to his arms. She had returned with fervor, fully connecting with him in more ways than he could have imagined. The fire between them roared stronger than ever, a fact Dorian had had no doubt of.

When he had finally thrust into her he had felt as though he could have exploded right then. He had not even noticed the time flying by, yet he did not regret getting a late start; rather he wished he could go back to the beginning and start from there.

He looked over at the woman beside him, who had placed her head back on the pillow and closed her eyes. He took her moment of peace to feast on her with his eyes. He could make out every curve of her figure under his black silk sheets, and he had to tear his eyes away or he knew he would get no work done. Reluctantly, he began to climb out of bed, and he felt her hand on his back. Her slumberous voice teased his earlobes.

"Leaving me already, are you?" she said, and he could hear the playful pout in her voice that subtly promised more of what they had experienced earlier.

He closed his eyes and leaned his head back, trying to focus. It was made an almost impossible task by Michelle, who was gently rubbing her fingers through his hair. Quickly he stood, desperately needing to break contact lest he drag her back to ecstasy.

She would be kicking and screaming, but definitely not in protest.

He tried to clear his mind as he backed slowly toward the bathroom that connected their two suites, but Michelle had switched to her side, watching him with a hunger he was sure was reflected in his eyes. He placed the tips of his fingers together, and pressed his lips to his index fingers. He needed to stop staring at the tempting naked body mere feet from him.

"God, Michelle, you have no idea…" he started, not sure how to put it. He needed to choose the correct words in order to keep that spark going in her.

"My darling, if I did not have a million business calls to make, I'd be yours to use all day." He reached the bathroom door and opened it. "I've really put it off long enough, sweetheart. Plus, you need to find something to wear. We have a charity auction tonight." He smiled as he began to close the door behind him. "I want you looking your best. Not that I don't mind you going like that, of course."

He heard her playful gasp and giggle as he closed the door, and he quickly crossed his large bathroom to turn on the shower. After he had fully cleaned himself, he stood with his face to the ceiling, letting the water pouring down from it cool his raging hormones. Lord, that woman did something otherworldly to him. Never before her had he experienced the mind-blowing pleasure she brought, and after she left he could not find a match to her insatiable passion. Other lovers he had encountered had only tried to impress him with their knowledge, over-playing the moans and sighs to the point of frustration.

But with Michelle it came naturally; she easily purred at his touch. Every gasp for breath, every moan of intense pleasure came from deep within her, and Dorian could feel every moment of it. It was no wonder some nights long ago he craved her, almost calling her name out into the darkness. She had been such a powerful, unseen force in his life over the past years; always only mere feet away in his mind, until he would open his eyes and realize it was a dream. Or worse, someone much less impressive. He knew what he had to do. He also knew that if he didn't do it, he'd never sleep a full night after their time was up.

He needed her as his mistress. Again. And he had to ask her immediately.

It was as simple as that. Dorian's mind resolved itself, and with a clear mind he turned off the water and stepped out. It would be nice to have her back at his beckon call, completely his whenever he wanted. Oh, yes. He could definitely get used to that.

He dried himself and started to wrap a towel around himself, but quickly reconsidered. He knew once Michelle heard what he had to say, she'd be dying for more of him.

To hell with business calls, he thought to himself as he flung open the door.

"So, I—" he started, but his sentence was quickly halted when he realized Michelle was not there. He cursed under his breath. Had he really been looking forward to her reaction? He chuckled to himself and went to get dressed, almost glad he did not find her with eager arms outstretched.

He really did need to make some phone calls.

He swiveled around his desk chair and picked up his receiver yet again, punching in digits he knew by heart. It rang twice, then a familiar female voice answered.

"Hello, Mr. Johnston. How was your flight?" Gwen asked, trying to sound chipper despite their time gap.

"Hello, Gwen. It was fine, thank you." He cleared his throat as the topic of their conversation became more serious. "Did you find the information I requested?"

"Yes, sir, I did," she said, sounding a bit perplexed. "But I'm not sure why you need it."

"I don't need you to. It's personal," he informed her, not wanting to sound rude. She was doing him a favor, after all.

"Hmm. I didn't think you had a 'personal' category in your life, sir. Be on the lookout for my fax. I'm going back to bed. Goodnight." With a yawn she hung up, and a few minutes later his fax machine roared to life. He rose from his chair and walked to it, carefully taking the paper it had spit out. He slowly read the personal information he had received about Michelle.

So, she was living in Maine...working for an interior decorating consulting firm that Dorian had never heard of. He assumed the reason she had moved was probably the reason she had accepted such a mediocre job, and was more than likely why she had come back to him. But what was it? He searched the documents, but there were no clues as to why she had come begging at his door.

She was indeed in school, as Gwen had attached Michelle's school transcript. By the look of things she was passing with flying colors, and was well on her way to finishing her degree. She had an 'A' in every class she was taking, and Dorian wondered how she was going to keep up her grades when she was with him for two weeks. He could almost feel a tinge of guilt eating at his conscience, yet a mischievous voice reminded him hat she knew exactly what she was getting into before she said yes. And when she accepted his offer to be his mistress she could stay wherever she liked, so she could finish school and accomplish her dreams. He would gladly fly to the moon and back to get to her whenever he wanted.

Thinking about her made him curious as to her whereabouts, and he slowly left his office in search of her. As he had closed the door behind him and came into the foyer, he noticed the open library doors. When he had crossed the threshold, a familiar figure greeted him with a smile. Michelle looked a vision in linen capris and a lavender tank top, and the sunlight coming in through the large windows danced in her hair as she flipped it out of her face. Surrounded by papers he was sure had to do with school, she looked as though she could have given his workload a run for its money. He found it oddly enticing, however.

"Finished with work already?" she inquired, putting her pen down. "Now that's not the Dorian I remember," she teased, and he couldn't help but smile.

"What are you doing in here?" he said, taking a seat across from her at the large round table where she sat. She looked confused, so he proceeded to explain further. "You're supposed to find something to wear."

He was surprised at her sudden outburst of haughty laughter.

"It's only eleven, Dorian. The auction doesn't start until five! How long do you think it's gonna take for me to get ready?" She picked up her pen again, as if about to resume whatever work she'd been doing. "I think I've got some time." She chuckled. "What kind of women do you deal with?" With that she turned her attention back to her textbook, and Dorian took it as his cue to leave. To give her privacy he closed the doors behind him, and smiled as he heard the soft "thank you" that floated out after him.

After he had settled himself at his desk again, he took a moment to reflect on Michelle's words. What kind of women had he been dealing with? But he knew the answer: he dealt with conceited, self-proclaimed fashionistas who needed at least half a day to get ready for dinner. He'd lost track of how many times he'd sent a car for a woman and she'd been late because she had not fully applied her makeup.

But not Michelle. She did not need hours of preparation to make herself beautiful. Had the auction's invitation not read 'formal attire only' at the bottom in neat calligraphy, he gladly would have taken her in her capris and tank top.

He did not know how long his restraint would hold if she dressed as she had the night previously. He could only imagine how stunning she would look that evening. Every curve, every subtle indentation that etched out the voluptuous waves of her body; he could already feel his hands running down them all over again.

He looked at his watch.

He probably could do some laps in the infinity pool before they needed to leave. He had to do something; just the thought of Michelle's body underneath his was fanning a fire deep down within him that he needed to get under control before he pulled her away from her work and every sane thought either of them possessed. He went to go change.

*****

Michelle stood in the open doors of the wardrobe, looking at two beautiful evening gowns. On her left hung a white and black one, with white front panels that were decorated with black roses. Its straps were black, and it came with a white wrap that hung lazily beside it.

On her right there was a champagne dress, strapless and beautifully outlined. Her bodice stopped just under her breasts and dropped to the floor in loose fabric giving a dramatic effect, long and flowing like a golden river. Luckily Andrew had included lingerie, shoes, and accessories with all her outfits, so she had nothing to do but her hair and makeup.

Thinking about Andrew reminded her that Dorian had purchased everything for her. She sighed. What was she doing here? She didn't belong in his world, and yet she felt so comfortable near him, as if she'd been by his side night after night. Speaking of night...she involuntarily blushed as she remembered what they had shared the night before. He made her feel so free, so unashamed...he truly worked a spell on her. A spell she wasn't necessarily rushing to have broken.

She looked at the clock in her room, which said three-fifteen. Biting her lip, she quickly decided on the white dress and went to get ready.

As she was applying her last bit of makeup, there came a soft knock at the door. She felt her heart leap as she called out, "come in!" She looked in the mirror and saw Dorian enter, dressed in a black tuxedo. He looked as at ease in his formal attire as some men did in a t-shirt. The fabric clung to his powerful frame in dramatic angles, making him seem like a dark, troubled superhero. He straightened his tie and said, "are you ready? The car is here." He stepped inside and pulled on the tails of his jacket to straighten it out, but there was no need. He looked immaculate.

She turned and slid into her shoes, grabbed her wrap from the edge of the bed, and came to stand beside him. He was so much taller than her usually, but with her heels they stood almost at eye level. She smiled up at him.

"Yes, actually, I am," she replied, putting her wrap around her shoulders. "How do I look?" she asked him, holding her arms out to give him an adequate view for inspection. She was taken by surprise when he pulled her into his arms and kissed her, and for a moment, an unbearably small moment, she let herself think she actually meant something to him. She could feel herself falling deeper and deeper in love with him, almost to the point of losing herself completely under his power. But somehow she did not mind. It was somewhat liberating, actually, being able to let herself be swept away by emotion. And even though she knew she would have to return to her normal life in a couple of weeks, she relished the fact that she could let herself get lost in the moment. Even if it was only a mere moment.

He led her to the waiting limo, and she slid over mere inches to let him sit. Since she was going to have him all to herself, she figured she might as well get in all the physical contact she could before she had to leave. As he slid in next to her, he noted the closeness.

"You know, I can't have your body pressed against me if you expect me to get through this evening," he informed her with a playful tone in his voice. She saw a smirk form in the corner of his mouth, an action that slightly changed the angles of his face. It made him appear light-hearted and carefree briefly, even though she knew he could not possibly be. Underneath that beautiful exterior there was a troubled man with too much on his mind, so much so that it superseded his personal life. She did not pretend to know how he found time to run an international company and appear almost every week in the gossip magazines, sporting a different woman on his arm each time.

    She felt a pull of unfamiliar jealousy, and she was immediately shocked at herself. But a small, dark thought began to expand in her mind: what if one of those beautiful women saw them together? She was suddenly very aware of her less-than-perfect physique. Round in the hips and a bit top-heavy, she knew she could not compete with women who worked with personal trainers on a daily basis; women who ate crackers and called it a meal. It was just unnatural. She, however, could sit down in front of a good movie and devour a pint of ice-cream without a second thought, after which she would usually have to fight tooth and nail to keep it from spreading into her hips.

    Her self-confidence dropped to nil. How could she try and hold a candle to wealthy socialites who spent hours in front of a mirror? They would be going on and on about who was wearing whom, whereas Michelle barely knew she was wearing Versace. Had she not seen the name sprawled on the box as well as the tiny tag she found inside, she wouldn't have had a clue. She hoped she could merely disappear in Dorian's shadow and not have to say much.

Dorian placed his hand on her knee. As if he had read her mind and heard her thoughts, he lifted her chin with his other hand and raised her to meet his gaze. She struggled to meet his eyes as he said, "don't doubt yourself. You're gonna make all these spoiled brats green with envy." He placed a light kiss on the tip of her nose, and she closed her eyes to keep her tears from spilling out at the pure emotion she felt from that tiny gesture.

His words lit a fire inside her. How could she have possibly had any worries? He had chosen her, hadn't he? Dorian Johnston had had Russian supermodels and Italian ballerinas on his arm before. He could hand-pick any woman in the world that he wanted, yet he had decided on her. Surely, she had to find solace in that fact. If he wanted other women, wouldn't he be with them instead of with her? Why would he waste his time? His time was precious, not to mention expensive, and she highly doubted he'd lose money over something trivial. He had to have confidence she'd be able to hold her own, or else he wouldn't have had her escort him. He had faith in her—she hoped—so she had to have some in herself. On top of that, she knew she possessed a razor-sharp wit worthy of any vain, conceited woman they could come across. She refused to let any woman let her feel inferior. Even if she knew she didn't look as though she had just stepped off the runway, she knew she could hold her own.

Their limo slid to a halt in front of a large hotel, and Dorian's door was quickly opened. He got out and reached in to offer his hand, which she cautiously took and slowly stepped onto the pavement. Dorian gave her hand a reassuring squeeze, and he put a comforting hand on her back to motion her forward. As they ascended the stairs Michelle felt butterflies beginning to form deep in her tummy, and she looped her arm through Dorian's for support. When they reached the top stair and began to walk inside, Dorian gently kissed her on the cheek. "Relax," he said calmly, and already she felt better.

They stopped at the front desk, and an older gentleman lifted his head. "May I help you?"

"Yes, the Trump ballroom, please," Dorian spoke up.

"Oh, you're here for the auction. Twenty-eighth floor, you can't miss it. Have a wonderful evening."

They headed to the rows of elevators, and Michelle was vaguely aware of the stares they were getting. After Dorian pressed the up button a pair of doors whooshed open not too far from them and they stepped into the cool space, and Michelle caught sight of her reflection in the mirrors inside. She looked so natural standing beside Dorian as he stood leaning against the wall, eyes to the ceiling. They almost looked like a couple, but Michelle knew better.

The spacious elevator did not provide enough room for her to escape the heat that was radiating from his powerful frame. She could almost feel herself being scorched all the way the way down to her soul, but she couldn't seem to pull herself away. She was content to be consumed by the raw power of him.

At last the elevator slowed to a stop and as the doors opened Michelle steeled her spine. In front of them there were a set of double doors, with a small sign beside them that read "Trump Ballroom". A small desk was placed in front, with a smiling woman sitting at it. As they approached it, she sweetly said, "name?"

"Johnston," Dorian said, apparently not needing to say anything to accompany it, and it seemed to hang in the air for a moment. The woman checked the list in front of her, and, upon seeing his name she replied, "thank you, Mr. Johnston. These are for your bidding," she said, handing them both a white paddle with a number on it. "Enjoy your evening," she added, and Dorian held one of the doors open for Michelle as she stepped inside.

Once on the other side of the double doors she saw there were rows of chairs set up, with a stage and podium in front. The people that had already arrived were seated quietly, and Michelle noted every woman in attendance was fashionably dressed. They chose two seats in the back, and she could see Dorian looked focused. She leaned over to him and said, "so, what is this for?"

"The Eric Trump Foundation. They take the proceeds and put them towards St. Jude's research for children with life-threatening diseases."

She was taken aback. She did not realize he was involved in charity events or that he was even passionate about such things. How did he fit it into his already heavy schedule? She was amazed that he would be able to find time to invest his money in his personal interests, but her mind quickly reminded her that he owned the company and could do as he pleased.

She marveled at the different layers of him: the ruthless businessman, philanthropist, and semi-family man. Not to mention what a lover he was. If he could only open up his heart and learn to love, he'd be almost perfect in her eyes. But it did not matter. She knew he could not possibly fall in love with her in the small amount of time they would be spending together, so she refused to get her hopes up.

A small woman walked up to the podium and banged her gavel twice, getting everyone's attention. She quietly cleared her throat, and the room fell silent.

"We want to thank you for coming out this evening..." she started, and Michelle listened as she explained the rules and protocols. When she finished she stepped aside to let a tall, stocky man step into her place. He quickly introduced the first item and began the bidding.

Michelle watched as thousands of dollars were bid by the minute but noticed that Dorian had not raised his hand once. She whispered to him.

"You're not bidding?"

"No," he replied, without hesitation.

She was confused. "Then why come at all?"

"Because Gwen said I needed to show my face more. She said I couldn't be the dark, unapproachable CEO that never comes out of his office," he said with a light, almost forced chuckle.

"But you are the dark, unapproachable CEO that never comes out of his office," she reminded him jokingly.

He turned his dark eyes to her. "I'm out now, aren't I?" He casually lifted one eyebrow. Before she could respond, he added, "I donate a bit afterwards." He said it with a sigh, as if making a public appearance was the last thing on his mind.

She settled back into her seat and folded her hands in her lap. Slowly she let her eyes wander downward to glance at her left hand, where her faux engagement ring sat. It lightly sparkled from the overhead chandeliers, and Michelle's hand had already grown accustomed to the weight of it. She barely noticed it was there anymore. Now, why was that? She knew it was not authentic. Her senses and her damned heart, however, could not tell the difference.

Somewhere in the back of her mind she let herself pretend that what they had was real, but only for a moment. She knew such ludicrous thoughts were no help when she was trying to stay in control of her grasp on reality, but something about the man sitting next to her put her entirely out of character. Her better judgment told her the sooner she was out of his magnetic power, the better. Her heart was not listening. It pleaded to stay, to sap up more of what his incredible body could give her.

She couldn't get enough.

She stifled a yawn that erupted out of nowhere, trying not to look disinterested. Dorian, however, caught the action and commented. Leaning into her ear, he whispered, "you want to get out of here?" She looked up at him, trying to see if she had heard him correctly. The mischievous glint in his dark eyes confirmed it.

She felt her blood rush with adrenaline. With a sly grin she lightly nodded, and a broad grin spread across his face. He stood and took her hand, leading her out. Her legs felt a little unsteady as she struggled to keep up with his long strides, and she tried to compose herself. It was all so spontaneous, so unlike him. What had come over Dorian Johnston? She pondered over this as they reached the elevator doors and he pressed the button for their descent.

As she was waiting, Dorian spun her around into his arms and kissed her. The action caught her off guard and off balance, and she felt her center of gravity shift as she fell into Dorian's embrace. Never breaking his lips away, he dipped her so low her hair almost grazed the floor. When he lifted her, she heard a small noise behind them: the nice woman they had spoken to earlier at the desk was clearing her throat.

Fully embarrassed, Michelle felt color flooding her cheeks. Looking into Dorian's face, she found him grinning back at her. She felt so alive, as if molten lava was running through her veins. She had never experienced the kind of intense feeling he brought just by merely being near her, and she was fairly certain she'd never feel the same way again. It was as though he had brushed the lonely cobwebs off her very soul, opening her up to feel all the sensations she thought she'd never feel after he had so carelessly disposed of her and her emotions towards him.

She turned her attention to the woman, who was smiling.

"Newlyweds?" she asked, not knowing how far from the truth she actually was. As Michelle opened her mouth the doors behind her slid open, the cool air hitting her on the back and sending a shock down her spine.

"Almost," Dorian answered, leading them both inside before the woman could manage to respond. As the doors sealed shut, Michelle could barely register what he had said before she felt herself being pushed against the wall, Dorian's hands on her waist. He stared down at her with a gaze that threatened to consume her.

"I've been aching to get you out of this dress since we left the house," he said huskily into her ear and kissed her neck. Instinctively she reached up her arms and looped them around his neck as he lifted his head to claim her lips.

She was barely aware of where they were, only the blood rushing through her veins as Dorian deepened the kiss. As his hungry tongue darted in and out of her mouth, Michelle felt her legs begin to weaken. Almost instantly Dorian pressed his body firmly against hers, supporting her. Before she could become completely lost in the moment, the elevator began to slow to a halt. Dorian pulled back, and she gave a moan of protest.

"Oh, there's more. I promise," he said against her lips. He quickly turned to face the doors just as they opened, and together they stepped out into the cool lobby. The gust of wind from the opening doors brought Michelle back to reality, and she lifted the hem of her dress to keep up with Dorian's brisk walk to the front doors.

It felt almost surreal, as though any moment she would awake to find William and James jumping on the foot of her bed, as they did almost every morning. Thinking about the boys made her remember that she had not called to check on them, and she felt a pang of guilt. She knew she would have to be discreet if she wanted to get away while Dorian was preoccupied with work to call them from her cell phone.

She barely realized that Dorian was holding the limo door open for her, she was so lost in her thoughts. She quickly composed herself and slid inside, smiling up at him.

They rode home in silence, Dorian staring out the window. She was curious what went through his mind when he got silent like that, but she didn't have the courage to ask him to share his feelings with her. Powerful men tended not to like people imposing on their personal thoughts.

They pulled up in front of the house, and a man quickly opened Dorian's door. As he stepped out he offered his hand to her, and Michelle immediately took it, gave it a quick squeeze, and exited. She looked up at him with determination, reassuring him that it was what she wanted. Her body craved it.

He began to run in the house, and Michelle lifted her long dress with her free hand to keep up with him. They sprinted up the stairs, both laughing, and for a moment, she felt completely free. She felt like a carefree young woman, and she listened to their laughter echoing throughout the large house. It all seemed so magical, as if he were her handsome knight who'd swept her away to his enchanted castle in the sky.

As they reached the entrance to his side of their adjourning rooms, he stopped and twirled her into his arms, and softly kissed her on the forehead. He placed his forehead against hers, and she closed her eyes. She was in the thick of it now, completely his. She knew exactly what was coming, she just had to hold on for the ride.

"Do you want me as much as I want you?" he whispered against her lips. His light breath on her face set her hair on edge.

"More," she replied, and that was the last coherent thing either of them spoke for quite some time.

Chapter 7

Dorian blinked hard, trying to focus on what his board members were saying, but he couldn't. The only thing occupying his mind was the beautiful woman he had left fully content in bed that morning. She flooded his thoughts; her beautiful face seemed to seep into every train of thinking. She intrigued him by the little things she did that made her unique. Once again she had requested that they make love in the dark the night previously, which he liked. He liked having to use his hand as his eyes, and by the time his eyes adjusted to the darkness, he was already deep inside her sweet warmth.

But something else about her seemed to have him captured: her dark, deep, endless eyes, her beautiful laughter, her feisty personality; they all had him transfixed. He couldn't quite determine what to call how he was feeling for her, but he knew her did not want to call it love. Love was a friend he had not yet met; when he had thought a woman had freely given it to him and he had tried to give it back, he had gotten his heart returned to him in tiny scraps.

Since then he had learned to put his emotions on hold, dam them up. Then Michelle, with her beautiful personality, was slowly cracking the cement around his heart. He did not want her to; he was a better businessman when he was ruthless. As his account manager delved into their profit margins, a sudden realization caught him by surprise: this was exactly how he had felt before, when he had ejected her from his life. Then he had been running scared. Not now. He wanted her in his world, damn the consequences. He couldn't imagine her not there, him rolling over to not see her in his bed, peacefully sleeping.

And although it may not be love, what they had was definitely something he liked.

He smiled to himself, looked at his watch, and realized he and Michelle had an engagement in a few hours. He knew she didn't require long to get ready, but he was ready to use any excuse to get back to her.

He held up a powerful hand to cut off Robert, his senior account manager. Immediately he stopped talking, and the other members turned to give their attention.

"Gentlemen, I know I'm still making you all filthy rich, thank you Robert." The group let out a light chuckle in different places around the table, and Dorian stood. "Now, if you'll excuse me, I have somewhere I need to be."

He gathered the files he had spread in front of him, and walked out. The looks of shock on the faces of the men he had made wealthy gave him more than enough satisfaction. He walked back to his desk, and upon seeing him Molly, his London assistant, hurried over to him.

"Meeting over already?" she asked, glancing at her watch.

"For me, yes. Will you call Liz and tell her to let Michelle know I'm on the way?" He closed his laptop and slid it into its case. As he passed Molly she said, "you're leaving already? Boy, she must be something special."

When he had stepped inside the elevator, he turned around and smiled. "Yeah, she is." The broad smile that spread across Molly's face only added to his happiness.

As he maneuvered his car through the winding streets, he took the time alone to think about Michelle. He wasn't sure what to call what they had together, but he felt a deeper connection with her than just sex. Somewhere deep within him, he felt as though they shared something besides their physical attraction. He couldn't quite put his finger on it, but something in his deepest reserves of emotions told him it was important.

When he pulled up into the drive, he barely waited for the engine to cut off before he jumped out. No one was there to greet him, but he didn't care. He only wanted to see Michelle.

She lit him on fire with the mere thought of her: the way her eyes sparkled, the way her lips felt on his, everything about her drove him insane. She blocked out all other thoughts from his mind, making him a pool of raging hormones. When he was not near her he immediately began to think about her, as if his mind would not tolerate being without her. On top of everything else, she was a phenomenal lover. She took him so effortlessly to heights of pleasure he had never experienced before; it was as though she understood his every aching need completely. No other woman he had taken to bed was so in tune with his body, so totally aware of what he needed. It was a much-needed change from the women who tried too hard to sexually impress him.

He rolled his eyes at the thought. If he saw one more blonde reach up and run her fingers through her hair as she straddled him in a pathetic attempt to look sexy, he was going to scream in frustration. But not Michelle. Every movement, every breathless sigh was genuine; she didn't need to overdo anything. Her authenticity undid him every time. She truly did lose herself under him; she gave herself and her willpower over to him freely and willingly.

He didn't understand why he never before realized how wonderful she was, how complete she made him feel. It was as though his fear of emotion had him blinded to how perfect she was for him. She was sweet, caring, diligent, beautiful, smart...all the things he had told himself he wanted in a woman.

As he stopped outside her door, he took a deep breath. So many things were hitting him at once; it was a little overwhelming. He needed to calm himself down before he saw Michelle and she excited him all over again. An idea struck him, one he couldn't believe he hadn't thought of sooner: he wouldn't ask her to be his mistress. It was too impersonal, and she deserved more than that. He'd ask her to be a part of his life, not as a mere play toy, but in a legitimate relationship. He wanted to see where their future could go together, and the thought made him stand a bit straighter.

He should have done this the first go-round; he could've had her all to himself for all these years, standing beside him, supporting him, building a life with him...and possibly bearing his children.

The thought of Michelle as the mother of his heir caught his breath in a way that shocked him. He struggled to push the powerful image from his mind and focus on the present.

With one last deep breath, he knocked on the door. As he waited for a response, he realized why he was so enthralled with Michelle's personality: she was just like his mother.

They both had the same infectious way about them, drawing people in with a mere smile or laugh. He remembered times, when he was younger, just sitting and listening to his mother on the phone. How alive she was, recounting whatever story to whoever was on the other line, often laughing heartily and talking with her hands. It was such a shame that a beautiful light such as his mother's had been snuffed out at such a young age.

Before he could start to elaborate in his head the door opened, and Michelle was beaming at him.

She was a vision in a soft gold—champagne, maybe?—dress that clung deliciously to her breasts with a tight bodice. When the material reached the underside of her lush mounds, it dropped straight to the floor, where the dress hung barely over the tips of her shoes. She looked like a goddess with her hair loose and flowing, the way he liked it. It was strapless to show off her smooth shoulders, and Dorian was glad. It would also show off the gift he had for her.

"You're back early! Liz told me you were on the way, but I didn't think she meant immediately! I'm almost ready, I just have to put on my makeup," she said, walking toward the large vanity that sat in the corner of the room. Though the dress did not emphasize her curves, one could not miss the voluptuous bottom that sat beneath her waist. He watched it sway as she walked away from him, and he stepped inside the door and closed it behind him. As she sat and opened the makeup box he'd had Andrew send over, she said, "how was work?"

As she opened a small case and covered a large brush with the powder inside, he replied, "long, as always." He noticed her rushing with applying her makeup, and he quickly spoke up. "Take your time with your makeup. We've got time, darling."

He sat on the edge of the bed, watching her. "You work too hard," she said, blunt. She dusted her face with the brush gently, carefully taking long strokes to cover it entirely. Her hands seemed to flow so effortlessly, her fluid movements working together to form a slow, blossoming transformation. Her makeup was light and not overdone, whereas so many women amongst London's elite tended to over-exaggerate their features with heavy creams and powders. Michelle had naturally what they spent countless money trying to obtain, and Dorian loved that.

It wasn't until she was applying her last bit of lipstick that he spoke. He stood, came up behind her, and withdrew a long jewelry box from his inner breast pocket. Before the board meeting he'd cut short, he'd had it sent to his office by express from Cartier as a way to mark his property that evening, to set her apart from all the other women who would be there, but he realized it meant much more than that. It was a symbol of the beginning of their relationship.

As she looked up from her reflection, she noticed the black box. Her eyes widened. "What is that?" she asked, smiling. He opened the box and gently lifted the necklace out, then snapped it shut and tossed the box softly on the bed behind him. With reverence, he dropped it around her neck, and she lifted her hair to allow him to clasp it. As she let her hair loose, her hand immediately lifted to her neck. He watched her eyes soften, and small tears formed in the corners, threatening to spill down her lightly powdered cheeks.

The diamond and pearl necklace lit up her face, and she looked angelic. He smiled as he placed his hands on her shoulders. "It's a symbol," he said, bending to say it over her shoulder. She tilted her head to let him nuzzle in the crook of her neck, then met his gaze in the mirror.

"Of what?" she asked.

"Of a beginning," he answered, coming to kneel beside her. She turned and looked at him with questioning eyes. Before she could ask, he quickly said, "of our beginning. I want you to be with me, Michelle. I wanna see where this goes between us."

"Are you serious?" she asked, her eyes sparkling. She happily looped her arms around his neck, and he squeezed tight. He hadn't felt completely happy in a long time, and he was glad Michelle could give that to him. As he pulled her back from him, he noticed tears slowly falling down her cheeks.

"Don't cry, dearest. You'll ruin your makeup," he said, smiling gently.

"I'm sorry," she replied, quickly turning to fix her streaked cheeks.

"Don't be," he reassured her, then looked at his watch. "But I guess we better go ahead and head out. Jeff's house is a little over an hour from here, and that's with good traffic."

As he moved toward the door, she said, "I'm ready if you are," and came to stand beside him. Somehow he knew she was talking about more than their evening, and he reached out and grabbed her hand as he opened the door. "I am."

He opted to drive that night, as he had a feeling they might leave early. Not that he would mind, of course. Rather than ride in silence he sparked a conversation with her about one of her passions: decorating.

"So, why interior design?" he asked.

Her face scrunched in confusion. "What do you mean?"

"I mean, it's such an under populated field."

"Well, it's always been a passion of mine, making things beautiful. Plus, my grandmother always kept a beautiful house, and it inspired me I suppose. When I started taking classes for it, I discovered just how fun it could be, and I was hooked for life. I knew it was what I wanted to do forever." When she talked her face was so animated and radiant, and Dorian found it hard to focus on the road. Luckily, he knew the way by heart.

"Any ideas for the estate?" he asked, turning a corner into Jeff's neighborhood. Immediately her eyes lit up.

"Oh, yes..." she said, her pitch already beginning to heighten with her anticipation. She turned in her seat as much as she could to face him, and although he couldn't fully focus on her, he saw enough in his peripheral to heat his blood. He made himself concentrate on what she was saying.

"In the foyer, what do you think about a baby grand under the stairs?"

He envisioned it in his head: a stylish, classy black piano would be a wonderful addition to the house; his father might even pick up playing again since he'd entered his form of retirement. He liked the idea. Why had no one thought of it before? He smiled at her before making a right onto Jeff's street. "That sounds wonderful," he replied, slowing in front of a sprawling house.

It sat back from the road, but it couldn't be missed among the trees. Beige and pristine with black shutters, its dramatic effect was a complete opposite to the man who resided there.

Jeff Matthews was the most relaxed man ever to run a Fortune 500 company. The only truly ruthless aspect of him was how he handled his business, which was the reason he was truly powerful as a CEO. No one expected such a carefree guy to be so much of a bulldog when things got down to business, so his intensity tended to completely blindside people. Starting as merely an accountant in a shipping firm, his intuitive knowledge of the inner workings of the business caught the attention of his employers and skyrocketed him to the top. So when he was named as successor to the retiring CEO, he jumped in the driver's seat with no hesitation.

Having put an entire company under his belt at the ripe old age of 26, the gossip columns held their breaths as they waited for him to pick out a bride. He hadn't, and after almost five years it seemed the world finally collectively exhaled.

Dorian gave Michelle a quick kiss on the cheek as valets opened their doors, and Dorian took his ticket as well as Michelle's hand as she came around to meet him. With grace she grabbed a bit of her dress and lifted it, making sure she would not fall up the steep hill to the front door. She looked so natural in her formal attire, it fit her like a second skin. She flashed him a dazzling smile as they began their ascent, and he squeezed her hand.

When they reached the front door, Dorian had barely put his hand back at his side from knocking before the door was swung open with a flourish.

"Dorian! So glad you could make it!" Jeff exclaimed. He was dressed in a suit, but wore no tie and had his top button open. Dorian laughed to himself. It was about as 'formal' as Jeff Matthews was going to get.

"I wasn't gonna come," he replied, grabbing Michelle's elbow and pulling her in front of him. "But I wanted you to meet someone."

"Well, well, well, who is this?" Jeff asked, reaching out to grab Michelle's hand and plant a kiss on it.

"This is my fiancée, Michelle," Dorian informed him, and he noted to himself that he said it with a bit more conviction. Jeff looked at him with wide eyes.

"Did you say 'fiancée'?" He put his hands on his hips. "So, Mr. Never-Gonna-Commit has finally found Mrs. Right, huh?" He turned to Michelle. "Or should I say Mrs. Johnston? You must be something mighty special, darling."

She smiled and looked over her shoulder at Dorian. "I like to think so, yeah," she sweetly said, leaning her head back into his chest. He took a moment to inhale her scent before wrapping his arms around her waist and pulling her close to him. The action seemed second-nature; he barely realized he was doing it before Michelle's back lightly touched against his chest. His arms curved around her waist so naturally that when his hands clasped together at her stomach and she immediately placed her hands on top of his, he felt as though he'd done the same motion hundreds of times before.

At their embrace, Jeff laughed. "What? Physical contact? In public? I can't believe this. What is this world coming to?" he joked, laughing and shaking his head.

As Dorian was about to reply, a familiar yet unwanted voice floated towards him. He was afraid to turn his head, for fear that his eyes would confirm what his head and heart were beginning to dread immensely. He didn't need to, however; she soon came into view.

"Baby, there you are, I've been looking all over for you. You left me with those dreadful women over there, all they want to talk about is the environment..." Nicole Orman said, placing a small hand on Jeff's shoulder.

Still a platinum blonde, she had her once long hair cut into a fashionable bob that hung just below her cheekbones. She was dressed in a long dress as black as her very soul, with a high spilt up one thigh. Once upon a time, the sliver of leg that showed would have enticed him, but not anymore. She had left a bitter taste in his mouth, and she merely disgusted him. He knew the kind of woman she was, the deceitful, conniving, devious snake that would strike at anyone who got in her way.

As she placed a soft kiss on Jeff's cheek, Dorian immediately and whole-heartedly felt sorry for him. He could only hope Jeff would learn the truth about her before it was too late for his heart.

"I was being a good host," he replied. "My friend Dorian here and his fiancée just arrived, and I came over to say hello."

At the sound of Dorian's name she quickly turned around, apparently not noticing them upon her first arrival. He wasn't surprised she hadn't realized two human beings were standing behind her; she was so wrapped up in herself it was a wonder she noticed the rest of the world at all.

When she met his eyes, he returned the gaze with such a fury he did not know he possessed. She was here, she was here and she was about to ruin this evening. He cursed in his head. This could not be happening. With his eyes he dared her to say something he didn't like, and relished the opportunity to knock her down to size.

"Dorian..." she said smoothly, slimily, holding her arms out for a hug. He did not move. She drew her lips up in a mock pout. "Oh, still bitter, are we? Well, no matter." She turned her eyes to Michelle, and he could feel her tense from where he held her around the waist. He gave her a reassuring squeeze, but he noticed it did not help. He only hoped her wonderful wit would not fail her.

"Fiancée, huh?" Nicole scanned Michelle with her eyes. She raised one eyebrow, then looked at Dorian. "Looks like you're scraping the bottom of the barrel these days, love. Feeling a little desperate, are we?"

Before he could snap back, he heard Michelle chuckle. "Now, that's funny. I was just gonna ask Jeff the same thing about you."

Jeff's jaw dropped, but not lower than Nicole's. The look on her face gave Dorian a feeling of satisfaction almost unparalleled. Almost. There was a certain feeling of satisfaction, however, that could never be matched. He immediately thought of how he would repay that razor sharp intellect of hers. *Take that, Nicole*, he thought to himself.

As if almost on cue a friend called out to Jeff and he walked away, leaving Nicole to only gawk at the woman who dared to challenge her. She laughed a light evil laugh.

"He didn't tell you we were lovers, did he?" she said casually, trying to push Michelle's buttons. "But it's not such ancient history, is it, Dorian?" With that she winked at him, and he felt quite sick to his stomach. Before Michelle could reload and fire back, Nicole slithered away, laughing. Quickly Michelle turned to him, her eyes blazing with anger. She didn't have to say a word.

"I'll go get the valet."

*****

Michelle was furious.

How dare Dorian not warn her in advance that there was an evil blonde in his past? She felt completely defeated, as if she had been sent to the plate without a bat. She could only replay in her mind what Nicole had said just before she had walked away; it seemed to taunt her. What had she meant by 'not ancient history'? Did that mean that she had seen Dorian recently? Her head was swirling.

She discreetly sneaked a glance of him, and noticed his knuckles were almost white as he gripped the steering wheel. His jaw set in stone, he focused intently on the road. He looked almost as pissed as she felt. As he swung dangerously fast into the driveway after some time, Michelle decided she would ask him about it after they were inside. She needed to be sure.

As she got out the car and began to walk inside, she could feel her stomach tightening. She couldn't understand why she felt the tingle of jealousy that was eating away at her slowly. She knew he had not been celibate in their time apart. Yet she did not realize she would be as affected by that fact as she was.

Entering into a relationship with Dorian Johnston meant that she would be faced with an endless parade of his ex- lovers, but she never expected the first run-in to be so harsh. How could he ever have been interested in such a vile woman long enough to get her clothes off? She seemed to radiate venom from every pore on her body. Even though she was beautiful, her personality tainted her good looks.

When she reached his side of their master suite and stepped inside, Dorian was not far behind her. He slammed the door behind him, threw off this coat and tie and sat on the edge of the bed. Raking his hands through his hair, he let out a long breath. Michelle slipped out of her heels, feeling the plush carpet under her bare feet as she walked towards the bathroom to get to her side of their large connecting rooms. Before she could reach the golden knob, she stopped, dropped her shoes on the carpet, and went to stand in front of him. She had to do this now, before she lost her nerve.

Slowly he looked up and met her eyes. When she opened her mouth to speak, he quickly began to talk.

"I know, I know, I owe you an explanation," he said, sighing. "But I didn't even want to consider the possibility of running into her. I didn't want to think about her, period."

"What did she do to you?"

He sighed again, deep and weary. "We were together before you ever came to work at the Towers. Everything was great in the beginning. We had met through a mutual friend and had hit it off. In a couple months I was swept up in whirlwind of lust, chasing it as if it was love." He chuckled, but there was no humor in his voice. "Well, I thought it was. But then something changed. She got mean and spiteful. We started to argue all the time. One night I told her I was leaving." He paused.

"And…?" she inquired further.

"She quickly announced she was pregnant. Naturally, I was floored. I wasn't ready to be a father—hell, I'm still not—but what could I do? I told her I'd stay. I was going to ask her to marry me, even. But the day before I was going to pop the question, she had a doctor's appointment. On the way there she confessed. She admitted she was never pregnant, and begged me not to leave." He ran his hands through his hair again, thoroughly disheveling it.

"I was so furious. I pulled over right there and let her out. I didn't come back for her, either. I should have listened to my father."

"What do you mean?" she asked, sitting beside him.

"He always seemed to be intuitive about the women I let into my life. He could size them up from a mile away. Whether they were spoiled, or prissy, or talked too much, or whatever the case may be. The moment I introduced her to him, he immediately disliked her. But against my better judgment, I pursued the relationship anyway." He closed his eyes for a moment. "What kills me is, I was starting to look forward to being a father. But she pushed the entire thought of family out of my head. All I focused on was business. I mean, the way I figured, if that was love, I wanted nothing to do with it." He lay back on the bed, letting his feet stay on the floor. "About six months ago I was here for a board meeting and we ran into each other. And I had to admit, I was curious to see if she had grown up or not. We had dinner, but there was nothing there. No spark, no lust, no feelings whatsoever. Well, none that were positive anyway. The whole time I kept thinking about work, completely ignoring whatever she was saying. She was the same vapid, shallow, self-centered woman I'd known and despised. I didn't even eat, just had some wine and left. All the while I was driving back to my hotel I just kept wondering how I could've been chasing after a woman like that in the first place." He let out a deep 'whoosh'. "I don't know how I was so stupid."

She took a moment to let his words sink in. No wonder he was so jaded when it came to relationships: he'd had his heart ground into mush by a woman who cared nothing for him. He was so affected by her treachery that he had boxed up his heart. But, somehow, she had slowly chipped away at the wall he had built, and he had begun to open up to her. If they were going to pursue a relationship, she would have to tell him about the boys soon. She did not want him to think she was purposefully deceiving him, even though she was. She needed to fess up.

She took a deep breath. "I have to tell you—"

A muffled buzzing coming from her handbag cut off her words. It immediately caught Dorian's attention; and she closed her eyes and swore inwardly. She'd forgotten she had left her purse in his side of their suite the day before when he'd surprised her and left work just to take her to lunch. A phone call on her cell could only mean an emergency.

"What's that?" Dorian asked, as she got up to answer it.

"Um, my phone, hold on."

She quickly rummaged through her bag and found her phone lying near the bottom, holding it up to read the caller ID: Candice.

Something was wrong with the boys.

Immediately her heart was caught in her throat. She thought the worst out of maternal instinct, and as she frantically answered, she felt horribly guilty. Here she was, losing herself in a whirlwind of frivolous passion halfway across the world, and her boys needed her at home. Immediately she regretted coming, despite all that had happened. Even though she had finally broken through Dorian's rough exterior and had begun to see a softer side to him, she was a mother first. Somehow she had forgotten that in the heat of the moment.

"Hello? Candice? What's wrong?" Already she was seeing a thousand possible perilous scenarios playing in her mind.

"Hey, Michelle, I know you're supposed to be relaxing, and I wouldn't be calling you if it wasn't serious, but is there any way you could come home?"

"Of course, what is wrong? Please, just tell me."

"Oh, don't think the absolute worst! It's just that William's contracted some kind of nasty virus. He's scared here at the hospital and wants you. James is sensing William's fear and wants you, too. They're almost inconsolable."

Michelle let out a small sigh of relief. Sickness she could deal with. She didn't even want to think about alternative scenarios that could have happened. She returned her attention to Candice.

"Tell them both to be patient. It's gonna take me a few hours, but I'm on my way. Thank so much, Candice.

"No problem, hon. I'll hold down the fort until you get here."

Michelle disconnected the call, and turned to face Dorian. She swallowed hard and decided she might as well tell him. She couldn't hide his sons from him anymore, especially since he was going to meet them in a few hours.

He looked genuinely worried, and she hated having deceived him for so long. She cleared her throat, but she knew she was stalling. She had to face the music.

He came to stand in front of her, putting his hands gently on her shoulders.

"What's wrong?" he asked, concerned.

"I have to go home," she replied.

His eyes darkened with worry. "Is everything alright?"

She tried to mold her wording, but there was no use. It had to come out, and there was no way she could make it sound better than it was.

"My son is sick." The words hung in the air for a moment, then she added, "one of them." An infinitesimal flicker of time passed, then Dorian blinked hard.

"You have children?" he asked, both eyebrows raised.

"Twin boys."

When he heard this, she heard him take in a small breath. It seemed to affect him more than anything, and he dropped his hands.

"I'll drive to the hangar."

She watched him go to the bathroom and slam the door behind him, then shortly afterward, she heard the shower turn on. She flopped on the edge of the bed and dropped her head in her hands. She tried to stop them, but the hot tears flowed down her cheeks regardless.

Dorian Johnston was about to meet his sons. And he was not going to be happy about it.

Chapter 8

Dorian had so many thoughts in his head, he was unsure how to begin his line of questioning. He noticed she kept her head down, as if ashamed. How dare she not tell him she had children? She probably had a husband too, or at least some man in her life. No man could possibly let Michelle bear his children and then leave her.

His head was swirling. It seemed surreal that only a few hours ago he had been baring his soul to her, and now they were getting ready to land in Portland International Airport to take her to a son he'd never been informed of. How had Gwen missed this in her research?

Two sons. Twin sons.

How could he have let himself begin to fall for a woman who couldn't even be honest with him? He steeled his spine. It was like Nicole all over again. At least this time he had not fallen so deep, and had found out the truth before it was too late.

As they loaded into the limo that had been waiting for them, the door had barely closed before Dorian began his interrogation.

"How old are they?" he asked forcefully, not meeting her eyes. He was pissed, and he wanted the truth. He watched her take a deep breath, then finally spoke.

"They just turned three last month."

"Where is their father?" He felt his jaw clench involuntarily.

"He doesn't know about them," she informed him.

"Well, didn't you tell him you were pregnant?" He was becoming more furious with each sentence. What kind of woman didn't tell a man he was going to be a father? The Michelle he thought he knew dissolved, and all that sat in front of him was yet another dishonest woman.

"He's a bit difficult to get in contact with," she replied, then turned to look out the window. As they pulled in front of the hospital, the limo had barely come to a stop before she threw open the door and got out. By the time he had gotten out and inside, she already had the room number from the front desk. She said nothing to him, but instead walked to one of the elevators and pushed the appropriate button.

As they stepped inside he said, "this conversation is not over." In the reflective doors, he watched her eyes darken with anger. Quickly she turned to face him.

"My son is sick. Your little game of twenty questions is insignificant to me," she spat at him. With that she turned back around, and the doors slowly opened.

He stood still, shocked for a moment. Even though he was upset, he was turned on by her anger. Usually women were scared to make him mad in fear of losing him, often walking on eggshells to please him to the point of annoyance. It was refreshing to find a woman who wasn't afraid of him.

He watched her hurry away down the hall, and he stepped out of the elevator slowly. He wondered how she could possibly be feeling: fiercely protective of someone no matter the cost. With a sudden thought he realized why she had chosen to come to him out of desperation...she needed money for her children. He sighed and caught up with her.

She almost sprinted down the children's ward, which was decorated with colorful aquatic murals down the walls. There was a front desk at which she signed in, and the smiling nurse pushed a button that unlocked the double doors leading to the patient rooms.

After a brief moment of walking, she knocked on the door of 709 and entered. He hung back, not sure what to do. But in the end his curiosity won, and he stepped inside slowly.

With the privacy curtain pulled he could see nothing, but it served as a perfect way for him to observe unnoticed. The first thing he heard was a female voice, not Michelle's.

"Oh, I'm so glad you're here," the voice said, sounding relieved.

"Sorry it took so long," Michelle replied. "Any word from the doctor?"

"Actually, she just left," the other unidentified female informed her. "She says he's doing fine, and she's gonna discharge him today."

Michelle breathed a sigh of relief, and Dorian was shocked when he felt himself doing the same. Why was he so concerned? He held no responsibility for this child, yet he felt a strange feeling of protectiveness, almost the same he felt for their mother. He chalked it up to his already unstable emotional psyche, and continued to listen.

It had become oddly quiet, and he realized that while he'd been wrestling in his mind trying to assess his feelings, their conversation had continued and stopped. He supposed the silence must have come with the acknowledgement of his presence. The privacy curtain moved a bit to one side, and Michelle stepped in front of him. Her demeanor from the elevator had changed, and she looked much more in control. After a brief silent moment, she spoke.

"Come on," she said, motioning him to follow her.

"Why?" he asked, immediately confused, but a small flicker of something he couldn't quite identify was beginning to stir inside him, an almost knowing, an understanding that the deeper recesses of his mind were beginning to put together before the rest of his brain could catch up with the realization.

"Because I want you to meet your sons."

He barely had processed what she'd said before she pulled the curtain back, and he found himself staring at a pair of miniature versions of himself. His breath left him as the realization hit him that he was looking at two boys he had fathered. He had so many feelings pouring into him, he was having difficulty deciding on which one to assess first. But one in particular stood out: a deep, stirring emotion was building inside him, powerful and all-consuming. He realized it was love, an overwhelming love for the small figures he had helped create. Just by looking at them, he knew he would swear to protect them with his very soul.

He had missed out on so much, how could he get that time back? Quickly he became angry, and he glared at Michelle as she began to wake them up. Seeing his own flesh and blood asleep in a hospital bed only fueled his anger. How dare she keep his sons from him? Before he could lash out, a tiny voice of reason spoke up in his mind. He had ignored her calls, deleted all of her emails, thrown away the seemingly endless notes from his PA...several times Gwen had tried to bring her up, and Dorian had stopped her dead in her tracks. Old news, he had told her. If only he'd known his sons would have been the topic of discussion! He realized she had tried to tell him, but he had blocked her the entire time. When she'd stopped contacting him he'd assumed she'd stopped trying to get back into his life, not that she'd given up trying to tell him he'd become a father.

How had he not realized the truth when she had told him their age? They had to have been conceived in the span of time she had been his mistress. He knew he would not need a DNA test; they were his spitting image. Why had she not told him in the first place? Whatever the reason, it made no difference: he should have known better than to trust a beautiful woman. He would have to guard his heart, lest he be hurt again. For he had to admit, not knowing he had sons hurt, but finding out like this broke his heart.

His mind was made up even before he approached the tiny figures; he would move all three of them in with him. If Michelle opposed to that, then he would fight tooth and nail for his sons. He refused to miss out on another moment of their lives. Even if he had to marry her, he would do it to be with his boys.

He approached the bed slowly as they began to wake up, almost fearful to enter the new role that was being thrust upon him. He watched quietly as they awakened and realized who was there, and their eyes lit up as they both wrapped Michelle in a tight hug. They looked so natural, and Dorian could only hope they took to him so easily. As they began to chatter excitedly despite one of them being sick, Michelle raised a finger to her lips to silence them. Immediately they quieted, and she said, "boys, there's someone I want you to meet."

It was only then that they turned their faces towards him, and he could see a glint of mischief in their eyes. He could definitely tell they gave Michelle a hard time on a daily basis. They were just so beautiful: with dark, infinitely deep eyes and adorable dimples, he knew they'd have him wrapped around their fingers in no time.

Michelle met his eyes and attempted a smile, then placed a hand on one boy's head.

"This is William, and this is James," she informed him. Immediately he tried to memorize their faces. "Boys, this is your daddy."

Their eyes lit up yet again, and Dorian could almost feel his heart melting. If any part of him had not been ready to be a father, that small action certainly erased any doubt. He smiled a sheepish smile, and was not prepared when they both crawled to the edge of the bed where he stood. They both stared intently at him for a moment, as if trying to process who he was. Hell, he was still trying to process who he was.

"Are you really my daddy?" William asked.

"And mine?" James chimed in. Their eyes almost pleaded.

How could he deny such pure innocence? His eyes almost began watering as the realization hit him that he'd be watching these beautiful boys grow up. They would be able to come to him with questions about girls and whatever else, and he could finally have someone to teach the business. He ran his fingers through their unruly hair.

"Yes, I am," he said, pulling them in close for a tight embrace. "I am."

To feel their tiny bodies pressed against his chest in a bear hug drove the reality home that he was a dad. He could almost sense their quiet heartbeats as he squeezed them tight, and he tried to hold back the tears he knew were threatening to fall any moment. He hadn't felt such overwhelming emotion since his mother had passed, and he was having difficulty adjusting. He heard James gasp.

"Are you gonna marry mommy?" he asked, snuggling into Dorian's chest. He didn't miss a beat.

"Yes, honey," he replied, and he noted Michelle's shock. "I am. Very soon. With a wedding and everything."

"Yea! Do I get to be in it?" James asked, excited. William quickly chimed in, pulling his head back from Dorian's chest.

"No, I wanna be in it!" he exclaimed, getting upset. Before an argument could ensue, Dorian quickly spoke up. "You're both gonna be in it," he informed them, and they gave each other a jubilant high five. They both sat back on the bed, and Dorian took a moment to note their tiny differences.

James had a small birthmark on his left cheek, whereas William did not. It was the only significant difference between them, and Dorian was sure he'd be using it to differentiate between the two for some time. They both smiled bright, vibrant smiles, and in an instant he was reminded of his mother. How he wished she could lay eyes on her grandchildren. His father would be completely overjoyed—after he overcame his initial shock, of course—and he couldn't wait to fly the boys to London to meet him. He only had to figure out how he'd explain their existence.

As his mind was already planning what to say, the female he had heard earlier cleared her throat.

"Oh, I'm sorry!" Michelle said, slapping her forehead. "This is Candice, my neighbor and good friend. She was looking after the boys while I…while I was gone." He noticed the quick correction, but did not comment on it. Instead, he offered his outstretched hand.

"I'm Dorian," he said smoothly, and she smiled up at him as she stood to shake his hand.

"I know who you are," Candice informed him. "Nice to meet you." She began to gather her things. "Michelle, I'm headed home to get some rest. Call me when you get home and get the boys settled in, ok?" With that she exited, leaving Dorian alone with Michelle.

The unspoken tension passing through them was so intense it could easily have been cut with a dull knife. Dorian opened his mouth to speak, but there was a soft knock on the door. A smiling woman who Dorian assumed was the doctor poked her head in.

"Hi there! Parents, I assume?" she asked, motioning to him and Michelle.

"Yes," they answered in unison.

"Oh, good." She stepped inside and closed the door behind her. "I'm Dr. Bellard. I was looking over our little trooper over there. He's all set and doing wonderful, I've put in his discharge order; a nurse should be coming any minute to give you his papers. As soon as you guys get those, you're free to go. He'll be fine, really. It was just a run-of-the-mill stomach bug, but I've included a prescription for antibiotics just in case. If it'd been something more serious, James would have it too. Nevertheless, if anything persists, of course bring him right back. Any questions for me?"

They both stood silent until Michelle finally spoke up. "No, thank you doctor."

"You guys take care." She turned to leave, and almost ran into the petite nurse coming in behind her.

"Oops! Sorry about that, Amanda, I'll take those. Here ya go, dad." She turned and handed Dorian a couple of pages of paper, then smiled and left.

He quickly handed the papers to Michelle, then called down to his limo driver, who was parked in the parking deck. After he disconnected the call, he turned his attention to the boys on the bed.

"Come on boys, we're going home," Dorian said, and he noted how comfortable he felt with it already.

"Yea!" they both exclaimed, and he stood them up one by one on the edge of the bed. They only had on pajamas and socks, so he lifted William into his arms. Almost immediately James raised his arms to be picked up, and Michelle quickly scooped him into her arms. With her free hand she put the discharge papers in their bag, put it on her shoulder, and together they headed out into the hallway. By the time they got downstairs and to the limo, both boys were asleep. Dorian laid both of them on a seat together, and then turned to face Michelle.

"You lied to me!" he spat at her, scathing. She looked taken aback.

"I did not! How was I supposed to tell you? You put so much on me at once." His mind flew back to when she had walked into his office, dripping wet. He was so blinded by lust he hadn't pressed the reason for her sudden reappearance. But it didn't matter. She should have found the time to tell him he had helped bring two beautiful boys into the world.

"I should have known you'd be no different than all the rest." He said it to hurt her, and he found it hurt him to say it. He knew it to be untrue, she *was* different from all the rest, but she'd kept this monumental thing from him, and he didn't appreciate being left in the dark.

"What? What do you…where is all this coming from? I don't understand…" she trailed off, her dark eyes filling with tears. He hardened his heart.

"You know what I'm talking about. Were you ever going to tell me about them?"

"I meant to! But…" her voice faded.

"But what? I've explored every intimate crevice on your body, yet you couldn't find time to tell me you bore my damn children?" He could feel himself getting furious, and he had to tell himself to calm down.

"I—"

He held up a hand to cut off her words. "There's nothing you can say to me except your address."

Head hung in silent defeat, Michelle climbed into the limo. They rode back in silence, and Dorian let his mind wander dangerously. Already he was planning when to bring the boys to meet their grandfather, birthday parties…he worried for a moment. He didn't know anything about two children he'd created, he knew nothing of any allergies or fears. He supposed that was what Michelle was for, to help him, guide him, and show him what to and not to do. He only hoped his paternal instincts would kick in and give him some kind of inkling about what he was meant to do as a father.

As he sighed deeply they pulled into a small, dismal apartment complex, and the driver stopped beside the rental office. Michelle got out, grabbed William, and he quickly followed with James on his shoulder. He noticed that she hurried past a closed door on the first floor of her building, with the word 'LANDLORD' on a brass plate over a deposit slot. As they began to ascend the stairs, he called out to her. "Why the rush?"

"Behind on my rent. Not all of us are seated in the lap of luxury, you know."

"Oh, but aren't you content in my lap, my dear?" He purred it at her, and only a lover could have noticed the slight pause in her breath as she digested what he meant. He smirked. He couldn't help himself. Even through his anger, his trepidation, and his discomfort, he could still feel his lust for her unwavering. It was ridiculous; he should be furious beyond recognition at her for keeping his flesh and blood from him. Yet, in spite of everything, he couldn't wait for the next time he could get her undressed and alone. However, he realized that it would now be much more difficult, since there were two people who would require a significant amount of their time and attention.

He needed to hire a nanny as soon as possible.

*****

Things were not going the way Michelle had planned. But honestly, what had she expected? She wasn't going to delude herself into thinking that as soon as he saw the boys his heart would melt and they would be one big happy family. She should have known he would automatically start making accusations. She cursed herself for not telling him about them as soon as she walked in his office that night. But it was too late now. His impenetrable wall was back in place, she'd never get through again.

As she neared the door to her apartment, she remembered she had not cleaned before she'd left. There were toys strewn across the floor, a few dishes in the sink, and other things she had promised to get back to once she got home. She just never expected to come home with Dorian Johnston trailing behind her with one of their sons asleep on his shoulder. If someone had told her this was how the scenario was going to end, she'd have laughed in their face.

She let her mind play over what Dorian had said in the hospital room to the boys. Had he been serious about marrying her? Or had it merely been something to keep the boys calm? He couldn't possibly want to marry her after he had found out she'd been lying to him. She had dreamt of such a thing happening somewhere in the deep fantastical recesses of her mind, but she knew it was now impossible. Dorian would never marry her, he didn't even want a family.

She turned her key in the lock and heard the familiar 'click', but before she could open the door it was flung wide by Dorian, who immediately sidestepped her into the apartment. As if surveying the area, he scanned her tiny living room and kitchen with harsh eyes. She noticed the look of disgust forming on his face.

"Where can I lay him?" he asked, as if not sure there was more apartment beyond the living room.

"Follow me," she replied, and led him down the hallway to the boys' room. She lay William gently on his bed, and Dorian followed her lead and slowly placed James on his bed only a few feet away. Like a pro, she tucked them both in and quietly tiptoed out with Dorian behind her, and she heard him softly close the bedroom door. Once they were both back in the living room, he exploded.

"You expect me to let you raise my children in this hovel? I can't believe my sons are being subjected to this on a daily basis. This is not how Johnston heirs are meant to be raised," he said, looking around. She immediately became defensive. Who did he think he was, questioning how she took care of her children?

She held up her hands, palms facing him. "Wait, wait. You didn't even know you were a father until a couple hours ago. So where do you come off telling me how they should be raised? We've been doing just fine for the past three years," she said angrily. How dare he sneer down his nose at her! William and James stayed clean, dressed, and well fed, regardless of how well she was taken care of. There had been countless times she'd bought something the boys needed while she went without.

He scoffed. "It doesn't seem like it. From where I'm standing, you're doing pretty pitiful." He walked towards her, his large body filling the tiny space.

"Dismal apartment, shabby furniture," he wandered over to her kitchen table, where there were quite a few late notices laying open. She'd been sitting at the table the night before she'd left, looking at them, crying, wondering how she was going to make it for her and her boys' sake. There were probably still tear smudges from where they'd fallen on the despairing unpaid notices.

"Late on your bills...it's no wonder you came to me for help," he finished, almost scowling.

Before she could respond he said, "pack your things." His sudden command caught her off guard. "What are you talking about?"

"I'm talking about I'm not letting them stay here. You all are coming to live with me. You are also going to quit your job and plan the wedding."

Her mind was a whirlwind. The gall of him, coming and barking orders at her! Uprooting the boys was a bit drastic, wasn't it? Although a small part of her was mildly excited about living with Dorian, she didn't let herself read into it. She understood full well why he insisted they move in with him: now that he knew he had sons he needed to secure his heirs, which only angered her further. Were his sons not worthy enough to live with him simply out of love? Or did he see them as merely clones he could mold into his image; yet another pair of potential ruthless businessmen he could pass his multi-billion dollar company down to when he retired?

Before her mind could go on a tangent, the last part of what he said rattled her: wedding? So, he *was* serious about marrying her, after all. Why would he put himself through it? She knew he was furious with her. She could rationalize moving them in, but why marry her? Especially if it was not for love, which she knew it was not. This was just another way for him to build the image he needed. She couldn't believe she and her sons were merely pawns in his own personal game of life! Didn't they deserve more than that? Apparently, in his eyes, they did not.

She closed the distance between them and met his gaze fiercely. "What do you mean, 'wedding'?" she asked, fuming. She was nearing her boiling point, she could feel it. She didn't take kindly to being ordered around by a man who obviously thought so little of her.

"You heard what I said," he said, positioning himself so that he stood straighter. His chest brushed against her chin briefly, and she took a step back. Even through her anger, she felt her body respond to the closeness. She cursed herself.

Without warning he grabbed her by the shoulders, and her eyes immediately closed as she tried to get herself under control. "I will not take the chance of me going back to New York and you disappearing with my sons. And if I have to marry you to ensure that, so be it. Now, are you going to start packing or what?"

With that final command he let her go, and moved away from her to sit on her couch. As he pulled out his phone, she took a moment to collect herself.

She couldn't believe what she was hearing! In the span of mere minutes he had, yet again, turned her life upside down. It seemed as though the entire world moved at the snap of his fingers, and she did not want to become yet another woman who obeyed his every word. But what choice did she have? If she didn't agree, Dorian would fight until the end for the boys. She knew she didn't have a fraction of the money he would have available for court costs. She would lose her precious boys, the little tikes she had been trying to mold for the past three years.

The thought created an icy cold manacle around her lungs, and for a moment she couldn't breathe. Even though their life had been difficult, she wouldn't let them go for the world.

She hadn't even realized he had finished whatever conversation he'd been having on the phone and was staring at her until he cleared his throat deeply. "Well?"

"We don't have any boxes," she pointed out.

"You think I'm letting you take this crap?" he scoffed. "Just pack the boys' suitcases. I've called ahead, so their room should be ready by the time we arrive."

Just like that. Yet another example of what unlimited money could accomplish. "Where are we going?" she finally asked.

"I have an estate on the outskirts of New York. Any other pointless questions you need to ask?"

She put her hands on her hips, flabbergasted. The very course of her life had been taken out of her hands. What kind of woman had she become? She never would have let any other man dictate to her.

Then again, Dorian Johnston was not any other man. Not only was he the father of her children, but he was almost everything she wanted in a man: tall, handsome, smart…but she could definitely live without his ego. Her eyes began to roam over his impressive physique despite of herself, and the sheer beauty of him made her throat dry. Instinctively she swallowed hard, and then went to pack the boys' things before her mind could wander into unwanted territory.

As she was loading as many pieces of clothing and favorite toys as she could into their tiny overnight bags (for when they spent the night at her mother's), she looked over at their sleeping forms. She was so happy they did not know what kind of man their father truly was: controlling, arrogant, and merciless. He had no idea how moving the boys so suddenly would affect them, nor had he cared to ask. How was she supposed to get back and forth to school? Had he even considered any of these problems?

She sighed deeply. It wasn't as though it made any difference; she was done packing and there was a mighty foreboding man sitting on her couch waiting. As she was standing up and grabbing the handles to their bags, a deep voice came from behind her.

"Are we ready now?" Dorian asked, startling her. She turned around to see him leaning against the doorframe, arms folded across his chest. He had a smirk of satisfaction on his face as he reveled in the fact that he had won, and it took every ounce of her willpower not to slap it away. As she tightened her hands on the bags to stop herself from doing just that, she sighed, thoroughly defeated.

"Yes, but what about my clothes?"

He stepped closer to her. "You are going to be Mrs. Dorian Johnston. I can't be seen in public with your wardrobe," he scoffed. "Since Andrew already knows your measurements, I'll have him send over an appropriate accompaniment to my lifestyle. He has good taste."

She noticed his slight emphasis on the word 'he', but she chose to ignore it. What could she do? He had placed her between a rock and a hard place, and was steadily squeezing them closer together. He was back to his usual arrogant self; the sliver of a good man that had started to surface had disappeared just as quickly as he had shown his face. However, she knew that if she had to endure much more of it, she would not be able to make it through their farce of a marriage with her self-esteem intact. She needed to start standing up for herself, or resolve herself to a life of being talked to like a subservient.

She chose not to respond but walked past him instead, heading towards her front door. She felt as though she was walking to an unspoken doom, a darkness that threatened to consume her and rip her soul from her body, leaving her null and void.

"How are the boys being transported?" Dorian asked, as if they were mere cargo. She huffed.

"Just handle their bags. I've carried them both asleep before," she replied, dropping the bags by the door and heading for their room. She gave it one last look before stooping to pick William up, feeling him squirm in her arms before finally settling back down and drifting off to sleep again. Before she could bend over to lift James into her free arm, there was a rustling noise behind her. Dorian moved past her smoothly, and quickly scooped James into his strong arms. When he shifted his weight to one arm, it was William who let out a small cry.

"Daddy?" he said quietly, lifting his head. Dorian quickly spoke up.

"I'm here, darling," he responded, reaching out to rub his back. For a small moment Michelle almost let herself believe they were truly a family, but her logic immediately cleared its throat. What they had was a business arrangement, nothing more. He was only marrying her for her beautiful boys; it was just another way for him to be in control.

After a moment of uncomfortably intimate silence, William reached out his arms to Dorian. He looked perplexed for a split second, and then took William into his free arm. After readjusting the weight, he looked at Michelle impatiently. He cleared his throat.

"Well? I don't have all day, and I'd like to get the hell out of Maine," he said with disdain, walking towards the living room. Michelle opened her mouth to retort, but instead she closed it tightly and took a deep breath. When she entered the living room prepared to retrieve their luggage, she saw that it was gone.

"Where are their suitcases?" she asked.

"In the car," he replied quickly, sounding frustrated. Quickly she moved past him and opened the door, and he blew past her as quickly as he had blown into their lives. He cared zilch for their convenience, concerned only with the pieces of his puzzle and how he could use them to create the picture he desired.

As she walked behind him down the stairs, she noticed the way his muscles moved beneath his clothes. Even though she was furious with his complete disrespect of her, her body still responded just as effortlessly to him. She wanted to reach out and touch him, to let him know that she had not deceived him maliciously, but she knew she could not. The tiny window of hope for a shift in his personality had closed forever. She found she had her arm nearly outstretched, and she dropped it slowly with a sigh of resignation. He was back to the old Dorian, and there was no chance he'd change.

They loaded the boys into the limo and began to drive silently to the airport, until Dorian cleared his throat. Michelle felt herself tense.

"I'm going to pay your bills off and terminate your lease. I'm also going to call your employer and explain the situation."

"Situation?" she asked, incredulous. Was that all this was to him, a situation? Something to be dealt with, handled, resolved? Did he consider this some sort of ugly mess he was now forced to clean up? She was boiling on the inside.

"Yes. You've rekindled your relationship with your long lost love, and we are moving to New York to be closer to my home base of operations. You'll be on leave until further notice." He didn't even have the decency to look at her; he merely stared out the window.

Michelle huffed and sat back in her seat. She felt completely powerless.

Chapter 9

Dorian took one last look at his beautiful sleeping sons before finally closing the door to his airplane's master bedroom. They'd had a long day: he imagined finding your father was quite draining for two toddlers. He still couldn't believe he had acquired an entire family in a matter of a few hours, and with the last woman he had expected in a million years.

The same said woman lay sleeping on her back on the couch across from his desk, her arm draped lazily above her head. Even though he was intensely angry with her, he still found her utterly beautiful. The anger he felt at her deception could not snuff out the memory of her body pressed against his, her breath hot on his neck.

His eyes roamed down her body, finally resting on her stomach. He quickly realized that she had been a vessel for his children for nine long months. As he sat down at his desk and continued to watch her sleep, a pang of guilt began to form in the pit of his stomach. He had no idea if she'd had a tough pregnancy, nor had he been available for support if she had. Nevertheless, she had given him healthy, gorgeous sons, and for that, he was thankful.

He could barely comprehend what was happening to his life. One moment he had everything by the reigns, the next it was being turned upside down by two tiny figures he had created.

With their mother, of course...

He had his reservations about his feelings for Michelle. Their physical attraction was as strong as ever, if not stronger. Just watching her enticing form peacefully sleeping was sending shock waves to his loins. With each rise and fall of her swollen breasts, he could feel a fire stirring inside him. No matter if they ever had another emotional connection, he wanted her in his bed again. He needed to feel her under him, to have her luscious form wrapped in his in a dance they knew all too well. She was the only woman who could hold her own against him sexually, and he wasn't about to let that get away. He had no problem having a physical relationship without an emotional one. Hell, he'd been doing it most of his adult life, and it had suited him just fine.

Michelle let out a small noise in her sleep and rolled away from him, giving him a wonderful view of her shapely figure and her lush bottom. He shifted uncomfortably in his seat as he felt his loins reacting instinctively. He had never had any woman in his life that could stir a fire in him so easily, nor did he understand how it could happen after all they had been through together. It was as though his body had a mind of its own, and didn't listen to his sense of reasoning. It frustrated him almost as much as it excited him. To stop himself from taking her where she lay, he turned on his laptop and decided to do some work.

After thirty minutes of getting nowhere, he realized it was quite impossible to get any work done with Michelle merely feet away, his for the taking whenever he pleased. He knew it would take a mere touch, and she would melt into his hands. But he couldn't, not with his sons on the plane with them. If they were alone...he stopped his mind before he drove himself crazy. He couldn't seem to focus on anything except what he knew was resting between those succulent thighs.

He slammed his laptop shut and leaned back in his chair, letting out a breath that came from a resigned piece of his soul. He wasn't sure how much longer he could restrain himself around her. As he turned his eyes to the ceiling, he tried to plan what would happen when they landed to get his mind off Michelle. He looked at his watch. He had a business meeting in a few hours, since he'd called Gwen and demanded that she force the McAndersons to meet with him as soon as possible, and in his New York office. He knew it was short notice, but he didn't care. Luckily, they wanted the whole ordeal over as bad as he did, and agreed. With any luck, he could be home with the boys by lunch. If he wanted them to truly accept him as their father he needed to bond with them, not dump them in a large house while he stayed in the office all day. He knew the feeling, and he didn't want his sons to go through that.

With a thought popping into his mind, he picked up the receiver of the phone on his desk. He punched a few numbers, then waited.

"Hello?" A familiar clipped British accent rang into his ear. The head of his 'house management' staff—he didn't like to say 'butlers' or 'maids'; he always thought it didn't adequately describe the extent to which they kept the house running—Maureen, had been with their family since before he was born, and had been hired shortly after Liz. They ran the estate together when it'd been Dorian's father's, and when Edward retired to London (taking Liz with him to run the homestead), Maureen elected to stay behind and help maintain it. When Dorian's father announced that he was giving him the New York property, he would have no other woman than Maureen take over as head of the household staff—not that she would have left anyway.

"Maureen, it's—"

"Hello, Dorian. You think I don't know your plane's number, as many times as you've called and asked me what I was cooking for dinner? How far out from the airport are you, hon?"

"Maybe forty minutes or so, give or take, we're making good time. Listen, did you get a chance to finish what I asked earlier?"

"They're moving the last bit of furniture in now. I hope you appreciate this. Do you know how difficult it is to convert a large bedroom into a room for a pair of toddlers? It takes an awful lot of pulled strings and called-in favors. You owe me big, mister."

"Don't I always?" He smiled to himself as he hung up. If there was anyone he could count on to get a job done for him quickly it was Maureen. When he wanted to convert his father's estate into a home for himself, it had been Maureen who had made the arrangements, making an old-fashioned grandiose mansion into a more modern, 21st century-friendly home that he could escape to from time to time. His suite at the Waldorf could accommodate them quite comfortably, but he did not want the boys to be raised in a hotel as spoiled brats. He wanted them to value working for what they wanted in life, as he had. So what better place to bring them than his father's family estate? His newly acquired family deserved the best.

Even that mother of theirs. She had carried his children, after all. That had to earn her at least his respect, if not his love.

When his pilot announced their upcoming descent, Michelle began to stir and wake up. She slowly sat up, and Dorian couldn't help but watch as she lifted her arms above her head and stretched. The sensuous action made her breasts rise and fall dramatically, and by the time she had dropped her arms to put on her seatbelt Dorian was already burning to touch her. If he continued to stare at her, he knew he had no chance of keeping her composure. So instead he stood and walked towards the back of the cabin, choosing to ignore Michelle's gaze that he was sure was following him. Just knowing that sent shock waves up his back, and he had to steel his spine in order to ensure his self-control. He slowly opened the door to the bedroom expecting the boys to be asleep, but as it creaked wide he saw that he was sadly mistaken.

Two rowdy toddlers were happily jumping on the bed, laughing together as if they had not a care in the world. Unnoticed, he watched from the doorway for a few moments. What he wouldn't give to be that carefree, not having to worry about the very real problems waiting for him every day. James spotted him first, and when William caught his sudden distraction, he also turned his head towards Dorian's direction. Simultaneously, their eyes lit up. One after the other they leaped off the large bed and wrapped their arms tightly around his midsection.

"Hi daddy!" Their eager voices rang out in unison, their little bodies so full of excitement that they continuously bounced as they gripped him even tighter. The pure love he could feel radiating from them was almost enough to bring a tear to his eye. He never knew he could feel so loved without question, reserve, or ulterior motive. Being a father was one of the best feelings he had felt in a long time. It was something he couldn't quite explain...but to him, it needed no explanation.

He basked in their embrace for a moment more until he cleared his throat and said, "alright, boys. Time to get your seatbelts on." He practiced sounding firm yet loving, and found it came easier than he'd expected. He could definitely get used to being a dad.

They ran past him and bounded towards Michelle, reminding him just how much energy toddlers possessed.

"Mommy!" he heard them squeal, and immediately they began to chatter excitedly about everything they loved on the plane. Dorian smiled to himself and closed the door behind him, moving to sit behind his desk and put on his seatbelt. He dared not meet Michelle's eyes, on the chance that she might be looking back at him. He could almost reach out and touch the sexual tension between them, and he wondered how long either of them would be able to stand it.

After they had put the boys into the waiting limo (much to their awe and wonder), they rode in near silence to the estate, excluding the boys' occasional commentary on their surroundings. Michelle seemed content to merely stare out the window, apparently deep in contemplation. He could understand; he had become lost in his thoughts a long time ago. He had no idea how he was going to do this: not only stepping into a full-time father's role, but a full-time husband's as well.

It hit him that soon he'd have a wife to answer to, and rowdy children running around the house. Was he ready to settle down, truly? His ego quickly spoke up. Of course he was ready! He was Dorian Johnston! His name alone made ripples in the business world. How could he possibly be timid? He couldn't believe he was doubting himself. Honestly! Sitting up a bit straighter, he reassured his shaky nerves. If he could address a boardroom full of unapproachable CEOs as cool as a cucumber, he could surely handle his own children and their mother.

"This is it, boys," he said as their car pulled into the gate. They immediately popped their heads up into the window, both letting out a gasp at the same time. They quickly began to bombard him with questions.

"Is this where we live?" James asked, in awe.

"Can we play under that big tree?" William questioned, pointing to the large weeping willow that sat in the front yard.

"Yes, and yes," he replied, chuckling.

Dorian's father had had the estate built when he made his first few millions, as a present to himself and his wife. After a couple of years, he'd commissioned the enormous weeping willow to be planted in the front yard. The branches hung so low to the ground that they formed an enclosed space, a place to escape from the hectic world. Dorian had been there many times to scream, or simply sit and think, and, on one rare occasion, he'd cried. It had given him clarity when his entire world seemed hazy.

The house itself always seemed to remind him of the glamorous mansions of the roaring 20s, with Gatsby-worthy parties late into the next morning. He remembered as a kid trying to stay up and listen to the revelers, but Maureen and Liz kept a watchful eye, and always escorted him back to bed. With its grand foyer and majestic chandeliers, it was like something out of a dream. And though Maureen had altered it a bit, it still held its old-fashioned charm.

Pulling into the large circular drive always brought him back to his childhood, when he would stare up at the house in awe, as if it were a large, foreboding force. The large columns that sat in front seemed to serve as a gateway to another world, a pathway to somewhere where normal rules did not apply.

He stepped out of the limo and took in the air. He had grown up inside the large walls; he'd rode up and down the banisters, been grounded at 12 when a rogue tennis ball from a game with Alex had soared through the library window...he missed those days.

He turned around just in time to watch Michelle climb gracefully out of the limo. He blew out a long breath and turned back to the house, his body already beginning to respond to her lush figure.

God, sometimes he hated being an adult.

*****

Michelle let out a chuckle as she watched the boys ask Dorian permission to go play, then run off towards the weeping willow they had passed while pulling into the driveway. She still couldn't believe where she had ended up. As she lifted her eyes to scale the tall mansion, she felt a bit dizzy. But she wasn't sure if it was from the height of the building or the reality of where she found herself. It all seemed to hit her at once: she'd soon be Dorian Johnston's wife, they'd all be living under the same roof...it was as though the fairy tale she'd dreamt of had been terribly skewed, like she'd made a wish from an evil wishing well. One that gave you exactly what you asked, with a few strings attached.

She barely noticed the men rushing to get their things out of the trunk, only the searing heat when he lightly touched her elbow.

"Come on in, let's get the boys' stuff settled," he said to her, leading her forward. It felt almost surreal, as if her mind could not grasp what was happening to her. Her body felt as though it were on autopilot, moving of its own accord without her input. She barely realized she was walking up steps into Dorian's massive house.

Three steps that extended to the far ends of the front of the house led up to a pair of black mahogany doors that sat propped open, but uninviting. As she entered the doorway, immediately she saw what filthy rich looked like.

Black steps aligned a wall to her left, leading up to a large balcony that looked over the foyer. Straight ahead of her she noticed an entrance to a formal dining room, while on her right there sat a mysterious closed door. It intrigued her, but she was afraid to press further. She followed Dorian upstairs, close at his heels as they passed door after door. As they reached the end of the corridor, he stopped in front of the last room on the right. He turned to face her.

"This is the boys' room," he informed her, opening the door.

It was like something out of a dream: two identical racecar beds sat in the middle of the room, surrounded by a complex racetrack that looped around and under their beds. A large bookcase stood against one wall, packed with children's books. On the opposite wall was a large toy chest, overflowing with a wide assortment of toys. A teddy bear almost as tall as Michelle rested in a far corner, along with several other, smaller teddies. The room itself—which was probably larger than Michelle's apartment—was painted deep blue with red trim, with an assortment of racecars and trucks covering most of the walls. Instead of a grand chandelier to hang from the ceiling, a large mobile dangled playfully with several miniature sports cars hanging from it.

Stepping past Dorian and into the room, she was amazed. It was everything she had imagined for the boys and more, set out before her as though she had designed it herself. How had he known what the boys were interested in? As she turned around to ask him, a tall, smiling older woman greeted her instead. She wore a simple, black, short-sleeved dress that fell just below her skinny knees. She looked at Michelle with patience that looked perfected, as if she had seen her share of long days in the Johnston household. Her hands clasped in front of her, she stood with an unquestionable authority. After a moment, she said sweetly, "you must be Michelle. I'm Maureen."

Michelle noticed her accent and laughed to herself. Was no one who worked for the Johnston family American? She wondered with brief absurdity if maybe they'd just gotten under the skin of every American they dealt with.

Maureen held out a slender hand, which she took quickly in a firm handshake. When she turned to leave the room, Michelle was soon right behind her.

"So, how long have you worked for the Johnstons?" Michelle asked, following her back down the stairs. As Maureen carefully descended, she clasped her hands behind her back and chuckled over her shoulder.

"What makes you think I work for them?" she asked lightly.

Before Michelle could respond, she added, "I don't consider myself a subservient. I see myself as an equal member of the family, as does Dorian and his father." She laughed a light laugh. "Sometimes I wonder what they'd do without me," she said, picking a miniscule piece of lint off her dress. She didn't say it with arrogance, but instead with an amused tolerance. They reached the bottom step together, and Michelle was compelled to follow her, like an unknown magnetic force was pulling her. They walked a bit further, until she finally spoke up.

"Where are we going?" she asked, noticing that they were venturing further into the house. She found herself walking through the large dining room she had spotted earlier, with its large rectangular table perched in the middle. Over it hung two grand chandeliers, each one seeming to sparkle brighter than the other did. She imagined it had seen its share of formal dinners, with plenty of pretentious conversation to accompany it. She was having serious doubts about whether or not she and the boys would be able to merge into Dorian's world, where money was no object and anything could be accomplished as long as you knew the right people. They'd lived such a simple life before, and suddenly they were being thrust into the opposite side of the spectrum. She only hoped the boys would be alright.

Maureen stopped and turned to face her. She let out yet another dry laugh. "Well, I assume you'd like to see a bit around the house?" she asked, as if it were absurd to be asking. She held out her hand to Michelle, pulling her to her side. "Darling, I've got a lot to teach you if you expect to keep up with this busy man and his hectic lifestyle. Let's start with a tour of the house, and we'll go from there." Her tone was so warm and inviting, almost motherly.

"What about the boys?" she asked.

"I assure you, they're well taken care of." Immediately Michelle was reassured, which was odd since she usually worried excessively about her children. She couldn't explain it, but an inexplicable feeling in the pit of her stomach had her at peace in Maureen's presence, the same feeling that told her she was a good person to have on her side, someone trustworthy. She smiled to herself, and felt her nerves calm a bit. Maureen gave her hand a quick squeeze, and together they walked through the house.

Michelle tried to take in all Maureen said, but it was almost impossible. The house was too vast for her to possibly remember everything in one tour. She tried to focus on the important places: kitchen, her bedroom, the boys' room...but after a while, they all seemed to run together. She decided she'd try to figure it out after dinner, after she'd given the boys a bath and put them to bed. She noticed they were headed back to the foyer where they'd started, so Michelle quickly spoke up.

"Thank you so much, Maureen. I'm gonna try and remember as much as I can, but I can tell you right now I'm going to get lost a few times before I get it."

"Don't worry, I didn't get it the first time through, either," she admitted with a hearty chuckle. "Now, if you'll excuse me, I'm going to go see about lunch." With that she turned and gracefully walked away, and Michelle was left standing alone in the foyer. Unsure of what to do, she tried to remember her way to her bedroom—a bedroom right next to Dorian's. Something about that tiny fact rattled her somewhere deep in the pit of her belly.

Somehow she found her way, and as she opened the door the large comfortable bed caught her eye. It was then she realized she had not had a good amount of sleep in a while; since she had been running halfway around the world and had been thrust into a chaotic frenzy of events, her mind had barely had enough time to overcome the jetlag. She bit her lip. Could she sneak in a quick nap? She looked over at the clock that hung to her right, crunching the numbers in her head. She could easily sneak in perhaps an hour or so and be fine, as long as she set her alarm to get up in time for lunch. She looked over at the bathroom door, knowing that Dorian's bedroom was just on the other side. Would he try to come to her tonight? If he did, she wasn't so sure she'd resist…

The Billionaire's Captive Mistress * Jessica Simmons

She slipped off her shoes, feeling the plush carpet under her feet as she walked to the large balcony beside the bed. As she opened the doors and stepped out into the brisk fresh air, she looked down just in time to see Dorian's limo pulling out of the drive. She knew he was in the backseat, probably scanning through items in his phone. He was always focused on work, always thinking about his next business move. She figured that must be exhausting, never taking a break to simply relax. He just threw himself into his work. It was almost as though he were trying to block something out by being consumed in his job. As she stifled a yawn, she decided not to wonder further. Men of mystery tended to want to stay that way.

She opted to leave the balcony doors open, letting the breeze flow through the room. She sat on the edge of the bed for a moment, thinking. Her mind was being pulled in a million different directions, each one more confusing than the last. For a minute she thought she should check on the boys, but Maureen's reassuring voice played over and over in her head, a soothing balm to her worry.

She let her mind rest and finally climbed into bed, feeling the soft pillow under her head like a warm, inviting friend. It wasn't long before her eyelids became too heavy to handle, and she drifted off to sleep.

When Michelle found herself reluctantly waking up, she almost forgot where she was laying. It wasn't until she sat up and looked around that the dramatic, sudden changes being made in her life began to rush back into her head. At the same time she noticed the room was dark, with the exception of the bedside lamps that cast a soft glow into the space. Immediately she looked at the clock on the wall, which stated that the time was after nine o'clock. She gasped.

Had she truly been asleep for that long? Why had no one awoken her for lunch? Or dinner, for that matter? And what about the boys? How had they been handling things without her? She knew they must be scared to death, and immediately she felt bad for sleeping so long. As she stood up quickly and was rushing to get to the door, she nearly collided with a tray that was sitting beside the bed. Lifting the silver lid, she found herself staring at what she assumed had been served for dinner: barbeque ribs, with mashed potatoes, corn, and a large dinner roll that looked as though it had been soft and buttery before the meal had gotten cold. She had expected filet mignon or chicken a la orange or some other expensive meal to complement Dorian's expensive tastes, but she was relieved to see the house ate food for the average Joe.

Next to the plate was a piece of paper crisply folded in half, her name neatly written across the front in beautiful handwriting. Michelle picked it up and read what was inside.

You'll have to find your way to the kitchen

for dessert!
Maureen

With a smile she replaced the lid and the note, trying to remember where Maureen had told her the kitchen was in the massive house. She opened the door and stepped out into the hallway, nearly knocking someone over.

"Oh, just the woman I was looking for!" Michelle exclaimed, wrapping Maureen in a tight hug. "How are the boys?" she asked immediately.

"Oh, they were angels," she calmly replied, beginning to walk down the hall with Michelle close behind her.

"Were?" she questioned, confused.

"Yes, they've had dinner, baths, and now they're in bed. I read them a story, and last I checked William was fast asleep, with James not far behind. His eyelids were looking too heavy for him, poor thing." She chuckled, leading Michelle through the house, and too late she realized she hadn't been paying attention enough to get back. But somehow it all seemed to fall to the backburner as she realized her sons were in better care than she could have ever dreamed of. To have her two bundles of endless energy fed, bathed, and in bed—not to mention asleep—by nine was nothing short of a miracle. Slowly but surely her fears of the boys adjusting began to melt away, as she saw there was practically nothing to worry about.

As Maureen swung open the double doors that led to the kitchen, Michelle could feel a weight lifting from her shoulders. But just to add to her peace of mind, she decided she would peek in on them after she had some dessert. When she looked up, she almost could not believe what she saw.

The kitchen was just as magnificent as the rest of the house: polished black marble countertops and glistening stainless steel gave the room a bit of a sparkle. It could easily hold its own against any of the largest hotel chains' kitchens, complete with state-of-the-art appliances, and—she was sure—a full staff. There was a large island in the middle of the room, on top of which sat a plate of chocolate chip cookies. Immediately Michelle's mouth began to water—she could not remember the last time she'd had fresh baked cookies. She quickly sat down on one of the barstools, hoping Maureen did not notice her eagerness. She felt almost like a child, being given a treat after doing a good deed.

As Maureen smoothly sat, a plump smiling man approached them with two glasses of milk. When they had been set on the island gently, Maureen spoke up.

"This is Rod. He's our head chef." She introduced him and he beamed, quickly grabbing her for a hug. He was warm and smelled like cookies, and she had a feeling he had baked them from scratch. She inhaled deeply before he pulled away.

"Anything you want to eat, anytime, your wish is my command. Anything for the woman who tamed the lion that is Mr. Johnston. How did you do it?" he inquired, taking a seat on one of the stools at the island. They both looked in her direction.

Michelle wasn't sure how to answer: had she truly tamed him? It was true he had agreed to marry her and raise their children, but she didn't have his heart. Not anymore. Not ever again.

"I'm still asking myself the same thing," she finally answered, giving a small chuckle to ease the tension she felt as they awaited her response. Quickly she took a cookie and bit into it, hoping her vague answer would appease them. After a heartbeat too long, Rod smiled and said, "well, that does it for me. And those boys are his spitting images."

"And a couple of angels," Maureen added, taking a cookie as Rod stood.

"Well, I'd hate to miss what I'm sure will be a riveting conversation, but—"

Michelle quickly interrupted. "No, please, stay." She wanted a man's perspective on her husband-to-be's psyche, so she could figure out how to at least try and make this marriage work. Rod seemed pleasantly surprised, taking his original seat with an even larger smile on his face than before.

"So, what was Dorian like as a child?" Michelle asked, taking a sip of milk. She noticed Maureen take a slight pause before finally saying, "nothing like how he is now, if that's what you're thinking." She, too, took a swallow from her glass.

"He laughed. A lot," Rod added, staring off into no place in particular as if he were remembering to himself. She wondered what kind of memories they had stored of Dorian, carefree as a child, running and laughing. It almost seemed impossible to picture: the powerful business influence of Dorian Johnston being hidden underneath a boy only interested in climbing trees. The thought brought a tiny smile to her lips.

"Hard to imagine, isn't it, considering the man we know today. But it's true," Maureen insisted. "His heart was much lighter."

"He was very curious," Rod said, taking another bite out of a cookie. "He asked a lot of questions." He chuckled. "I guess there's one trait he took into adulthood."

A thought struck her. "What made him change?" Some kind of catalyst had to have changed him from a typical little boy into a hardcore businessman with such efficiency.

She noticed them exchange glances before Maureen quietly said, "the accident."

"What?" Maybe she had heard wrong.

Rod sighed and shifted in his seat as Maureen cleared her throat. It was her who finally spoke.

"When Dorian was younger, maybe nine or so, he was in an accident with his mother and brother."

A mountain dropped on Michelle's throat and took the air from her lungs. Brother? Dorian had never mentioned any siblings. Hell, what else didn't she know about him? Why had he never told her? But then again, their personal lives had never come up in conversation, and the nature of their relationship hadn't exactly encouraged divulging into details about their backgrounds. She had simply been a play toy, why would he tell her anything personal about himself? She decided to let it go. It was all in the past anyway, right? She tried to reassure herself.

"What happened?"

"Well, they were riding together and they came around a blind curve. Another driver lost control and hit them head on." Maureen took a pause as tears began to well up in her eyes. She took a deep breath and continued. "Dorian blamed himself for his brother's death. Still does, I think. Just a bit."

"Why would he blame himself?" Michelle asked, curious.

Maureen let out a deep sigh, as if reliving the memory of the whole incident was too much too talk about, too intimate, but she softly said, "because he unbuckled David's seatbelt."

Michelle could not help but gasp. Probably no more than rowdy boys playing in the backseat, but...goodness. It had to have been the one experience that changed his life completely, shifting his perspective.

"What was he like afterwards?"

"Distant. Very serious. Edward was a mess," Maureen replied. "I think he likes to just pretend it never happened these days," she added. "We don't speak of it."

Michelle tried to picture strong, charismatic Edward Johnston 'a mess', but the image couldn't come into focus. It was difficult to imagine such a tragedy rippling through the Johnston family and business, and she wondered how they had bounced back. Her mind was racing, and getting tired fast. Slowly she stood and stretched.

"Well, I'm gonna call it a night. It was wonderful to meet you, Rod," she said, coming to loop her arms around his neck. Once again he flashed one of his mile-wide smiles, and after giving Maureen a hug she bid them both goodnight. As she was leaving she heard Rod quietly say, "she's gonna be a good addition to this family."

"I know," Maureen replied. "Much better than that Nicole character."

Michelle smiled.

Chapter 10

Dorian thanked his driver and began to walk up the steps into the house, loosening his tie. He looked at his watch, noticing the time was after midnight. He knew Maureen had left him a plate from dinner, but he wasn't hungry.

Well, not for food...

Before stepping inside, he looked upward to see if a light shone upstairs. *She must be asleep*, he thought to himself. Michelle had been on his mind all day, so much so he could barely concentrate at work. Several times he had slammed his laptop closed and began pacing around his office, unable to focus on the screen in front of him. She had seemed to infiltrate every train of thought, every productive direction his mind had tried to go towards. He couldn't wait to get home to her.

Somehow, 'her' and 'home' just seemed to fit together in the same sentence...

He took his shoes off as soon as he crossed the threshold, grabbing both of them and holding one with each hand. He felt almost like a teenager sneaking up to Michelle's room, trying to be as quiet as possible so as not to wake the house.

He didn't understand why she excited him so, but he was beginning not to care. She was his, dammit, no one else's, and he was about to have her for the rest of their lives. With any other woman the mere thought would have been simply unbearable, but with Michelle it seemed doable. He laughed to himself. She had come crawling back into his bed, now he had her there permanently. He never imagined their love affair would end in marriage, but it wasn't completely a loss. He'd gained the family he thought he'd never have, in spades. Not only had he acquired a wife he could deal with, he'd gotten two heirs included in the package as well.

Somehow, by fate or divine intervention or both, Michelle had given him two sons, two beautiful sons, whom he already loved beyond comparison. He never thought his heart would be able to emit the kind of love they evoked from him, but somehow it came pouring out every time he saw them. Their smiles and bright faces reminded him so much of a time when he, too, was innocent and pure, seeing the world through hopeful eyes. He hoped he would prove to be a good role model for them, learning from the mistakes he'd been through and passing down the knowledge. With any luck he'd shape two of the finest minds the world would ever know. He held that knowledge somewhere deep in his heart, and it made his spine a bit straighter.

As he drew nearer to her door, he felt his heartbeat quicken. It seemed as though the hallway got longer with each step he took, as if he were walking in quicksand. It was absurd of course, but thoughts of her running through his head tended to push all rational thought from his mind. When he finally reached the door and threw it open, however, Michelle was not there.

He was not prepared for the disappointment he felt. He should've been furious with her for not informing him that they'd become parents over the course of her absence, but he just couldn't seem to stay angry with her. She made it nigh impossible with her beautiful eyes alone.

He took off his coat and threw it on her bed, frustrated. How was she supposed to fit into the role of willing wife if she was not where she was supposed to be when he needed her?

Stepping into the hallway, he nearly collided with a young woman, Maureen's oldest daughter, her hands full of folded linens.

"Amelia! Where is Michelle?" He almost demanded it, his voice forceful.

Frazzled by his tone, she quickly answered, "um, I think she's still down in the laundry, sir."

Quickly he made his way down, stopping in the doorway to watch her for a moment. She transferred a bundle of sheets from the washer to the dryer, then started it and sat down on top of it. With the same textbook he had seen at the hotel, she began to read. Her hair fell slightly in front of her face, making her have to swipe it out of her view periodically.

She was beautiful without trying: even at her most casual in a tank top and lounge pants, she still set fire to his loins. She drew her knees up to sit cross-legged and leaned further forward, so that her lush bosom nearly toppled over the scooped edge of her shirt. He felt a chill travel down his spine as he imagined being under her and those mounds in his face, their warmth encircling him from the neck up. His sudden intake of breath was louder than he had expected, and her attention was drawn from her book.

She gasped, startled. "What are you doing down here?"

"Could ask you the same," he replied, leaning against the doorframe. She rolled her eyes.

"William wet his bed. He gets a little afraid in a new place."

He was slightly taken aback. He saw a completely different side of Michelle, one he'd never had the pleasure of experiencing before. He saw her as a mother, willing to stay up all hours of the night tending to the needs of her children. It was different, but refreshing. She continued to chip away at his anger for her, damn her.

Could he step up to the plate? Would he be willing to sit with one of the boys after a nightmare when he'd just gotten home from a long day at work? His self-doubt was cut off as she began to speak.

"After I gave him a quick wash down and changed his pajamas, I told him to get in the bed with James while I washed his sheets; he ends up doing it anyway most nights, they like to be near each other. I found my way down here to the laundry after getting lost twice, and I saw that you have a 'sanitize' setting on your washer. I thought that'd be great, you know, it could really get the smell out of his sheets." She let her legs dangle once again, and Dorian was sorry to see the angle change.

"Little did I know the cycle was two hours! So I figured if I was going to be up, I might as well study." With that she returned her attention back to her book, but he was not about to be dismissed that easily.

He cleared his throat. "Look, I think we need to discuss some things," he said, coming to stand beside her. Her knees lightly grazed his side, and that tiny contact had him ready to devour her. He was on edge, and he couldn't promise he'd be able to hold himself back for much longer. He could feel her tense at their closeness, but she did not slide over.

"And those would be?" she asked, not looking up. He could hear her trying to sound aloof, but he knew she was just as intimidated by their current situation as he was. She was never good at hiding her feelings from him; he always knew how to read her, how to know what she was feeling even when she was deploying every defense mechanism to hide it.

"We need to talk about the wedding." He could almost feel her breath catch in her throat. "Now, as you know, money is no object. But please don't turn this into the social event of the year. I don't—"

"Look," she interjected, cutting him off. "I don't need much, honestly. Hell, I don't even need a wedding. So don't worry, there will be no 'social event of the year'. I'm not after your money."

He scoffed. "You could have fooled me. Isn't that why you're here in the first place? Isn't money the reason you graced my office doorway in the middle of the night?"

She slid down from the dryer and faced him, her beautiful breasts jutting against his chest. "No, your rapidly growing sons are what drove me to your door. Had it not been for them, I never would have seen you again." She grabbed the textbook and slammed it shut. "And that would've been just fine with me." She turned in a huff and began to leave, but he grabbed her arm.

"Stop running away from how you feel," he said. She turned her eyes up at him, and the simmering anger he could feel boiling just under the surface of her cool exterior sent chills down his spine. She snatched her arm away and glared at him.

"I'm not running away from anything. I'm here, aren't I? If I was running I would have said no to your marriage proposition in the first place." He noticed she said proposition instead of proposal, and he knew she'd done it on purpose. He watched tears well up in her eyes, and he felt an unfamiliar stab of guilt. "I said yes for our sons. Plain and simple." With that she turned and left, her lush bottom swaying behind her.

He stayed in the laundry room for a while, just thinking. Michelle had him completely bewildered. He was offering safety and security for her and the boys, everything they could ever want, yet she was ungrateful. Hell, she didn't even want a wedding! She was unlike any woman he'd met. Every woman he knew would jump at the chance to be Mrs. Johnston and plan the wedding of the century to flaunt it to the rest of the world, yet she was shunning even the idea of it. She actually felt trapped! It intrigued him as much as it excited him. He had been looking for someone not cut from the same cloth as all the other women he'd dated, but he'd never expected to find it in Michelle.

Somewhere in the midst of his thinking the dryer's cycle ended, the loud buzzing snapping him back to reality. Without hesitation he took the sheets out and made his way upstairs, heading to the boys' room.

As he approached the open doorway, something about the situation seemed natural. It was as though everything was as it should be, like he'd walked up the stairs numerous times to see the boys.

After he'd made William's bed he tried to coax him into it, but he refused. He gave off a little whimper, like a sad puppy watching his master go off to work. It was so adorable; Dorian couldn't help but let a huge grin spread across his face at the miniature sound.

"But daddy, I wanna stay with James..." he protested sleepily. Not wanting to disturb him, he stepped back and simply watched them for a moment.

They were so gorgeous, so peaceful ...they had no idea the problems that were facing their parents, or the building tension between them; they were content to merely cuddle up together, facing each other with their hands under their heads. Dorian remembered their tiny beds at home, and wondered how they managed to squeeze together. He made a mental note to get rid of their individual beds, and buy them one large bed. He could have it custom-made to look like a life-sized car, instead of their current mini racecars. He smiled to himself. He loved being a dad already.

He began to exit and as he reached the doorway, he heard a small voice cry out behind him.

"Night-night, daddy."

He could almost feel his heart melting. He never knew such a powerful love could exist.

"Goodnight, baby," he replied quickly, before he could let his son hear the tears in his voice. The overwhelming emotion caught him by surprise, and he cleared his throat deeply as he walked back to his room.

He stopped at his door with his hand on the doorknob, debating on whether or not to bring Michelle to his bed. He knew she would not say no; the attraction between them was simply too powerful for her to ignore. He knew she had to want him as much as he wanted her. On the other hand, he didn't want to take her by force. He loved her willing and ready beneath him.

With a willpower he didn't know he had, he forced the door of his room open. Across the foot of the bed was the coat he had shed in Michelle's room, and he smiled as he closed the door behind him. How thoughtful of her to bring it back, even if she was angry with him. She couldn't stay mad at him for long, just as he had to put aside his anger and surrender to his carnal desires. He wanted her almost to the point of madness; her body alone drove him wild. But it paired with her personality was enough to make any man insane with lust.

He slung the jacket over a chair by his wardrobe, and he began to disrobe. When he had hooked his thumbs in the waistband of his boxers to pull them down, he heard a small 'click'.

He froze. Slowly, the door to his bathroom creaked open.

Michelle appeared in front of him, naked. Dorian's breath was stolen. Her hair loose, it cascaded around her shoulders in teased curls. Her luscious breasts sat in perched globes above her slender waist, leading down into her thick thighs that held her femininity between them. There was a small dark patch of hair there; one Dorian fully intended to kiss. Immediately he was rock hard for her. Slowly, to tease her, he slid his boxers down. The effect she had on him could not be missed. It stood out erect, almost pointing at her. Almost beckoning her.

"I can't sleep," she said softly, her sweet voice dancing over his ears. Without a word, he pulled the covers back and slid into bed. Patting the empty side, he said, "so come sleep with me." Without hesitation she moved to get in beside him, pressing her warm body close and bringing her nose inches from his. Her light breath on his face made his entire frame tingle with anticipation.

"Kiss me," she whispered against his lips.

He obliged without question, furiously taking her mouth with his. Immediately he received her tongue, fiercely passionate and willing. Her breathy moans and sighs only added to his excitement, bringing his readiness to fever pitch. He ran his hands madly over her body, feeling every curve and storing it into his mental rolodex. He wanted to memorize every ounce of her with his hands.

It was almost as though things had been building up to that moment, their tension mounting until finally it was exploding between them. He couldn't wait to be all over her, inside her…his body craved her. Every minute he spent not inside her seemed almost unbearable, but he endured it, as he needed to taste her as well. It was as though his body could not decide which way to experience her deliciousness.

He knew his frustrations were not alone; he knew she felt the same eagerness. He could feel it reciprocated in the way she moved, the way she raked her fingers through his hair with wild abandon. She was on fire for him, too.

Gently he pushed her flat on her back, eager to explore her. He moved his lips from her mouth over to her ear, hearing her slight gasp as he flicked his tongue over her lobe. Softly he nibbled on it, feeling her wiggle beneath him. Her hands clutched at his lower back, making him arch towards her. The feeling sent shock waves up to his neck, and he lowered his head to capture her mouth again. When he returned his mouth to her ear, he let his tongue trail just beneath it, almost on her cheek. It felt so primal; he caught himself before he almost growled in her ear. God, what was she doing to him?

He placed one light kiss on the tip of her nose, and she let out a small giggle. A tiny twinkle appeared in the corner of one eye, and for a moment he was transfixed. She truly was gorgeous, inside and out.

His physical attraction for her pushed her transgressions to the backburner of his mind; he knew he had forgiven her a long time ago, even if involuntarily. He needed her body, damn her mistakes.

He rubbed his cheek lightly against hers, feeling his slight stubble rub against her smooth cheek. He loved the contrast, the delicate softness of her skin against his rough hairs. Everything about her made him want her more; the longer he denied himself of her...he wasn't sure how much more he could take. He had to force himself to slow down, however; the feeling was just too delicious to rush. He had to take his time, savor every moment. He deserved every ounce of her; she was his.

Trailing kisses down her neck, his hands found her warm breasts and cupped one in each hand. A low moan escaped her, one that pooled lust deep in his loins. He felt the soft skin beneath his fingers, each mound too big for his hands to hold. He took each nipple between his thumb and forefinger, rolling the tight flesh lightly. Immediately they came to hard peaks, and he lowered his head to lick each one gently. He saw Michelle shiver and she arched her back beneath him, taking in a rush of air. He opened his mouth and took the entire dark circle into his mouth, sucking on it gently as she wriggled against his hips; she was begging him for more without saying a word.

Without warning she began to lick his ear, and the sudden action sent a cold chill down his back. Her warm tongue against his earlobe and her breath on his neck was almost too much for him to handle. He found himself panting and moaning against her neck, his body craving much, much more.

She gripped his neck firmly with one hand, the other placed on his lower back, pulling him tight to her. Her warm thighs were pressed against his stomach as he lay between them, and it took everything he had not to slide himself into her. He had to move their differentiating parts away from each other, or he wasn't sure how much longer he'd be able to restrain himself. He lifted himself an inch or so to move down her body, but she held him tight. He kissed her in the crevice between her breasts, and she released her grip on him as she realized he meant to go lower.

His breathing became rapid as his kisses lowered, trailing down her belly, feeling the skin smooth under his lips. Each touch brought a sigh from Michelle, an unchained response to the ecstasy she felt. They were light and airy, like fluffy clouds on a beautiful day. They seemed to hang in the air, lingering in the open space.

When he had reached the tops of her thighs, he inhaled her feminine scent, sweet and hot. Carefully he spread open the folds covering her bud of womanhood, running his tongue over the fold of skin slowly. Dorian lifted his head just in time to see Michelle arch her back, watching her breasts bounce as she sat herself back down. A shockwave of lust shot through his bones, and he immediately thrust his tongue inside her.

The taste of her in his mouth sent him to another world entirely. He was lost in the salty sweetness, licking and sucking on her until she began to melt beneath him. Her thighs quivered around his collarbone, becoming slicker by the moment.

He lost track of how long he feasted on her, alternating between fast, light licks that drove her insane and deep, powerful thrusts of his tongue that brought her to the brink of explosion, stopping her immediately before her release. He did this repeatedly, hearing her struggle louder and louder not to cry out in anguish. When he was finally ready, he let her erupt beneath him, her body trembling as her orgasm coursed through her. Her heavy panting gradually slowed as the waves subsided, and he took it as his cue to come up and gently press his weight on top of her.

Immediately she linked her arms around his neck, pulling him close. He wasted no time in spreading her legs with his knees and guiding the head of his shaft to her slick opening. For a brief moment he held it there, slightly pressing it against her flesh, antagonizing her. He could hear her beneath him, her breathing becoming unsteady as she waited for him to enter her. She wiggled her hips beneath him as an incentive, but he held fast. He wanted to relish the moment; he loved having her lose all self-control and completely give herself over to her desires.

When she couldn't stand it anymore, she pressed her lips to his ear and whispered, "take me, Dorian."

The urgency in her voice added with the feel of her breath on his ear drove him to near insanity, and he thrust deep into her.

The feeling of her silken sheath wrapped around his manhood was almost enough to make him explode immediately. It was incomparable, inexpressible, the feeling he felt when he was making love to her. He wasn't sure what made it so amazing, but it had blown his mind from the first time he'd taken her. Every time he found something new about it he loved. He was never disappointed, never left unsatisfied. When they were joined, it was as though no words needed to be spoken; their bodies knew more than their words could ever express.

Not wanting to be overpowered by the feeling of her around him, he began to withdraw, hearing her faint sound of protest. With a satisfied smirk he plunged back into her warmth, setting a rhythm that she easily, willingly matched.

Together they rocked back and forth, settling into a familiar groove. With every change in pace she was right there with him, her legs linked behind his back, along for the ride. He looped his arms under hers, bringing her in closer to him. He could hear her moans in his ear, a vocal reminder of the passion she felt for him, the pleasure he made her feel, and the intensity of what they shared. Having her breathy sighs and sounds of content so near to him helped his raging hormones none; they served merely as fuel for the flame that was raging inside him, their hungriness making him wild with his need to fill every bit of her.

With his thighs he spread her wider, pushing himself deeper inside her. He pushed himself up on his hands, so he could watch her; he had to see her beautiful face as he possessed her. He took his time with each thrust, letting her feel his shaft inch by inch, and he watched her face contort with pleasure as he filled her. He leaned back, grabbed her calves, and brought her legs up, crossing them at the ankles. This allowed him to enter her at an angle, causing her to arch her back towards him. Ooh, he liked that.

There was nothing he was afraid to do with her, yet she'd set ground rules early on in their arrangement and he'd always respected them. He knew there were just certain things she wouldn't do—not many, though, he'd found out—and he'd never pressured her to do them against her wishes. What she did do, however, was more than enough for him. He could place her in any position he pleased; he'd learned through stray pillow conversation—after a particularly gymnastic night that'd left him slightly sore the next morning—that she'd taken ballet all through middle and high school, so she was as flexible as he needed. It was as though she'd been engineered to match him perfectly in the bedroom.

Time seemed irrelevant and non-existent as they were entangled, switching from position to position with the skill and familiarity of old lovers. One moment he was behind her, hands on her hips as he plowed into her, the next moment she was astride him, her breasts swaying in his face. With each position he found a new way to explore her, to find out what pleased her the most. He loved to watch her on top, but he could tell she loved to be submissive under him.

They were in their own world, made up of only them and their longing for each other, oblivious to what was going on around them. She would lock eyes with him and he could almost see the sparks fly between them. She set him aflame merely by looking at him...when their bodies met he was a raging conflagration.

Over and over he brought her to climax, feeling her intimate warmth pulsing around him as each orgasm sent her cascading over the edge of oblivion. It was as though he could feel each one along with her; it took every ounce of self-control he had not to explode alongside her. But as the hours ticked away, he found his willpower disintegrating the longer he stayed inside her.

When he finally could not contain it anymore, he released himself, and was flung into mindless ecstasy. He'd never felt anything as exhilarating as when he came inside her; it was almost as though every part of him was released as well. He collapsed beside her, struggling to steady his breathing. He heard her trying to regain composure as well, and he smiled to himself as he placed a light kiss on her cheek. As he flattened himself onto his back she put her head on his chest, her head slightly rising and falling as his breathing slowed. He couldn't see her face, but he could feel her smile.

He ran his fingers through her hair, slightly damp from her sweat, feeling the texture between his fingers. It was soft and smooth, and hers—another fact he loved about her. Nothing was fake; nothing was added, implanted, or suctioned to make her look the way she did.

Being with her was nearly indescribable: every woman he'd bedded had fallen tragically short of how she made him feel, yet she never flaunted her sexual power over him. Rather she let it linger and simmer around him, gradually overpowering him without her knowing it.

A fact he was thankful of...he shuddered to think how she might make him behave if she knew just how much power her sexuality had over him.

He prided himself on his ability to retain control in tough situations, yet when it came to Michelle all logical thought escaped from his mind. He was almost completely out of control when he was in her presence, a fact that thrilled him. It was as though he could lose himself, forget about his obligations or responsibilities, even for a moment. He knew he'd do anything to keep that outlet of freedom in his life.

He looked over at the woman now curled in his arms, so peaceful as she slept. As he watched her sleep, he realized that she was the mother of his twin boys. She had raised two beautiful, smart, well-mannered boys by herself for three years. Was he truly ready to take on the full responsibility of being a father? He'd seen other fathers and sons together, and they always seemed so natural. Would he be able to slip so comfortably into parenthood? He was so used to being only concerned with his well-being; now, there were two people—three, if their mother was included—that depended on him for their survival. He was no stranger to responsibility, but he was stepping onto foreign territory. He didn't know the first thing about what to do when it came to taking care of children, especially his own.

He sighed, putting his head back on the pillows. Dorian hated being unprepared.

*****

Michelle woke up rested, temporarily unaware of her surroundings. Sunlight gleaming in her eyes, she stretched deeply, raising her arms above her head. She closed her eyes for a moment, relishing the unbroken silence. Just as her mind began to settle, a realization hit her like an atomic shockwave: she was in Dorian's bed!

Quickly she sat up, checking to see if he was still beside her. To her astonishment he was, fast asleep, with the arm closest to her behind his head, and his opposite hand on his stomach. He looked immensely peaceful, almost at ease as he slumbered. She took a moment to gaze at him, watching his chest rise and fall. He was, she had to admit, devastatingly gorgeous, a wonderfully chiseled work of physical art. In any other circumstances, she would have been more than grateful to have a man like him in her bed: tall, strong, handsome, smart, amazing lover...he was what she had prayed for numerous times, but never had she expected to find it in Dorian Johnston, of all people!

She slowly maneuvered her way out of bed and tiptoed to the bathroom, closing the door behind her. With a sigh, she sat on the edge of the large tub, and the sudden coldness on her bare flesh reminded her of the night before, and a rush of scandalous memories flooded back to her at once. She'd behaved wildly, throwing herself at him without care. Her cheeks—both sets—became hot as she remembered what they'd done, apparently late into the morning.

Why had she acted like that? It was completely out of character for her. She'd never considered herself a seductress by any means, but something had happened to her last night. Even as she tried to rationalize, a small voice spoke up in her mind. She knew why: she just couldn't take it anymore.

After she had stormed away from Dorian in a huff, she had gone back to her room. As she had opened the door, she'd noticed his suit jacket on the bed and bit her lip. She picked it up, feeling the expensive material in her hands and inhaling his scent. A debate arose in her mind whether or not to keep it in her room as an incentive for Dorian to come after her, but she quickly decided against it. She was not some lovesick girl, and she was sure he would not chase after her anyway. With resolve she had laid it across the foot of his bed, and had returned to her room to lay down.

She had found, however, that she couldn't sleep with thoughts of Dorian on her mind, and she had tossed and turned endlessly. She sat up, draped her legs over the edge of the bed, and had an argument in her head. What could it hurt, right? After all, they were getting married, so she'd have to share his bed sooner or later. He already knew about the boys, so there was no reason she couldn't show off her body to him, unafraid. She was done making excuses.

No one made her feel the way he did simply by looking at her, undressing her with his eyes. He was always hungry for her, always ready to take her, a fact that never ceased to excite her from head to toe. She wasn't gonna find anything like it and she knew that, and with a slight smirk of self-satisfaction she had stood and went to the bathroom door.

The tile had been cold under her feet, but it wasn't the reason she had chills. She was nervous beyond words; she felt almost like a virgin bride being presented to her suitor on their wedding night. But when she had opened his door, expecting the room to be empty so she could climb into bed and wait for him, she found herself staring at him half naked—just as surprised at her as she was at herself.

What had happened next, well...

She blushed just thinking about it.

But what did they possibly have beyond the bedroom? He cared nothing for her but that she had given birth to his sons, other than that she could've been nothing more than one of the countless women he'd dated. She looked at the large diamond that sat on her finger. She'd become so used to the weight of the extravagant stone that she barely noticed it anymore, but did it mean anything? She felt merely like a houseguest.

She needed to talk to Dorian about where their relationship—or lack thereof—was going, figure out where his emotions were in relation to her. She couldn't possibly stay in a marriage where her husband did not love her, no matter how much he loved their children. It wasn't fair. The boys could tell when she was upset, and if she were unhappy, it would affect them. She couldn't do that to them.

She stood up, grabbed a black robe hanging in the bathroom, opened the door to tell him precisely that, but he was not there. She scoffed. How long had she been in the bathroom? She noticed a magazine on the bed, with a note and credit card placed on top. Carefully she picked all of them up, reading the note.

Start planning. I'm bringing in help.
D.

The magazine she held had a beautiful blonde in a wedding dress on the cover, smiling broadly. Suddenly a stone dropped in the pit of her stomach, and she plopped down on the edge of the bed. She had completely forgotten she had yet to plan the wedding. Even though she knew she had an almost unlimited amount of funds, she still had no idea where to start. She'd never planned a wedding before. There were so many details involved…the thought of everything began to overwhelm her.

As she was beginning to make a mental list, there came a soft knock on the door. She was halfway to answering it when the second part of Dorian's note came to the front of her mind. Bringing in help? God, she hoped he didn't bring in one of those snobby wedding planners.

Her hand on the knob, she took a deep breath. *Don't let her take over*, she told herself. She opened it slowly, preparing herself for the worst, but what she found on the other side was the last thing she expected.

"Andrew!" she squealed, wrapping him in a tight hug. Enthusiastically he hugged her back, laughing. Before she could begin to ask a slew of questions, he held up his hands to stop her words.

"Before you even start, beautiful, Mr. Johnston put in an emergency call last night and I was here in a flash. I've been waiting down in the dining room forever, what have you all been doing up here—oh, never mind, why did I even ask?" He laughed, throwing his head back. "I can't believe you snagged Mr. Johnston! Do you know how many women would kill to be in your shoes right now? When I saw you guys, I had no idea you were in a serious relationship! How long have you two been dating? And how have you kept it under the radar?" he asked, moving to sit on the edge of the bed.

"Oh, it seems like forever sometimes," she sighed, sitting down next to him.

"Well, just don't let the press get wind of it until you're good and ready. The media would have a field day, knowing the world's most eligible bachelor is getting ready to come off the market." He glanced behind her. Picking up the bridal magazine off the bed, he let out a deep gasp. "Oh, God, tell me you're not reading any of this garbage." He threw it on the floor, quickly standing up and pulling her to her feet.

"No, no, no, missy. This wedding is based on what you want, not what the runway says. Now, don't get me wrong, I love a good runway, but it has no place in a wedding. So…" he said, walking to the wardrobe and flinging it open, "put on some—oh." Michelle chuckled as she watched him flip through Dorian's suits. Huffing, he turned around, hands on his hips, eyebrows raised.

"Well, where are your clothes, dear?"

"Follow me." She led him through their connecting bathroom and stood in front of her wardrobe, holding her arms open with a flourish.

"So, why the separate rooms if you two are together?" he questioned, heading over to open the wardrobe doors.

"Dorian's father is old-fashioned. No sleeping together until we're married, all that jazz." Her cheeks became hot. They really didn't sleep much though, did they?

"Ah, I see. Oh well. You won't have to wait too long, then you can be curled up beside him every night."

Michelle thought about that. There would come a day, when she would give herself to him before God and witnesses, when she wouldn't be able to run away from their physical attraction any longer, or use her separate bedroom as an escape. She'd be in his bed every night, and there would be no way he'd let a night pass without making love to her.

As Andrew reached for the handles on the wardrobe, a thought struck Michelle.

"Wait, Andrew, I have to tell you something. I have—"

Before she could finish her sentence, the door burst open and a familiar sound met her ears.

"Mommy!"

William and James bounded into the room, hugging her around the legs. They both began talking excitedly.

"Mommy, our new house is great—"

"There are so many new things to play with—"

She looked up to see Andrew grinning. As her focus changed the boys' did also, and noticing another presence in the room they quickly became silent.

Michelle addressed Andrew. "Like I was saying, I have two children. Well, we have two children."

He gasped. "They're so beautiful! And they're the spitting image of Mr. Johnston. You didn't have to tell me that."

Before she could enter in to full 'mommy mode', Maureen came in.

"Good morning, Michelle. I see the boys have found you. Should I make them some breakfast so you can focus? I know you've got a lot on your plate with the wedding and all."

She breathed a sigh of relief. "You don't mind, do you?"

"Oh, of course not. Come along boys, let's let mommy have some time to herself."

They immediately followed, each one grabbing one of Maureen's hands. Michelle was so grateful they had taken to her so easily; usually they were very shy around strangers. She almost felt guilty for pawning them off on someone else, but she had raised them alone for three years. Couldn't she use a little break?

She turned to face Andrew. "Look, hon. I know you live in a world of glitter and diamonds, but I'm not used to all that. So I don't want anything too extravagant. I mean, I know it's expected, marrying Dorian Johnston, but I just don't want the whole thing turned into a social event." It all ran out of her mouth so fast, she was amazed he understood her. Quickly he nodded.

"Gotcha, babe. It'll be an elegant affair, not too over the top. But there is one thing you absolutely have to splurge on," he informed her.

"What's that?" she asked, confused.

"Your dress."

She took a moment to think. She hadn't even put a thought into what kind of dress she wanted. She realized if she didn't have help, she'd never make it through the whole process. She looked hopelessly at Andrew. He gasped.

"You don't even know what kind of dress you want, do you?" he assessed. Slowly she shook her head. Andrew's eyes widened in shock.

"My gosh, girl, what am I going to do with you?" With that, he heaved the doors open, and stood standing in the doorway with his hands on his hips. He called out to her as she sat down on the bed.

"What kind of mood are you in today, darling?" he asked, apparently trying to pick out an outfit for her.

She thought for a moment. How was she feeling? Overwhelmed, anxious, tired...but at the same time, completely head over heels in love with the father of her children, a man who was marrying her out of obligation. Of course she couldn't let Andrew know that, so she let out with a sigh, "so-so."

"So-so, huh? Hmm." She could tell the wheels were turning in his head. After a moment he reached in, pulled out an outfit, and lay it on the bed.

"Put that on, and meet me downstairs. We are finding your dress. Today." He put an emphasis on the last word, cast her a firm glance, then left her to get dressed. After the door had closed behind him, she took a look at what he had set beside her: a black kimono-sleeved shirt, with tan flare-legged pants. Looking closer, she noticed the pants had small black pinstripes. She chuckled. That man could definitely put together one hell of an outfit.

After she quickly showered, dressed, asked Maureen to look after the boys (to which she happily obliged), and met Andrew downstairs, the rest of the day quickly became a blur. He pulled her in and out of one boutique after another, trying on dress after dress, but she couldn't find one she loved. It was almost surreal: trying on wedding dresses for her wedding to one of the wealthiest men in the business world, a man who could hand-pick any woman he wanted. And even though they had gotten engaged under circumstances she abhorred, it was still a bit exciting to be the future Mrs. Johnston.

"It's got to be a dress that takes your breath away when you step in front of the mirror," he said, pulling open a large glass door to enter a David's Bridal. "But I think Vera Wang suits you. She's got some wonderful designs that complement your figure in her bridal collection."

She nodded, smiling, but she didn't quite believe it. She had yet to find a dress that she thought was 'the one', and they had been to countless stores already. She made a firm decision as she stepped into the cool air of the store that she would find it, even if she had to try on every dress in the place. She was so tired of looking, she wasn't even sure she had the energy to find anything else.

She squared her shoulders and paid attention to the consultant that was speaking to her.

"So, when's the wedding?" she asked brightly, her nametag reading 'Barbee'. Michelle laughed to herself. How appropriate.

"Soon," Andrew immediately answered. She thought on the word 'soon.' When was the wedding, actually? She hadn't even talked to Dorian about it; she had no idea what type of timeframe he was looking for. She began to panic, until a thought struck her. Why did she need him to sign off on her decisions about the wedding, anyway? This was just as much her wedding as it was his, and he'd had little consideration for her opinions anyway. She steeled her spine.

"Next month," she said firmly. Both Barbee and Andrew's eyes grew wide. She smiled to herself.

"Well, our standard shipping time is twelve weeks...I'm not sure that's gonna be possible..." Barbee trailed off, a grimace of worry spreading across her face. "Unless you find one in your size here in the store, of course."

"I'll pay you whatever you need," Michelle added.

Barbee's jaw dropped. "I think we can maybe make that happen. But we have to find you a dress first!"

"Well, lead the way!" Michelle exclaimed, excited. She figured if she was being forced to get married to a man who didn't love her, she might as well have fun planning it. Before she could begin to follow Barbee, however, Andrew grabbed her arm.

"Are you having fun yet?" he asked, smiling.

She grinned. "Oh yeah. I need to start acting like the future Mrs. Johnston, right?"

*****

Dorian smirked as he glanced over his bank account statement on his computer screen. *She and Andrew must be having a blast*, he thought to himself. He couldn't believe he was going to be a married man soon, complete with kids to take care of. He smiled to himself, thinking about the boys. He had come home early to spend time with them but when he had arrived they were taking a nap, so he had decided to catch up on some work and answer a few emails. After a while, however, he found himself unable to focus. He looked at his watch, noticing it was almost five. He frowned. What could be taking them so long?

He opened the balcony doors leading out to the patio, letting the fresh breeze hit his face. Looking out onto the grounds of the estate, he had to admit to himself that he had a great life. Beautiful house, beautiful children, beautiful wife…

His train of thought was run off track with thoughts of Michelle. She was smart, beautiful, quick-witted…everything he had been looking for in a woman, yet he could not give his heart to her completely. The scar on his heart from Nicole's betrayal still had not healed completely, and subconsciously he was still afraid to let himself be vulnerable. Not to mention the fact Michelle had deceived him as well, no matter her intentions. And although she hadn't been nearly as devious as Nicole, she had still withheld vital information from him. Before his mind could relive the anger he felt, he watched a red car pull up in the driveway. He assumed it could only be Andrew's rental, bringing Michelle home, and he turned to go downstairs to meet them.

A thought struck him and he stopped. Why was he chasing after this woman? He never pursued a woman, much less ran to the front door to greet her like a lovesick puppy. He gripped the balcony railing until his knuckles were white. How did she do that to him? He never could seem to explain the hold she had over him; it was almost otherworldly. No matter how much he thought he had satiated himself with her, the moment he saw her again it was as though they'd never been intimate.

He could hear distant happy chattering in the house, and then he heard Andrew say his goodbyes and exit. His breath caught in his throat as he could hear her door close, with accompanying rustling as she moved around. He debated back and forth about whether or not to enter through the bathroom they shared; finally his lust triumphed and he made his way to her door.

He noticed his heart rate increased as his hand closed around the doorknob, and he frustratingly took a few deep breaths before slowly creaking the door open.

The first thing he saw was Michelle bent over the bed, starting to unzip a large, white, long bag. He took in her plump bottom but, before his mind could begin to fantasize, a creak in the door alerted her to his presence. With a jump she turned around, gasped, and moved to stand in front of the parcel quickly.

She held her hands up, facing him. "Don't come any closer!" she exclaimed. "You can't see what's behind me."

He let an amused smile creep to his face. He highly doubted the conventional rules of tradition applied, requiring him not to see her wedding dress before the big day, but he let her have her fun. "Alright, alright, if you say so. Did you have fun?" he asked, coming to sit in the overstuffed chair by her bed. She smiled, the action lighting up her face.

"Actually, yes, I did," she replied, sinking down onto the side of the bed. "It's strange. Even though these are not ideal circumstances, I did enjoy the whole experience. Thank you." She stood up quickly, reaching into the purse she had set on the bed. "Here. You might need this back." She held out his bank card to him.

He looked at it for a moment. "Keep it for whatever else you might want."

He noticed her jaw drop a little. She began to stammer her reply. "Oh, no, I couldn't—I couldn't take this…"

He quickly cut her off. "You are about to be my wife. My wealth is your wealth. Plus, besides an island or small country of some sort, I highly doubt you could buy anything that would put a dent in the Johnston fortune. So don't worry. Keep it." As he stood, he noticed her eyes dart to the side, to the dress by her. He chuckled to himself.

"Don't worry. I'm not going to look at your dress. Put it up somewhere, so you won't have to worry." With that he began to leave, but she quickly followed him into his bedroom. She cleared her throat behind him.

"So, last night…" she trailed off. He smiled to himself before turning to face her.

How could he even describe 'last night'? It had been beyond words, surpassing anything they had felt before. She had given herself to him willingly, almost pleading for him to take her repeatedly. He had taken her body to heights of pleasure he was sure she had never experienced before, and she had easily returned the favor. Last night, indeed…

"It was amazing. Was that what you were going to say?" he asked, noticing the color flowing to her cheeks.

"Um, not necessarily…I mean, it was, but that's not what I was going to say. You said something that I can't get out of my head." She began to close the gap between them, wringing her hands. "You said that you could easily fall in love with me. Now, did you mean that, or was it just something you said in the heat of the moment?" She sighed. "Or is this whole marriage going to be emotionally empty and one-sided?" She finished with a huff, putting her hands firmly on her hips.

He opened his mouth to attempt an answer, but his tactful thoughts left as the door swung open.

"Mommy! Daddy!" James and William ran into the room, each one giving one of them a hug. Everything Dorian had been thinking left his head for a moment to make room for his sons. They were so beautiful, so full of life and discovery, eager to meet the day head on. He remembered when he had been like that. There were some days he really missed his childhood.

But, then again, there were other days…

He couldn't imagine starting over from adolescence, ruthlessly climbing the corporate ladder all over again. He had worked his way up fair and square at his father's insistence, and had earned his place among the business world's elite. His mind raced back to the present, James squeezing him tightly around his knees. He looked over at William, who had Michelle squeezed just as tightly. He was so relieved not to have to answer her question about their marriage that he laughed aloud. When he did that, the boys both began talking at once.

"Daddy, what are we having for dinner?"

"Mommy, where have you been all day?"

"Are we gonna stay here forever?"

A flood of questions began pouring at them at once. Before they could become too overwhelmed, Dorian held his hands up.

"Hold on, boys. Hold on. Now, one at a time."

"When are we going to have dinner?" James asked, finally letting go of Dorian's knees as he sat on the bed. He pulled James into his lap and looked at his watch.

"Dinner is soon, I promise. I bet Rod is working on it right now, in fact," he added. "Would you boys like to see the kitchen?"

Their eyes lit up. "Yea!" Together they bounded to the door, almost running out of it until they realized they didn't know where they were going. As they reached the threshold, they turned around to face Dorian and Michelle for guidance. She stepped forward.

"Come on, let's go find that kitchen." She cast a questioning glance back at him.

"I'll catch up with you guys," he told her. "Just gotta finish up a few more things. I'll be along shortly." He was lying, he knew it and hated it, but he needed time to think of an appropriate answer to give

Michelle. He didn't want to lie to her; he hated giving a woman false hopes when it came to his emotions. He knew he wasn't going to be able to give her what she wanted emotionally, but how did he tell her that? What he'd said to her last night…he'd gotten caught up in the moment, losing himself in her sweetness, and he hadn't been thinking rationally.

In all other aspects of their arrangement he could deliver…especially sexually. But when it came to his heart, that was another matter entirely. Hell, he couldn't even believe he was marrying Michelle! He never thought 'Mrs. Johnston' would come in such an unlikely package.

He closed the laptop on his desk, took a deep breath, and went to catch up with Michelle and the boys.

Chapter 11

2 months pass...

  Dorian kissed a sleeping Mrs. Johnston on the forehead and headed towards his office down the hall. He had started going to work a bit earlier since they had gotten married so he could get home with more time to spend with his family, even working from home sometimes. But no matter how early he rose, the boys always seemed to get up before him.
  Since it was the summer and they did not start preschool for a couple months, they got up early and spent every waking moment playing outside. They usually only came in to eat, take a bath, and go to bed, falling into the house by the end of the day exhausted and thoroughly dirty. They took advantage of every square inch of the estate's massive grounds; climbing, running, playing, and exploring until their hearts and imaginations were spent.
  This morning was no different, and as he looked down on the front yard from his office's balcony, he barely could see them sitting under the large weeping willow as they often did. Sometimes he would come out onto the balcony to see them acting out something only they knew the meaning of, or

other times they would simply sit and talk. Being twins, he was sure they shared a connection that no one else would understand.

He knew from experience…

Dorian sighed. He knew he was running out of time before Michelle found out about David, and then confronted him for not telling her of his own accord. He couldn't put off telling her much longer, he knew that, he just couldn't bring himself to re-hash all the painful memories that came along with it. He hated baring his emotions at all, and he knew reliving the accident would do just that.

His mind was already beginning to replay the moment that had changed his life when he felt a strong sensation travel up his back. Without looking he knew Michelle was approaching; he could sense her. Sure enough in a moment she was beside him, resting her elbows on the railing. After a deep breath she said, "they're beautiful, aren't they? So alike yet so unique." He nodded silently in acknowledgement, not sure if she could see him. She turned around to face him, putting her back to the railing. Her face was gravely serious, though still stunningly beautiful. He could get lost in her features, which he found himself doing before she spoke again.

"They deserve a better family than this," she sighed, putting her hands on the railing behind her.

"What do you mean?" he replied, immediately defensive. "They have everything they could possibly want!" He spread his arms out to indicate the house and grounds. He resented the assumption that his fortune could be insufficient for any child.

"But not what they need. They need two parents who love each other. And I know that's not going to happen."

With that she left, leaving her fresh scent trailing behind. He stood rooted to the spot for a moment contemplating what she had said. *She is right*, he thought to himself. They'd been distant ever since the wedding, and Dorian took part of the responsibility. He admitted he didn't treat her like much of a wife, more like a guest who just happened to be the mother of his sons. He started to put his elbows on the railing, but reconsidered and went to sit behind his desk.

His mind was whirling. If he wanted the normal, orderly family he craved and the submissive wife he desired, he needed to mend the rift between him and Michelle. He didn't want the boys to sense any animosity between their parents. As he gathered papers into his briefcase, he told himself he'd make a conscious effort to smooth things out. With a clear resolve and a new attitude, he headed to work.

*****

Michelle raised her head from the toilet, where she had just thrown up. She leaned back on the tub, closing her eyes as another wave of nausea threatened to undo her. She inhaled deeply and tried to calm her stomach as well as her mind. She gave herself a moment to think.

She'd been feeling nauseous off and on for a little over a month now, but she didn't want to face the possibility of a pregnancy. The thought had crossed her mind however, earlier in the week, and she had broken down and bought a pregnancy test anyway. It seemed to loom in the back of her mind like a splinter she couldn't get rid of, nagging at her to take care of the problem. She bit her lip.

Giving in to her curiosity, she crawled on her hands and knees to get to her purse that hung over her chair at her vanity. She reached her hand in and scrambled through the contents until she found the tough plastic wrapper it came in. She had long since thrown the box away, fearful that Dorian would find it and begin to ask questions. She stared at the plastic wrapper for an unknown amount of time, debating in her mind whether to open it or not. By the time she had returned to the bathroom and sat on the toilet, the urge to pee had snuck up on her. She quickly clenched her pelvic muscles and held it while she frantically unwrapped the paper and held it between her thighs. As she released and felt it hit the test, she knew there was no turning back. She had to find out.

When she had finished, she placed it on the side of the tub and washed her hands. Already her breathing had quickened as she realized the next few minutes had the possibility to change her life. Without looking at the results she picked it up and placed it flat on her vanity, and found herself pacing back and forth wringing her hands. What if she was pregnant? How would she tell Dorian? She had already straddled him with two children he wasn't ready for, what would he say when he found out about another? Would he be upset? She couldn't bear to think of it. With a deep breath, she sat down and picked up the test.

Michelle sat at her vanity for what seemed like forever, staring at the tiny pink plus sign she held in her hand. It stood as a clear testament to the fact that she and Dorian were going to be parents yet again, yet again they were bringing a child into the world when they did not love each other—at least, she loved him and he reciprocated nothing of the sort—and that fact weighed on her heart like a mountain. How could they teach their children about family and love when they themselves were not an authentic family? Children deserved parents who loved each other, not parents who had simply gotten married because it seemed the logical choice.

She looked down at the hand she had subconsciously placed on her stomach, seeing her sparkling solitaire diamond and the band that rested underneath it. Immediately her mind flew back to their wedding. She had smiled like she was supposed to, posed for what seemed like a million pictures for the awaiting, relentless paparazzi—they'd sniffed out the nuptials as soon as she'd begun to make last-minute, pulled-string arrangements for the wedding: the name Johnston could not be missed, no matter how much she'd tried to keep it under wraps.

She had mingled so much at the reception she thought her head might explode with all the names she'd learned, mostly business colleagues of Dorian's and New York socialites. She'd known very few people there, as Andrew had taken over the guest list after she'd told him she didn't have much family or friends.

She smiled to herself as she remembered the look on Dorian's face when she had entered the cathedral; she was glad she had kept her dress out of sight, after all. With its strapless bust decorated with pearls and its skirt billowy and flowing, she had looked and felt just like a princess. The wedding had passed by in such a blur that she had barely registered they were married until they had gotten back to their room after putting the boys to bed. Dorian had made perfectly clear her position—well, numerous positions—as his wife, over and over again.

But even though they were officially married, she didn't feel any closer to him. Sure, he was home for dinner almost every night, but she didn't feel any more like a family. Outside of the bedroom they didn't talk much; he never talked to her about his day or how he was feeling. The only time he initiated conversation was when he needed to talk about the boys. Did he even care about her thoughts as a human being?

Just thinking about how Dorian didn't treat her as a wife began to infuriate her. She had borne his children, why shouldn't she be acknowledged in his life? And she wasn't going to bring another child in this world with him when he didn't even recognize her as his significant other. She made up her mind in an instant. She had to leave. She was getting nowhere telling Dorian how she felt, it seemed as though her words went in one ear and out the other.

She wished things didn't have to resort to such drastic measures, especially since the boys were growing accustomed to their new life, but she didn't see another way. She refused to trap herself in a loveless marriage, even if she had to raise the children by herself. He had, after all, given her the blank check as a wedding present, and told her to cash it for whatever amount whenever she needed. She'd do just that, and make a new start for her and her boys.

Steeling her spine, she turned her attention to the notepad and pen on her desk and decided to leave him a note. But how could she put how she felt into words? There were so many things she needed to say, things she needed to explain to him. She didn't want to break the news to him that she was leaving in a note, but she couldn't bear to tell him to his face.

After re-drafting and editing her note several times, she'd finally decided what to say to him. She left her and Dorian's room and headed down the hall to his office, holding the folded note tightly in her hand. As she rounded the corner, she almost ran into Rod.

"Whoa, where are you rushing to so fast?" he asked, chuckling.

She closed her eyes for a moment and tried to settle her mind. "Oh, nowhere, just headed to look for the boys," she fibbed.

"They're where they always are: outside enjoying the sunshine," he replied, heading down the hallway. "Try the gardens, hon," he added. "They love the maze."

"Thanks, Rod."

Michelle breathed a sigh of relief as he walked away; she hated lying to him even in the smallest degree, but she couldn't run the risk of someone going and telling Dorian her plan out of loyalty to him. She couldn't afford him coming home and sweet-talking her into staying; she needed to leave while she still had the guts to get away.

She creaked open his office door, holding her breath, half-expecting him to be sitting in the large chair behind his desk. She let out a whoosh of air as she saw that he wasn't, and she quickly crossed the large room to drop the note on his laptop. It landed with finality, as if a chapter of her life was closing. There was no way he could miss it, his office was usually the first place he stopped by when he got home. She half-thought about picking it up and just going back to their room, but she decided against it. She deserved better, and the boys deserved a real family. If she didn't leave right away, she'd never get out with her emotions intact.

She backed out of the room and closed the door behind her, then rushed down the hall to gather some of her and the boys' things. She stopped at their room first, grabbing a couple of clean outfits and a pair of pajamas for them. It felt almost as though she were running away from an abusive husband the way she was leaving so suddenly, but she kept reassuring herself she was doing the right thing. When they got back to Maine she'd get an apartment and find another job, since she had turned in her resignation when she and Dorian had gotten married. Even if she and the boys had to stay in a hotel until they got back on their feet, so be it.

When she had finally packed all of the valuable things she wanted to bring, she left his bank card and her wedding ring set on the vanity for him to find and tossed the pregnancy test in the trash. The closet where she and Dorian's clothes hung was still full on her side with her clothes, as she wanted to bring as few items as possible. She sighed deeply as she exited the room and closed the door behind her, symbolically sealing a part of her life. It hurt her heart, leaving everything they had begun to establish, but the boys deserved two parents who loved each other as well as them. She didn't want them growing up like she did: her mom and dad argued so much until her dad finally gave up and left them altogether. She didn't want her boys going through that, not when she had a chance to change it.

After she had purchased their plane tickets online and was walking down the hall, the boys flew past her. They almost ran into the bag she carried, and had the hallway not been large they surely would have.

Noticing her, they did a u-turn.

"Mommy!" they exclaimed.

"Hey, what did I tell you about running in the house? Never mind. Just come with me." With that, she put the bag over her shoulder and grabbed their hands. In a flash, she was at the front door, speaking with their driver, Travis.

"Mrs. Johnston, is everything alright?" he asked, concerned.

"Yes, the boys and I are going to visit my mother," she fibbed. "Could you drive us to the airport?"

"Of course, ma'am. I'll bring the car around."

"Thank you, dear."

She squeezed the boys' hands slightly for reassurance, and kept looking over her shoulder to see if someone was watching. She felt almost like a coward running away from her problems, but she couldn't turn back. She was so close.

After a moment Travis pulled up and jumped out, ready to grab the bag and toss it in the trunk. Quickly she opened their door and loaded the boys in, closing the door behind her and breathing a sigh of relief. As Travis pulled away, she took one last look at the house to make sure no one was running after them, but the driveway was empty. Sitting back on the seat, she looked over at the boys.

"I can't wait to see Nana!" William exclaimed.

"Mommy, when will we be home?" James asked, kneeling in the seat to look out the window. William followed his lead.

She felt tears well up in the back of her throat. How could she possibly explain to them what was going on? They couldn't comprehend the reasoning behind leaving, and she wasn't sure they'd take it too well. She decided to wait to tell them.

"I don't know, baby. I don't know," she finally said.

Michelle checked the cash in her purse, made sure the blank check was still folded neatly inside, and closed her eyes. She didn't want to imagine the hell Dorian would unleash when he got home, and hoped he didn't take it out on any of the staff.

Looking at the bright side, she realized the boys would be back in Maine before they were to start preschool, something she was glad of. She didn't want to uproot the boys in the middle of the school year, especially since they worked better with a routine.

When they pulled up at the airport, Michelle was almost at peace with her decision. She still had a few doubts, but it was too late to change her mind. As Travis set their bag on the sidewalk, she almost wished she could tell him to load it back in the trunk and take them back to the house. But as she leaned over, draped the bag over her shoulder, and straightened her purse, she simply smiled and thanked him.

"When will you be home, ma'am?" Travis asked, heading over to the driver's side and opening the door.

With a thought, she said, "I'll call." She tried to convince herself that she wasn't *completely* lying.

The boys waved goodbye enthusiastically, which almost broke Michelle's heart. She led them inside, and got in line to pick up the tickets she'd purchased for them. She felt the need to look over her shoulders periodically, almost expecting Dorian to be walking towards them. Had he been approaching them, Michelle didn't know what she would say. He definitely would not want to cause a scene, she knew that much. However, as she neared the smiling attendant at the counter, there was still no sign of him.

The boys were so excited to be on another airplane that they almost forgot where they were going. She just had to explain to them that they couldn't run to another part of the plane to jump on the enormous bed, though.

*****

Dorian pulled into the quiet courtyard, and in an instant was out of the car and beginning upstairs. He had worked much later than he had planned, and he hoped Michelle was not upset. He had tried to make it home at least in time to catch dinner, but traffic had been like a parking lot and quite frustrating. Several times he'd had to stop himself from getting out of the car and coming to blows with an idiot driver who kept him away from his family.

Family. It was a word he'd gotten used to, yet one that still got him a little nervous at times. He had to admit he'd gotten much better when it came to parenting the boys, though he still couldn't get them down for a nap to save his life. He tried almost every Saturday, and every Saturday he failed miserably. When they saw him, they thought nothing of sleep. Maureen, however, had the magic hands, and could make them do anything. They loved her to death, and he was so glad. Also, it didn't hurt that he came home to Michelle every night.

He stopped by his office to drop off his briefcase, noticing the house was unusually quiet.

Was everyone asleep already? He opened the balcony doors; it was a beautiful night outside, and he was in a better mood just being home. He wanted to feel the cool breeze. As he rounded his desk a note lay on top of his laptop, with his name across the front in Michelle's beautiful handwriting. He picked it up thinking it was a sweet note, but the words he read when he opened it left anything but a desirable taste in his mouth.

> Dorian,
>
> I've been debating how to say this for quite some time, but there's just no easy way. I've gotta do what's best for the boys. They need and deserve two parents who love each other, and I know you can't give me that. Now, I don't blame you. Instead, I feel so sorry for you, Dorian. You push people away because you're afraid to get hurt, but you're only going to end up alone. And that's what's gonna hurt me the most. To see you end up alone because of your own doing.
>
> I know that you think you can't confide in me, that you can't love me, and that those things will never change. I can't wait around to find out if you'll prove me wrong or not. I can't raise our children in a home where only one parent loves the other; it's not fair to them to watch their mother suffer, miserable...so, we're leaving.
>
> Please know that I have loved you so much for so long, and I always will.

Michelle

P.S. I know about David, I've known for a while. Guess you weren't ready to talk about it.

Dorian re-read the note again and again, hardly believing what was staring back at him. How could she just leave? As he sank down into the chair behind his desk, an unfamiliar feeling began to stir inside him. He felt empty, as if someone had split him open. A stark realization hit him like a boulder being thrown into his heart: he missed her so much already. Her smile, her light laugh, her feisty spirit…it was as though a light had been extinguished in his life. He and the boys hadn't even had a chance to truly begin their new life together, even if it hadn't began the way he'd pictured it or in a way he'd been prepared for.

He couldn't run from the truth any longer: he loved her. He was head over heels in love with her. He couldn't breathe without her, couldn't think when he wasn't around her, couldn't live without seeing her face one more time. He needed her. It was why he couldn't get her out of his system, why he couldn't get enough of her. For as much as he had tried to keep his feelings buried, they had erupted and taken over his entire being.

His breathing became rapid, and before he knew it he was pacing back and forth frantically. He couldn't sit still, it was as though his newly-realized emotion had scattered popping candy throughout his body. A gust of wind turned his attention to the open balcony doors. He needed fresh air. He couldn't breathe.

But even after twenty laps in the infinity pool, he felt no better. If anything, his heart rate had increased, and he had to sit down to catch his breath. As he put his elbows on his knees and hung his head, he felt almost like surrendering. It figured as soon as he realized that what he'd been looking for was right under his nose all along, she'd be gone. He guessed it was payback for the way he had been living: breezing in and out of women's lives with not a care as to if he hurt them or not. Deep down he'd known it'd come back to bite him in the butt, but he never expected it to feel so horrible.

He came into the room they had shared and sat himself at her vanity, trying to feel connected to her in any way. It was then he noticed his bank card and her rings, which dropped a mountain on his heart. She really wasn't coming back. Had she cashed her blank check already? He wouldn't mind if she had, after all he'd given it to her as a wedding gift, no strings attached. He leaned back in the chair, remembering how she'd sat in the same seat countless times: sometimes doing her makeup, sometimes simply staring at her reflection, as if looking for something in her beautiful face. It was in those times that he wondered what she was thinking, but he had never dared to ask. Now, looking back, he wished he would have.

As he cast his eyes downward, something in the trash caught his eye. He blinked hard, and then bent over to pick it up. Carefully he inspected what he held in his hand: a pregnancy test. A positive pregnancy test, he saw by the plus sign that showed in the window. He sank back in the seat, floored.

Not only was she gone, but she was carrying his child…again. He had no doubt that he was the father; he had kept Michelle so busy in bed she would needed to have been Wonder Woman to have another lover. So many things were happening at once; his head was a whirlwind of thoughts and emotions. He didn't even know how to begin to sort through it all to make sense of everything. He tried to tell himself he was in control, but he couldn't get a hold of himself. He had negotiated multi-billion dollar deals, broken up corporations with a mere suggestion…yet he could not get a handle on what was happening to him.

He hadn't had many major realizations in his life, and when they came to him he got over the feeling rather quickly. But realizing he was in love was something completely different, something he'd never experienced before. He felt such a great sense of loss, one that almost paralleled with how he felt when he'd lost his mother and…

His mind recalled her p.s.: she'd known about David all along and hadn't said anything. She'd patiently waited for him to open up to her and confide in her the truth about the accident, but he had never trusted her enough, never opened his heart to her enough to let her know. That sunk his spirits even lower: she'd never brought it up, never pestered him about it…she'd put the ball in his court and he'd missed the shot. He'd missed it big time...and he didn't have a chance for another one.

He sat up straight. Why couldn't he have another shot? He had to track her down and tell her how he felt. He had to make things better between them if it took everything he had. He knew she'd return to Maine to where she was comfortable, so that was at least a start. In a flash he was at the phone by the bed, dialing Gwen.

"Hello?" she answered.

"Gwen, it's me."

"Sir, is everything alright?" she quickly inquired, apparently noticing the distress in his voice.

Dorian sighed. "She's gone, Gwen. She took the boys and left," he said, his voice beginning to break with tears. He held the phone away from his mouth to collect himself. The thought of losing his wife AND children in one moment tore him apart. He recognized someone was speaking to him, and Gwen's voice snapped him back to reality.

"Sir...are you there?"

"Yes, I'm here," he replied, clearing his throat.

"What can I do to help?" she quickly asked, ever ready to help, as always. Even though she had been off for maternity leave, she'd never failed to get all her work done, working from home and still helping whenever he called. She truly was his best employee.

He cleared his throat once more, trying to hide the tears. "Yes, there is. I need you to find her."

"How do I even begin?"

"I don't know," he sighed. "She'll go back to Maine, I know that much. That's where she has some kind of roots planted. Start there."

"The entire state?" she questioned, chuckling. "Boss, are you alright?"

He paused, thinking. "I'm more than alright. I'm in love! And I want my family back. Thanks, Gwen." Without confirming that she could do it—he had faith in her—he hung up with a laugh and ran down to his office, a sliver of hope igniting a fire inside him. In his jubilation he nearly knocked down Travis, who appeared as though he were searching for something he'd lost.

"Oh, sir, thank God. Have you heard from Mrs. Johnston? I dropped her and the boys at the airport this morning and she said she'd call, but…"

Dorian cut him off as he was about to get upset. "Travis, calm down. They're fine. Michelle and the boys are gone."

"Yes, she said they were going to her mother's, but she didn't say—"

"Wait, her mother's? That's exactly what she said?"

"Yes, sir. Is everything alright?"

He breathed a sigh of relief. At least he knew where to start. "It's going to be," he replied, wrapping a confused Travis in a tight bear hug. He entered his office, called Gwen with new instructions, grabbed his keys off the desk, and made his way to his car. As he bolted out the front door, he swore he would get his family back no matter what it took.

By the time he was touching down in the airport in Maine, Michelle's mother's address in his pocket, he couldn't lie to himself and say he wasn't nervous. As he hailed a cab, he checked his watch. It was after eleven at night, would the woman even be up? He didn't want to wait until morning; he had to find his wife.

He told the driver the address, told him he'd pay double the meter if he stepped on it, and prayed Michelle's mother would be awake. Although, if she was any kind of precedent to Michelle's night-owl personality, he had a feeling she would be.

The driver maneuvered through quiet streets in a quaint, barely lit neighborhood, finally coming to rest in front of a small brick house. The grass was short and neat, with immaculate rose bushes by the front door. A sole car sat in the driveway, a pink Cadillac that Dorian assumed could only belong to Michelle's mother. He smiled to himself.

As he paid the driver, he had a second thought. "Could you wait here until I'm through?" He knew there was a possibility he'd state his name and get a door slammed in his face, and he would hate to be waiting for another cab with only his defeated pride to keep him company.

"The meter will be running," the driver replied.

"Of course it will." As he squared his shoulders and walked up the cobblestone pathway to the front door, a thought struck him. He'd come all the way there with nothing but his wallet and the clothes on his back. He had no idea of what to say, nor had he any clue as to what he was going to do next. But, somehow, his unpreparedness did not worry him. If he had to walk the entire state inch by inch just to find Michelle and the boys, he would. He needed them; he couldn't breathe without them.

The door inched closer and closer, and before he knew it, he was raising his hand to knock twice. Looking over at the front window, he noticed a small light come on, perhaps from a lamp. He breathed a sigh of relief. She was awake.

Within moments, she opened the door, looking confused.

"May I help you?" she asked, putting one hand on a hip. Looking at her, one could definitely tell where Michelle got her beautiful features. She was a stunning older version of his wife; tall and slender, she held herself with such an aura of confidence that she seemed to radiate from within. If she was any kind of preview as to what Dorian had to look forward to, he had not one complaint.

He put on his best charm, despite his stomach's butterflies. He tried to smile a comfortable smile.

"Yes, ma'am, I sure hope so. Are you Anjanette Ortiz?" He mentally crossed his fingers.

She raised an eyebrow. "Yes, I am…and you are?" she asked, folding her arms. It was then that he noticed an unoccupied ring finger. He sighed. Probably yet another woman scarred by a man.

"Well, I'm Dorian—"

She cut him off. "Wait, Johnston?" Immediately her stance became defensive.

He sensed the change and backed up an inch. "Yes…" he answered cautiously.

Her eyes narrowed. "I do not know where my daughter is. Even if I did, I wouldn't tell you." She began to close the door, but he slammed his hand against it.

She gasped in shock, but he didn't care. He had something to say.

"If you see your daughter, tell her that I love her. Tell her I'm sorry I realized it too late. And she could have made the check amount much more."

With that, he turned and started out to the cab that was waiting, when her voice hit him.

"Leave her alone. And that's coming from her, not me."

He turned slowly and closed the distance between them. "What are you saying?" He was almost terrified to hear the answer as he placed his hand back on the door.

"I'm saying that she doesn't want you in their lives. She told me you've hurt her enough, and to send you on your way should you come snooping around. I meant what I said. I don't know where she is. Now get off my property."

He took his hand off the door and she slammed it in his face, the loud crack ricocheting throughout the sleepy neighborhood. He swore loudly out of anger and frustration, not caring what the driver inside the cab was thinking. He made his way slowly, the distance between himself and the house steadily growing, but he dared not close it and bother her again. She made it very clear whose side she was on, and he couldn't blame her.

He reached for the door handle on the cab, but he couldn't bring himself to leave just yet. He sat himself on the curb, feeling the hard, cold cobblestone beneath him.

The passenger side window lowered, and the driver's voice came from the car.

"Sir, would you like me to leave, or keep waiting?"

"I know the meter's running. Trust me, I can pay. Just give me a bit, alright?"

When the window finally closed, he let himself get lost in his thoughts, putting his elbows on his knees.

She didn't even want to see him…God only knew how many other ways she planned to keep the boys away from him. So he truly had lost her, after all. All his prestige, all his reputation, all his self-assurance, money, power…it had done nothing to make Michelle stay. Everything he thought he needed to be indestructible made him unapproachable, selfish, inconsiderate…and he'd learned the hard way.

It seemed the cruel fate of powerful men to push away the ones they cared for on their path to greatness, trampling over the hearts of so many in their way. He wondered how many times he'd been inconsiderate of Gwen or anyone else in his employ, or his father…there was no telling how Michelle had felt, waiting for him to confess his love to her, waiting for him to talk to her about David, to confide in her.

She had probably been miserable, loving him unconditionally, silently, afraid to be rejected lest she tell him her feelings.

As he began to concede to his self-pity, a persistent voice spoke up from the back of his mind. He loved her, and he knew it. He wasn't just going to be told to stay away and simply leave without a fight. He fully intended to go to the mat for his family, come hell or high water.

Hell no, he wasn't going to leave his family, damn that. Especially not after he'd just found his boys, his beautiful boys, two out of the three people he'd come to love more than life itself. He couldn't let them slip away, he refused. They needed him as well, someone to show them what kind of men they were supposed to become; when he left the company to them—which he fully intended to do—he would know he was leaving it in capable hands.

He stood up, brushing off the back of his pants, and opened the door of the cab, his mind made up. The sound of the door closing behind him woke the cabbie, who'd been trying to catch a quick nap while Dorian got himself together. At that Dorian laughed to himself, glad for something to lighten his mood a bit.

As they began to pull off, he dialed Gwen. After the fourth ring, she sleepily answered. "Sir? You're cutting it awfully close with me right now."

"I know, I know, forgive me. Look, I have a plan to get Michelle and the boys back. It's gonna be difficult and it may take some time, but I need you. Ok? Please?"

"Come on, difficult is what I get paid for. See you in the morning, boss." Before she hung up she added, "try using 'please' more often. It's a good word to keep in your vocabulary. Goodnight."

Chapter 12

Michelle smiled as she stepped out onto the stoop of her building and felt the sunshine on her face. She had dropped the boys off at daycare—she was going to forego preschool and send them directly to kindergarten, to give them time to adjust to the move—but had forgotten her design book at her apartment and had returned to retrieve it. Almost three months had passed since she'd left, and as she looked down at her already swollen belly, she had no regrets. The boys had only asked for Dorian a few times, and once they had started daycare they'd stopped altogether.

With the check she'd cashed she'd paid up an apartment for a year, to give herself a comfortable span of time to find a job that would cover the bills when she ran out of money. Luckily, a job offer found her, with an excellent starting pay and room for advancement. Her work had already begun to catch the attention of her superiors, and she fully intended to keep up the high quality work. She was finally in control of her life again, a fact she treasured.

She had an ultrasound scheduled for later that day, a doctor's appointment she had rescheduled twice because she'd been dreading it. She was very nervous to find out what Dorian had put in her belly this time around. Whatever it was, it had exploded her tummy so much that she could barely see the tips of her feet. Whenever she went somewhere, people would always remark on her baby bump and her 'glow'.

A week or so previously, a woman had turned to her in the grocery store and said, "how many days do you have left? You look ready to pop!" When she had informed the woman that she was only about five months along, her jaw had nearly hit the floor. Michelle had simply smiled at her shock and kept going, putting cereal for the boys in her cart.

She had to admit she had a certain 'glow'; she thought it to be perhaps because she was carrying Dorian's child. Just knowing yet another life they created rested inside her gave her butterflies, but she didn't mind. It was as though she were holding onto a piece of him that couldn't deny her its heart. She'd been angry at him for so long, but she'd taken time to simply think about it: everything they'd done she'd consented to, so she couldn't be but so mad at him for simply being himself. In her heart she'd forgiven him, after all, she loved him too much to stay mad at him. They were connected, even though they hadn't worked out; she liked that. Dorian was brilliant, handsome…she was more than happy to pass down those traits.

As she rode the elevator to the floor where she worked, she took a few deep breaths to collect her thoughts. She tried to make a mental list of what she had to do that day, but she couldn't think unless she was at her desk. As soon as she sat down, however, three of her co-workers popped their heads into her tiny office.

Jean, Barbara, and Sandra grinned at her, each one looking more mischievous than the last. When she had started there, they had taken her under their collective wing, since they had been decorating with the company for years and knew the ins and outs. She owed them so much; when she'd entered into the lower management position, the few people under her immediately resented her. They'd been her fiercest supporters, always coming to her aide when someone was giving her a hard time.

They each had such vibrant personalities. Jean was a heavyset woman, with huge dimples and a smile that covered half her face. She had a thick New York accent, one that only thickened the faster she spoke. She was almost like the 'big mama' of the bunch, dishing out advice, criticism, and design tips all at the same time. As soon as Michelle met Jean she'd liked her, latching onto her refreshing sense of humor and silly nature. She had them all in tears laughing so often that their supervisor threatened them with disciplinary action almost every week— never seriously, of course.

Barbara, on the other hand, was a miniature firecracker. Short and skinny, she easily made up for it with her 'big dog' attitude. She could always be found in the middle of a conversation circle, feeding continuous bits of juicy news, and was always willing to share it as easily as a tabloid. But under that sassy exterior there was a woman who would go to bat for her in an instant; she had done so on several occasions.

Sandra was the one who seemed to pull it all together. Whenever they would get a tad bit out of control she seemed to be the one to rear them back into decency, and remind them where they were. Her sister, Jasmine, worked at the front desk, but they didn't get to see her much. With one son working in security and one in maintenance, Sandra kept a watchful eye over the people she cared for. They had instantly clicked when she found out Michelle was pregnant, since she'd just been blessed with a new grandson herself. Sandra made her promise to inform her the moment she found out the sex of the baby.

Michelle leaned back in her chair, resting her hands on her belly. "Good morning, ladies," she said, smiling. They looked at her expectantly.

Immediately she was confused. "Am I missing something here?"

"Well, aren't you gonna tell us?" Barbara demanded, coming to stand beside her.

"Tell you what?"

"Don't play dumb, missy," Jean added. "We know you're being offered the Smith estate that's up for renovation. Are you taking it or not?"

Michelle couldn't believe what she was hearing. She hadn't heard anything about the Smith estate since the rumor began floating around that it was going up for renovation, and that one of them might be offered the job.

She blinked hard. "What?"

"Wait, you haven't heard anything?" Sandra asked, then gasped as Michelle shook her head. "Pretend we didn't say anything!" she quickly said, just as the intercom beeped.

All four of them jumped.

"Michelle, could you come in here?" The voice of their supervisor, Dot, rang out into the office loudly. "And bring your portfolio."

In unison they squealed, and as Michelle began to stand quickly, Sandra promptly sat her back down. "Whoa, sister, let's not forget you're carrying a full load there. Take your time."

She heeded the advice and sat back down, taking a moment to steady her breath. She could barely settle herself down; she was so excited. The estate meant a lot of money for the company, and if she nailed the job, it could mean a huge promotion. A promotion she could definitely use.

Taking Sandra's hand she stood slowly, gradually allowing her weight to shift. When she had risen to her feet, she turned and grabbed the black case that held her portfolio off her desk, straightening her skirt.

"Do I look ok?" She held her arms out for inspection.

"You look good and pregnant," Barbara said, giving her a nudge out of the door. On unsteady legs she made her way to the elevator, clutching the handle of her portfolio for dear life. As she pressed the button and stepped inside, she took several deep breaths. She didn't want to appear like a nervous wreck in front of Dot; how could she trust such responsibility to someone who couldn't hold it together under pressure? She needed to be strong. Slowly the doors slid open, and the rush of cool air calmed her nerves almost instantly.

She had worked her butt off and she deserved a chance to spread her wings, to show that she could handle the job if only given the opportunity. After all she had been through, it was nice to finally have something go in her favor. Still, she couldn't help but feel a bought of nervousness as Dot's secretary helped her into a seat outside her office.

She rifled through her portfolio while she waited, trying to find a way to explain any weaknesses in her work. She went over a thousand possible scenarios in her head, wanting to make herself sound as promotable as possible. Dot was tough but fair, and Michelle was sure she could make a case for herself.

She had just started twiddling her thumbs when Dot poked her head out. She smiled, and Michelle was already beginning to feel better.

"Hey Michelle, come on in," she said, and Michelle slowly rose and began to follow. As she almost hit the doorway, she felt a strange, familiar tightening in the pit of her belly. She hadn't felt it in months, but here she was, feeling as though *he* were right around the corner.

Yet as she stepped into the room, the grip on her stomach only squeezed.

He was there. As arrogant as a Johnston, as beautiful as a Greek god...Dorian sat squarely in a chair at Dot's desk as if he belonged there. As if he had been invited.

Immediately her breath was stolen. She could barely speak his name.

"Dorian Johnston."

"Oh, good, you've met. Well, this should be easy. So, Mr. Johnston here has purchased the Smith estate and wishes to have it remodeled, renovated, and redecorated, and he's requested you by name. Go ahead and let him see your portfolio, sweetheart."

Michelle was so stunned she couldn't move.

"You alright? Come on and have a seat." She motioned for her to sit in a chair beside Dorian in front of her massive desk. "I know you get tired, carrying around that heavy load you call a baby."

Her body on autopilot, she carefully sat in the plush chair and started to hand Dorian her portfolio. Quickly he held a palm up with a shake of his head.

"No need, Michelle. I've seen your work up close," he smoothly said, his silky voice floating over her.

Dot raised an eyebrow. "So, I see you've been researching our little rising star here," she said, smiling at Michelle.

"You could say that," he replied, as Michelle tried to return a weak smile. She looked over at him and he flashed one of his killer grins, the kind that melted every ounce of willpower she had against him into a pool of hungry lust deep in her loins. She quickly looked at Dot, who was beaming.

So HE was how she had been recommended for the job. It hadn't been based purely on her talent, she'd had help. Her anger almost sent tears flowing down her cheeks. She took several deep breaths before addressing Dot.

"Are you offering me the account?" she asked her carefully.

"I am if you're accepting."

Michelle turned to face Dorian. "Mr. Johnston, I'm glad to be collaborating with you. If you'd like, we can meet at the estate and do a walkthrough, and you can tell me some of your visions for the place." She tried to sound as professional as possible, hoping it would mask the terror she felt from head to toe. Something about him made every hair on her body stand on edge. And here she was, big and pregnant with his child…again.

With his typical charm, he smiled. "That sounds great, but I'm kinda slammed. Is there any way you could possibly meet me at my office in New York sometime this week?"

Immediately she looked over at Dot, who simply smiled. "That's fine with me, just bring me your receipts so we can reimburse you."

God, he was doing it again. How could he have the world at his fingertips with merely the sound of his voice? Michelle began to protest.

"But I can't—"

"Don't worry, it's on me. I'll send the ticket and information here, is that alright?" He asked it lightly, almost daring her to object.

How dare he show up here like this, trying to steal her control over her life! She was finally starting to set roots where she was, yet he was trying to sweep her off her feet again. She couldn't let herself be controlled by him anymore. He didn't love her, so what reason would she have for staying in a one-sided marriage? Surely he couldn't make her stay, taking all that into account. Hell, she never should have been there in the first place.

On the other hand, she needed the account, and she couldn't just turn down an offer because she would have to deal with Dorian. She was a professional, dammit, and she could do this.

With a sweet smile she stood slowly, grabbing her portfolio from where she'd sat it on the floor beside her. "That's fine," she said to him, thanked Dot, and quickly left. Dot's secretary bid her goodbye, but she was too preoccupied to offer a response.

As she was reaching the elevator, his voice touched her ears.

"Michelle, wait, please," he pleaded, closing Dot's door behind him. "Just let me explain."

"Let you explain what?" She demanded it, furiously turning to face him. "Just couldn't let me be free, could you?" She nearly sobbed. Just the sight of him rapidly approaching made her knees almost weak. He had chased her down, gotten himself tangled into her business life...he used any method he could to get her back under his control. Well, not this time. She squared her shoulders.

Just as he had planted himself a few feet in front of her, she began to fuss him out.

"Let me tell you something, Dorian Johnston. Don't think you can just come in here and—"

"Just let me get this out, ok?" He let the words fly out of his mouth, holding up his hands. He sighed as they fell sadly to his sides, looking defeated. He closed the distance between them and slowly grabbed her hands, looking at them for a moment before finally raising his head. As she looked at his hands she could feel the heat radiating from them, but also the gentleness underneath. It was almost unnerving, feeling him touch her so softly, but she couldn't move her hands away.

When she looked up at him she noticed his eyes looked deep and sad, as if he had not been sleeping well. She took a moment to study his face, remembering his chiseled features. There was fresh stubble on his cheeks where he had neglected to shave, with saggy bags under his eyes. Even his hair was a bit disheveled, perhaps from running his hands through it a few too many times.

She'd been so floored before by his sudden appearance that she hadn't fully noted the change in his features. Looking at him closely, she saw just how much his face had become more serious since she'd left. She didn't want to lie to herself and believe it was because of her, though. Dorian Johnston never let any woman affect him that much.

She sighed and swallowed hard. "Make it quick."

The elevator doors opened, but she didn't step over the threshold. It was her method of escape, and she had ignored it.

He took a preparatory breath before speaking, and she found herself doing the same. She was almost afraid to hear what he had to say.

"Look, I know I'm not perfect. I'm arrogant, I'm selfish…I know this. But when I read your note…" He put his hands on her shoulders, and a shiver ran down her spine. "When I thought I'd lost you, I felt like someone had stomped on my heart. Like my whole world was ending. It was then I realized I couldn't live without you. I couldn't bear to spend another waking moment without you by my side, without the boys running around. I…" He sighed as he tried to find words to say, but Michelle was getting the picture.

"Michelle, what I'm trying to say is that I love you. I love you so much. I don't know what took me so long to figure it out, but I'm glad I finally did. I've loved you all along, honestly. I was just too stubborn to admit it." His breath escaped in a heavy whoosh, and he looked on the verge of tears.

"I'm sorry I couldn't talk to you about David…it's just that I didn't trust you enough to let you in and relive that horrible moment in my life. But I should have had faith in you, I'm sorry. My status and money made me feel as though I couldn't be emotional, like I couldn't connect with anyone or show weakness. But my wealth is nothing if I don't have you guys to share it with, I know that now. I'm sorry for not opening up to you, and every other pig-headed thing I've done. I'd be willing to apologize every morning I wake up, as long as I'm waking up next to you."

Tears were rapidly flowing down her cheeks uncontrollably, and Dorian reached out to wipe one away. She closed her eyes for a moment, simply feeling his hand on her skin. She had missed him so much...she couldn't believe the words she'd been waiting to hear were being said right in front of eyes by the man she thought she would never see again. She could barely contain her emotions.

"Please don't cry, beautiful. I can't bear it." Just as he said it, the elevator doors slid open again and a couple of men stepped out, headed for Dot's office. It was then she realized they were directly in the way, and Dorian picked up on it.

"Look, right here is not the time nor the place," he said with authority, stepping her to one side. "Just..."

He pulled out a tiny notebook from the inner breast pocket of his jacket. With an attached pen he scribbled something quickly on a sheet of paper, then tore it off and handed it to her. She found herself looking at a New York address she didn't recognize.

"What's this?"

"Just bring you and the boys to that address when you land in New York. I'll send the tickets here, ok? Please, just..." He glanced at his watch and gasped. "I gotta go, but please be there, ok? Please." He took her into his arms and kissed her fiercely, weakening her knees. Her head was swirling in a thousand different directions, but she was so happy she could barely think straight. He pulled away and she almost groaned, but then quickly remembered that they were still in the middle of the hallway.

"I'll be there—we'll be there," she promised him as he stepped into the elevator, and she meant every word.

*****

Three of the longest days of Dorian's life passed as he waited for Michelle. He'd paced back and forth numerous times, he couldn't sleep...it was as though merely their kiss had set him afire. He couldn't stop thinking of the future now that they were on the right path; every moment away from his family was killing him. Speaking of family...
Michelle was beautiful when she was pregnant. Already quite big and radiant, it was as though the tiny life inside of her was making her glow from within. Already he couldn't wait to meet whoever was in there. He only hoped Michelle liked the surprise he had planned.
He glanced at his watch, noticed the time, and rushed out of his office toward the elevator.
"Gwen, lock up when you're done, ok?" He called out over his shoulder to her, pressing the down button. Mouth full of cookie, she replied, "mm-hmm!"
As he raced through the streets towards the address he'd given Michelle, he could feel knots forming in the pit of his stomach. His mind was going in a million directions. Not only was he going to see Michelle but he'd missed the boys so much...the

house had seemed so empty he had temporarily moved back into his hotel suite.

It had taken pulling almost every string he owned and then some to find her, and he had quickly set his plan in motion. With the help of Gwen he'd researched her company and the properties they had their eyes on, and had snagged one quickly. He hadn't actually purchased the property, merely entered into a contract with the owner, Robert Smith, to have his name on the account as a temporary trustee of the estate. Smith, an old friend and colleague, had completely understood the need to do anything to get the woman he loved. After planting a bug in the ear of Michelle's superior of his possible interest in their company, he'd easily been able to hand-pick the consultant he wanted for the job. His name held quite a bit of weight.

He pulled into the garage, parked, and immediately ran upstairs. She wasn't there yet—the place was quiet—and he tried to calm himself while he waited. He straightened his jacket and tie so many times he felt as though he were meeting an important business client.

He took a few deep breaths, but his heart rate only raced more furiously. He couldn't stop smiling; his cheeks were almost starting to hurt. But he didn't mind a bit. It had been so liberating being unafraid to express himself in the last few months, there'd been a new spring in his step around the office. When he went to bed, however, thoughts of her nearly drove him mad. He was almost ready to explode with wanting for her. He'd read countless books about making love while pregnant, and he was fully prepared to be as gentle as possible. Anything to have her curled in his arms again.

His train of thought was skewed by the sound of quick footsteps on the stairs. Immediately his heartbeat quickened as he recognized the boys' laughter floating up towards him. Quickly he turned to face the door, and in a moment it burst open.

"Daddy!"

They yelled it in unison, and he dropped to his knees to receive their hug. He allowed himself a moment to inhale their scent, and he closed his eyes for a moment to stop his tears from flowing down his cheeks. They were beaming from ear to ear, dressed identically in jeans and long-sleeved collared shirts. He ruffled their hair, and finally noticed someone was missing.

"Where is mommy?" He cast an eye towards the staircase.

"Mommy says she has to go slower than us," James said.

"Because her tummy is so big!" William added.

"I heard that," a sweet voice called out. Huffing and clutching her swollen belly, Michelle slowly made her way to the top stair. When she finally came to stand in front of them, he slowly rose to meet her eyes. She was so beautiful, glowing despite her tiredness, and Dorian couldn't help but pull her into his arms and kiss her. Instantly the world around them disappeared, and all he could feel or think about was the press of her lips against his. He almost lost himself completely until he heard the boys snickering below him. With restraint, he pulled himself away.

"Later," she whispered against his lips, and he nearly melted. He cleared his throat and knelt to face the boys. "Why don't you guys go look around, ok? Pick out which room is your favorite," he said, and they immediately ran off. When he raised again to full height, he grabbed Michelle's hand and pulled her forward.

"So, what is this place?" She looked around, confused. "I know it's not the Smith estate, I've studied photos of every angle of that house looking for ideas."

He gave her hand a slight squeeze. "This is not the Smith estate, no. And the Smith estate is not actually mine, either. You have the account; of course, I'm just not the holder. You'll meet Robert, and he already loves your work. I just needed to see you." He looked around. "Before I explain any further, let me ask you…from what you see now, any ideas for the place?"

'The place' was a three-story brownstone, with a lower-level garage and an attached fenced-in yard. When he saw it was for sale he had bought it flat outright, paid in full, needing something much closer to his office and smaller than his estate. In his assessment of his life he'd realized the boys needed something more practical than a mansion to grow up in. Hell, they could get lost in that enormous house and they'd never spend any time together. The brownstone was completely bare, so Michelle could design it all her own from the ground up. That was his gift to her. She didn't have to answer to anyone but herself, with unlimited funds.

She had wandered over to the large windows by the front door, holding her arms high, palms spread open, as if imagining something in front of them.

"There are just so many possibilities," she said with awe, turning to face him. "But you still have me confused," she added, putting her hand on her belly.

Dorian grinned, then moved to take her hands in his. "This is for us. For you, the boys…this is so we can be together as a family, without too much house around us. I want you to put your own flavor to the house, every room, every bit of it. It's yours to fill to the brim with ideas."

Tears were welling up in her eyes, and a warm blanket spread out around Dorian's heart. It made him so happy that he'd been able to give her something she enjoyed so much. He wanted any way possible to show her just how much he loved her and their family.

"But what about your estate?" Tiny droplets fell down her cheeks, and he reached up to wipe one with the pad of his thumb.

"Well, I have another piece of news," he said, beaming, "my father moved back into it last month. He said he wants to be closer to his grandchildren, so he packed up the entire London staff, including Liz, and moved here."

"Wait, what? But—" She immediately looked worried, so he cut her off to calm her nerves.

"Now, now, before you start fretting, I sat my father down and told him the truth. I mean, the truth about everything. After his initial shock, he took it surprisingly well," he added, remembering how his father had completely forgotten his anger upon learning he had grandchildren. He had been ready to move so fast it had nearly made Dorian's head spin. Liz had cried with joy for so long she had gone through half a box of tissues.

Michelle could barely speak. She opened and closed her mouth as if preparing to say something, but in the end she simply wrapped her arms around his neck.

"Don't cry, baby…speaking of baby!" He pulled her back and put his hands on her stomach.

She placed her hands on top of his. "I'm sorry I didn't tell you in the note, but I didn't expect you to come after me."

"You thought I was gonna just let you slip away?" He chuckled, gently rubbing her belly. "Oh, I'm so happy you're carrying my child…wait, which reminds me, let me show you—"

"There's a room for baby sister!" James exclaimed from behind them, and Dorian sighed and playfully rolled his eyes as the boys ran to join them. Michelle's brow creased. "How did you know we were having a girl?"

"Well, I made a call to your doctor, simply explained that I was your husband and that I had missed the ultrasound because of work, and wanted to know the sex of my child. He happily obliged."

Her eyes softened. "That breaks so many HIPAA laws," she teased.

He laughed a hearty sound that erupted from the pit of his stomach. He felt almost like dancing, he was so happy.

"So, here you come, sweeping me off my feet again," she said, gazing up at him. He looked forward to getting lost in her eyes every day for the rest of his life.

"No, my sweet," he corrected, "it's you who has captured my heart."

Epilogue

"Lord have mercy girl, are you ever gonna pass those potatoes?" Lucy asked playfully. She, Alex, their daughter Sara, Jeff (without Nicole; they had long since parted ways), Michelle's mom, Dorian's father, and all their family were gathered around the formal dining room table for Christmas dinner. Alex cradled Sara in his arms, feeding her green mush from a tiny jar.

"Hey, don't mess with a pregnant woman and her food," Dorian spoke up, taking the bowl Michelle was reluctantly handing him and passing it to Lucy.

"When is that baby getting here, anyway?" Jeff asked, his mouth full.

"I'm only eight months!" With that she laughed, her belly bouncing slightly. Jeff's jaw dropped. "Are you serious? You look like we could be getting the call any day now," he said, laughing.

"Really, I've still got a few weeks," she said, patting her enormous tummy.

Edward laughed. "She's about to pop, isn't she?"

"Oh, be nice," Angie spoke up, snickering under her breath.

Gwen, her husband Caleb, and their children had stopped by to drop off presents, but had turned down Dorian's offer to stay for dinner since they were headed out of town. The sounds of silverware clattering and light conversation added a happy harmony to the picture. With their large Christmas tree merely feet away, it all seemed like something out of a picturesque magazine.

Michelle and Dorian looked around at their family and friends happily gathered, and they both smiled. James and William were in the adjacent den playing happily with the golden retriever puppy they had received that morning, much to their surprise and delight.

Everything was going so much better than anything either of them could have imagined, although things were not perfect. Dealing with her pregnancy, sometimes Michelle's hormones would rage out of control (one day she cried for an hour because William spilled juice in the kitchen), or she'd send Dorian to the grocery store in the middle of the night for odd combinations of food. He didn't mind; he was more than happy to do anything to keep her satisfied.

Their baby girl was growing so fast, she'd exceeded all the doctor's pre-conceived expectations. Michelle was going to deliver yet another big, healthy child, one who was already spoiled to death by all her family. Dorian's father had bought so many gifts the nursery was beginning to get crowded.

Dorian stood from his place at the head of the table and clinked on his glass with his knife. Immediately the room became silent.

"First of all, I want to thank everyone for being here to share this special occasion with us, and our growing family," he said, reaching out to grab Michelle's hand. She smiled and gave his hand a reassuring squeeze.

"Over the past few months, my life has been turned upside down quite a few times. I want to thank each and every one for being with us every step of the way. We wouldn't be here without you guys. Merry Christmas, everybody," he finished, holding his glass high.

"Merry Christmas!" They all replied in unison, taking sips from their glasses. As Dorian sat back down, he found Michelle staring at him with a content smile on her face.

"What, honey?"

"I just love you so much," she said, a glint of mischief sparkling in her eye, a signal that he had another, more carnal Christmas gift coming to him later that night.

"I love you, too," he replied, and he meant it with all his heart.

Printed in Great Britain
by Amazon.co.uk, Ltd.,
Marston Gate.